FIRE AND ICE AT SILVER RIDGE

CLAIRE CAIN

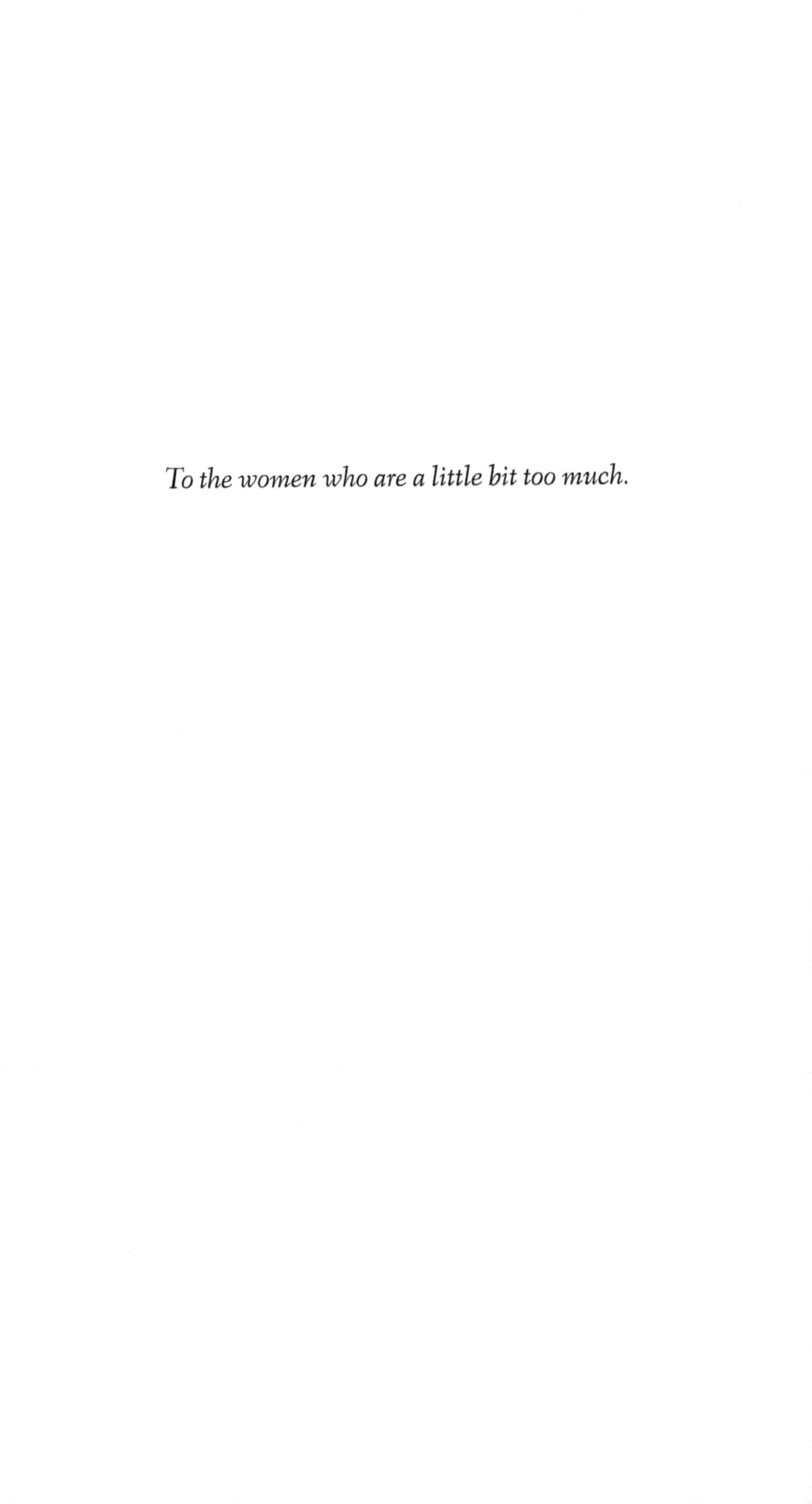

To the women who are a little bit too much.

CHAPTER ONE

Leo

T his was all good. Everything was *great*.

No, really. All good news. Nothing about this, what had been happening in the past few weeks, could be called bad news.

Danny was healing up nicely. He and Mia were engaged now, tied by Grandma's ring thanks to Grandpa Will's generosity. I'd determined not to feel that like the blow it was—Grandpa Will's gifting of a ring I'd always thought of as mine, being the only granddaughter and all that, to a brother I'd never expected to settle down before me. If I had to guess, they'd be married and moved in together by the end of the calendar year.

And Bel and Jamie had been in LA for a few weeks. They'd extended their time in Silverton, but had had to go eventually. I'd made peace with that. They'd be back.

And Wells and Liam were married. *Married.* Not a word about it until after the fact, but yeah, fine, I got it.

I closed my eyes against the blast of cool mountain air rustling in the trees and breathed in slow, slow, filling my lungs, willing the parts of me that felt hollowed out to solidify or disappear. I didn't want this—this miasma of feeling. Sadness and self-pity and all the nastiest things a woman could feel when her best friends and her siblings were all somehow marrying each other and running off into the sunset... and leaving her behind...

Even this real, actual, glorious sunset, with purples and pinks and oranges striping the sky to the west and illuminating the entire mountain range with a kind of heavenly glow, and which would normally make me feel that soul-expanding peace and gratitude, fell flat.

I clenched my teeth, pulling in another breath, refusing to let tears for myself fall. What a loathsome creature, to feel anything but happy for these people I loved so much. How could I stand here drowning in this ridiculous sense of loss when everyone I cared about was not only healthy and happy, but whole and moving toward wonderful new adventures?

A choking, aching sensation scratched at my throat, and I gripped the railing that bordered the overlook so idiots wouldn't wander right off and plummet to their deaths.

"Ms. Morrison."

Speak of the Devil, Ugh.

Well, I hadn't been speaking of him, or even thinking of him for once, but he'd materialized anyway, like an uninvited jack-in-the-box of ill will.

Of course I'd hear that voice. My sicko sad sack mind had probably conjured it in an effort to complete the sense of torment plaguing me.

"Ms. Morrison, are you all right?"

No.

That wasn't just my mind. It was real.

His crisp, perfect voice *would* interrupt my internal meltdown here at the top of the mountain where I'd come for privacy and a moment to myself.

And sure, it was a public place. I'd taken the gondola to the top of Silver Ridge Peak—or as high as it went—and skirted the lodge that welcomed people at the top of the mountain for lunch, bathroom breaks, and other needs, and found my way to the observation area on the far side of the ridge. From the back deck of the lodge, you might see a person standing out on the platform, which was built on an outcropping and reinforced now by steel beams and all kinds of feats of engineering, but not without really looking.

Since it was September and late in the day, not many people were up here. In fact, the gondola would close to the public in about an hour and only remain open for the workers doing various construction tasks around the lodge and on a new lift installment that led to one of the neighboring mountains.

So the fact that Jonas Bauer had found me—not just *found* me, but approached me—and was now speaking to me as I tried desperately to clutch at some semblance of calm, confirmed the Universe's decision to crap on my head today.

And unlike seagulls, the Universe crapping on one's head was not considered good luck.

Resigned to being unable to ignore him, I turned slowly. I had never attempted to mask my disdain for this man, nor did I have plans to start, especially when he exemplified everything that was wrong in the world.

He stood there, obnoxiously tall and just this side of

massive, really. But it all folded into a brutally perfect dark gray suit, white shirt, navy tie. I didn't scan to his feet because he'd no doubt have some sort of annoyingly perfect man shoe, undoubtedly the male equivalent of the Louboutin red sole to showcase his wealth and class.

Or something. I didn't know. But he always seemed perfectly composed. Inhumanly so, if one had to put a word to it, and it, like everything else about him, made my hands involuntarily clench into fists before I tucked them away.

"Bauer."

His gray eyes narrowed just slightly. "Are you quite well, Ms. Morrison?"

I blinked at him, slowly, irritated to find I noticed the close crop of his hair at the sides of his head and recognized he'd had a haircut. I shouldn't notice such things. I didn't care.

"Just fine."

"Would you accompany me down the mountain?" He turned to the side, one hand pressed against his suit jacket currently buttoned once, and gestured with his other toward the small mountaintop lodge and gondola station.

"I would not."

He didn't need to know why.

None of your business! my mind screamed.

He certainly didn't need to know I hadn't gotten a grip yet, and I was banking on these mountains, this view, *this place* returning some shred of humanity to me before I ventured back down and had to face myself and an entire weekend alone in my microscopic apartment.

"The gondola closes in moments."

Twine wrapped around my lungs. He didn't have much of an accent, but times like these, when his word choice sounded just slightly different from what you'd expect, showcased his not-entirely-American heritage.

"The gondola closes in hours, which I know because I've worked here and lived here and taken rides on this gondola *my entire life*. I'll be fine." My head snapped back to the view in front of me, praying he'd find the dismissal in the movement.

"Ah, but it closes to all passengers in seven minutes. They've changed the schedule due to a crew issue. I would hate for you to be stuck here."

Defeat filled me, along with a healthy dose of disappointment, which I wouldn't have thought I had room for after everything else. Of course my time here, in this safe place, would be cut short. Of course it'd be him doing it.

He already wanted to take everything else away from me... why not this, too?

I whipped around and stomped past him, aware I was acting like a petulant child, and not remotely interested in changing my tune. I walked directly to the gondola station, certain if I got there quickly enough, he'd lag behind, or at least get the hint, and I wouldn't have to spend the full thirty-minute ride down the mountain in a small, enclosed space with him.

"Have a good day, Leo!" Ricky, the gondola operator, shouted as the doors to the bright blue car ratcheted open.

"You too. Say hey to Athena for me." His wife was on bedrest for their third child. It'd been a few weeks since I'd dropped by. I should visit her again, and made a mental note to schedule that for the next week.

I slumped down on the hard plastic seat lined with a thin layer of material—not padded, but enough to keep people from slipping and sliding into each other—and leaned my head back against the glass window, shutting my eyes. The gondola bumbled along the curved path inside the station, and just before the doors clamped shut, the car bounced from the weight of another passenger stepping in.

I squeezed my eyes further shut as my heart beat a little louder in my ears. *It couldn't possibly be him,* I thought, grinding my molars to dust since I knew it would be. I cracked a lid open, just barely, to see the unmissable form of Jonas Bauer sitting across from me.

"Do you wish to discuss it?"

CHAPTER TWO

Leo

I ignored him for the entire ride.

Well, almost the whole ride, until he apparently decided he wouldn't accept my ignoring him. The twenty minutes of focusing my attention outside of the car, attempting to admire the sunset, the towering pines, the craggy rocks on the far face of the mountain adjacent to us, ticked by like hour-long seconds. Though I wore a digital watch, Bauer's was analogue, and I could have sworn I could hear the second hand progressing each time it moved, scratching hash marks in the air as we descended the slope.

Every little tick of time ratcheted the tension in my chest tighter, tighter, until the mere act of breathing the same air as him made me want to snarl. But today, I didn't want to let out all that animal rage at him. I just wanted to get out and get home and be gone from this man who had everything I'd ever wanted in his pocket.

My determination to freeze him out, avoid conversation, and exit the car as soon as the doors swung open, evidently meant nothing to Jonas Bauer. As the base station came into view, he spoke.

"Ms. Morrison—"

I whipped around. I'd tried to be nice—or as close to it as I could when it came to this man, but no. He kept pecking at me, like he *wanted* me to bite his head off. "Would you at least do me the courtesy of using my first name like a normal human would do after knowing someone nearly a year?"

If possible, he straightened where he sat, though his posture and bearing were military in their precision and strictness. I hadn't let myself look at him, seeing as I'd planned to ignore him and leave as soon as possible, but now that I beheld him, my throat dried out and my hands gripped the bench on either side of my hips.

"My apologies...." His dark blond and silver brows—the same confusing color as his hair—furrowed, and he leaned forward, ever so slightly, a hand smoothing down one side of his unbuttoned slate gray suit jacket. "I meant no disrespect."

Something about his response surprised me. I had expected something equally annoying to his usual *Ms. Morrison* which thus far had served as his greeting, farewell, question, answer... that was almost all he ever said to me. And now this... *sincerity*.

I nodded once.

"Thanks. Good." I reached around for something else. "It's fine."

Our exchange must have stunned us both into silence, because we sat, eyes jumping to each other's faces, then away as the gondola car rumbled into the station. The doors cranked open and Bauer held out his hand, palm up, waiting for me to precede him out of the car.

His manners were impeccable. Unimpeachable, if one cared about manners and used words like *unimpeachable*. That had to be leftovers from my most recent historical romance read.

I hopped out of the car and walked out of the station, down the stairs after a wave to Jiff in the control room.

As much as Bauer's manners were perfect, I'd also classify his personality as dogged. So I knew, whatever it was he had on his mind, he wouldn't simply stop trying to address me because we weren't in the car. And though I prided myself on avoiding the man, or if I couldn't do that, on avoiding screaming at him like a banshee when he made me angry—which was virtually every encounter we ever had—I wouldn't classify myself as a coward, which meant I couldn't run away from him knowing this.

The light pats of his fine leather shoes followed me down the metal safety grated stairs. Reluctantly, I turned, wondering for the thousandth time since his first attempt to speak to me on the ride down what he wanted.

His face remained serious, as usual.

"Ms.—" He stopped, his lips pressing closed and jaw ticking when our eyes met. "Leonie, could I trouble you to find time for me Monday?"

Air compressed in my lungs as his words echoed in my head.

Not good. Very bad.

All of time slowed down as the sound of my name on his lips, my full name no one ever called me, pronounced with more German accent than he normally had, clocked me in the side of the head, nearly knocking me off balance.

Not Leo-nee. Not Lee-*oh*-nee.

Lay-oh-nee. But delicate. Soft, almost breathy. Like the tip of his tongue only *just* touched the back of his teeth to make the L sound. Like the name was light and familiar, not peculiar and troublesome.

Some maniac must have run by and punched me in the breadbasket like Danny used to do when we wrestled. Someone had smashed my lungs in their fists. Someone had made sounds disappear out of the air. That was the only excuse for this breathless, aching feeling in my gut when he said my name, just like I'd asked him to.

That voice...

I cleared my throat. *No.* Not happening. This didn't matter, didn't affect me, didn't mean a thing.

"Time?" If my own voice sounded a bit thin, a bit high, well... I was practically faint with hunger at this point, having skipped lunch to head to the peak. Foolish, especially for me.

His gaze never wavered. "A half hour, if you can spare it. A short meeting. To ensure we can cooperate."

Ah, there we go.

I nearly groaned at the word *cooperate.*

A fresh and immediate rush of dislike washed over my mind, and without effort, a sneering smile stretched over my lips. "Of course, Mr. Bauer. Ten?"

I sprawled out on my double bed as the exhaustion pulled me down. I felt old. I'd turn twenty-five in a few months and somehow, I felt twice that. The stress from Danny's injury, and though I'd kept it together fairly well, the utter terror on the drive to the hospital, waiting through his surgery, and even during recovery... I'd aged exponentially in those hours.

Frankly, this whole year had been exhausting, and the busiest months were just winding up. Fortunately, they were also my favorite months of the year—the first hint of freeze as we rounded into October, the chill and a surprise snowfall or two toward the end of the month. Then November and the insanity of prepping the lodge, creating scheduling for the *kinderschool* and hiring seasonal workers for both the kids' program and the adults'. Usually, we tested new instructors out in the days of snow-making before the season started if we didn't get a nice big dump of snow to help out with the base required to cover the runs and make opening the day after Thanksgiving possible.

"But it won't be the same," I said aloud to the ceiling of my tiny studio apartment.

By all rights, it was far too small for me at this stage—it barely fit my books—and yet I had no desire to move. I'd moved in the summer after high school, bound and determined to prove my independence despite the fact that my employer was the family business. No interview required.

Granted, I'd been working there, in one way or another, for most of my life, and on payroll at sixteen, as soon as I was legally allowed to be at the ticketing desk.

This place, a little over-the-garage apartment on a family friend's property, had been cheap enough to allow me to rent an apartment in Ogden too. I'd attended Miller State University there, got my degree in three years instead of four because I was a badass who had no boundaries when I set my mind to something, and still had a place to land that wasn't Ma and Da's when I came home weekends.

And I did. I came home every weekend. I made no attempt to build a life in the city during the semesters because I always knew I'd come back here. This place, Silverton, was in my blood. It *was* my blood. I'll raise a family here, and it'll be their blood too.

Well.... It would be if Jonas Bauer didn't systematically destroy everything my family had built over the last sixty years and edge the Morrison name out of every nook and cranny he could. Because the more I learned about him, the more we worked together—or, alongside each other, because *together* wasn't a thing when it came to me and him—the more I could see what no one else could.

The Silver Ridge Lodge—excuse me, now *Resort* like some kind of pompous Aspen private mountain for the wealthy—meant nothing but dollar signs to Bauer. Yes, he'd come in at a time when Liam had been about to lose his mind, and when I could begrudgingly admit we had no other options. But in the ten months since he first visited, he'd insinuated himself into everything.

Literally. First, he consulted for us. Then, he found an investor. So far, so good... right? *Sure.* But then... *THEN.*

Then he somehow finagled his way into acting as a representative for the investor—see what he did there? No longer on our team, but on the investor's—where the money was. And okay, sure, he ended his consulting contract and wasn't being paid by the lodge anymore, but he convinced everyone he still acted on the lodge's behalf when he was *working for the investor.*

How did no one see the issue? Liam was too awed by his ability to find someone who actually wanted to dump several million dollars into a floundering family business and thereby free my older brother to follow his pretty pretty princess dreams of full-time work at his brewery. Jamie didn't seem concerned, but he hadn't been here through the whole sketchy process. Danny was half in love with Jonas because in his eyes, the man was a fitness god riding in on a chariot of mountain-loving sunbeams or something.

But now... he'd gone too far. Of course I knew it was coming, but I'd pushed it out of my head and pretended it'd be okay. I couldn't keep doing that.

Now he'd taken Liam's job as mountain manager full-time, thereby making himself *the* person in charge. The person in charge and yet, as far as I knew, still the person acting as a liaison for the investor. Yes, there was a voting board he had to answer to, but because everyone viewed him as God's gift to Silver Ridge and in many ways, by extension, Silverton, no one would go against him.

Hello conflict of interest. How does no one see this!!?

No one but me.

And more than the potential for him to be doing seriously sketchy things with his fingers in every pot around the business, he'd taken what I'd always wanted. First Liam had, though when he'd taken over five years ago, I couldn't have since I was still in college and admittedly not experienced enough, and so I'd been forced to admit it wasn't entirely his fault. But now, Bauer.

He'd taken the mountain manager job, and in doing so, he'd taken something that was *mine*. The resort, the mountain, the possibly shifty agenda he had... that had all been problematic these last few months, but now?

Just thinking of that smug, serious face made me want to scream. It was frankly amazing I hadn't yelled at him the entire way down the mountain, and I could only credit exhaustion for that.

And whatever it was that'd set me even more off-kilter in that instant he'd said my name today... *that* didn't matter. It had nothing to do with anything. It certainly didn't negate that he stood in the way of my dream, stupid crisp suits and glasses and face and *everything*.

"*Ughghghghg*." I pressed the heels of my hands into my eyes. Damn this teary-eyed version of me. I didn't want to cry. I wanted to do something. I wanted to change all this. I wanted Jonas Bauer to leave on the high horse he rode in on and never come back.

How to make this happen, though?

CHAPTER THREE

Jonas

Ms. Morrison came calmly to the meeting Monday. *Unexpected.*

Customarily, she arrived just short of snarling any time we interacted.

I'd grown used to it, and I'd grown to relish it with a kind of sick masochism I could only blame on the look of her and how it muddled my reason.

Today, she wore fitted olive green utility pants with pockets on the sides of each slender leg and that tapered over her calf and ankle. Her navy sneakers were not ones I'd seen before, and a little over six months ago, I'd noticed she had a rather extensive collection.

I didn't allow a moment to take in the top half of the woman, knowing I'd find a build, posture, and some delectably fitted shirt I wouldn't want to look away from. Not professional, so I wouldn't look.

Though in my peripheral vision, while making eye contact as she sat in the chair across from me at the conference table, I noted a white V-neck T-shirt. Impossible to blur it out entirely. Two shining blond braids with streams of moonlight stitched in framed her neck and that impertinent chin that would no doubt be jutting out at me any moment.

Anticipation curled in my gut.

"Thank you for coming Ms.—" I pulled in a quick breath, adjusting course. "Leonie."

Her eyes shuttered momentarily, then shot to me with a nod. "Hello, Mr. Bauer."

If I smiled, I'd lose this congenial air between us. That wouldn't be all bad, but I couldn't let that slide. "Ah, but if I'm to call you by your given name, then shouldn't you afford me the same familiarity?"

She swallowed, that slim golden neck growing long as she straightened. "Hello, Jonas."

"Very good. Now..." I folded my hands on the table, casual, calm. "How will we proceed?"

Her face didn't change except for a small jump of her brows before her eyes moved to the stack of paper in front of her, handily avoiding my own gaze. "Could you be more specific?"

"Forgive me for being blunt, Leonie." She looked away from me as I continued. "Our relationship has been... contentious thus far."

Those glacier-blue eyes shot to mine. Truly, it felt a little like being knocked back a step each time I saw them.

Then there were all the times she'd refused to give me her eyes. The times she'd studiously avoided me, sometimes even when she stood right next to me. My gaze found her in any room, on any city block, on any snow-slicked shoot. Her power seemed to be evading me, or perhaps genuinely forgetting I existed. This served only to create a tedious, cloying feeling in me I couldn't escape until I did see them again.

"I'm not sure what you—"

"If you'll do me the courtesy of honesty, it would be most appreciated. Thus far, we've successfully avoided confronting the dynamic between us, but I can ignore it no more. My position here has changed, as you know, and with that change comes certain implications about our working together. Let us discuss it now, and move on."

She grew three inches as I spoke, her spine straightening, neck elongating, entire body seeming to stretch and take up more space. Her jaw seemed to sharpen, and there came the chin, lifting in challenge. "Fine."

Clearing my throat, I tamped down the desire to shake my head or perhaps grab her and shake some sense into *her*. How she tried me... "As the acting mountain manager, your department, ski education and childcare, like all others, falls under my direction."

Naturally, reminding her she fell under my management would serve me about as well as stealing a cub while the mama bear watched, but I couldn't resist. Plus, it was true.

Her jaw ticked, but nothing else moved. No blinking, no breath. Utter stillness. Perhaps her parents, the senior Morrisons, had detected this ability in her at birth—her surprising skill at making one feel singular and prey-like under her still, severe gaze.

"The previous mountain manager, your brother, Mr. Morrison—"

"Obviously I know who the previous manager was." Sharp.

I nodded slowly, like her blade-like words and knife-edge demeanor didn't faze me. It didn't... at least not in the way she wanted it to. And the way it *did* wouldn't be information either of us could use. "He allowed you to function at will, with only final approval on yearly budget planning and new projects."

Her chin lowered, and there came the eyes again. "Because I'm the best. I know what I'm doing, and I do it well. My instructors are top tier, my *kinderski* program is the best in the state, if not the region, and my management of the kinderschool and its daycare is literally award-winning."

She knew her worth. This woman couldn't fool anyone into thinking her a shrinking violet. She often blazed into a room, all impetuous energy. Her tendency to challenge me on anything, even when she didn't know what I would say or do, made my lungs burn. But this—her clarity when it came to her professional self... this made me burn in other ways. Strong women and their tenacious temperaments— my Kryptonite.

I sniffed, clearing my head of that path. "Yes. I have no disagreement with you on this matter."

Her mouth dropped open just a touch, but for Leonie Morrison in the context of a conversation with me, this proved a comically large reaction. It was almost as delicious as her anger. Perhaps I'd try surprising her more often just to see those full lips open without planning to.

"You don't?"

"I do not. I only wish to clarify that I will need approval on such things and to work out a proper timeline. I'd like to extend you more money, particularly to grow the *kinderski* program, and I believe you may want to hire more instructors. Our projections for the coming season may be hopeful, but they are not unrealistic. If the numbers are even remotely accurate, we will greatly exceed supply."

"You—" She cleared her throat and leaned forward, elbows on the table, silken strands of hair fluttering down in front of her face before she jerked her head to flick them out of her way. "You want to give me *more* money?"

"Yes."

"And you want me to maintain control of the programs."

"Yes."

"And you'll give me free creative reign over said programs?"

A low chuckle escaped.

"Perhaps not entirely, but I have no desire to hamper your natural abilities. If you'd had proper budgetary support and the population had grown, your program would already have achieved renown. The fact that it hasn't is merely a reflection of the isolation this community has dealt with so far." I picked up the stack of papers in front of me and straightened it as I continued. "If I have my way, and I'll tell you without ego, I always do, then your program, and this resort, will be an inescapably attractive beacon drawing people the world over to Silverton."

Her focus shifted around the room, as though looking at me didn't make sense so she had to search for meaning in the darkened corners of the conference room. Then she picked up the papers in front of her and scooted back in her chair. She stood, so I did too.

When she spoke, her voice held less steel and more complexity than I'd ever heard when she directed it at me.

"Well, then, I hope you do get your way."

CHAPTER FOUR

Leo

I maintained calm all the way out of the conference room. I walked the hallway, my strides unusually long, and entered the small staff restroom just before the daycare rooms. I shut the door, turned the lock with a sharp click, and sank butt-to-heels against the panel, the papers he'd placed in front of my seat on the table and that I hadn't yet looked at crumpled under one arm.

Had there been an invasion of body snatchers? Had some benevolent alien life force taken Jonas Bauer's soul and replaced it with one less maddeningly mercenary?

No. Couldn't be. He was still there in all his familiar glory.

If I have my way, and I always do...

"Ughhhh." I let it out, that pent-up pressure.

If they hadn't snatched Bauer's body, then maybe they had taken mine. That was the only explanation for why his saying my name flooded me with awareness. It was the only possible reason why his stupid mannerly politeness and whacked phraseology made me feel a little lightheaded.

Surely, alien invaders were the only way to rationalize the fluttery, restless feeling that grew as he explained his plan to give me more money, more freedom, *more.* The dizzying effect of his gray gaze and his intensity and his...

My head fell to my knees, my eyes shut, and I blew out a breath. Then I pushed up against the door to standing again, a refreshing burn in my quads bringing me back to myself.

I'd walked into the conference room this morning expecting battle. I usually did when it came to him, because we'd always been at opposite ends. He represented everything I hated, and he disliked me. He'd come to make my life a series of small and large frustrations capped by daily disappointments and life-long dreams squashed. He'd busted into our family business, sold out to an investor, and attempted to take over the business as mountain manager.

Hadn't he?

Yet there he sat, his navy suit this morning looking irritating and requiring words like *bespoke* and *tailored* and *deliciously flattering.* Then the name-saying, the complimenting me professionally like that wasn't Leo Morrison's catnip number one, and suggesting if I left it up to him, he'd make *me* and my family's business more successful than we might ever have hoped...

Somewhere, he'd read a manual on me, and today, he'd brought out the big guns to lull me into submission.

Wear a suit that makes you look professional, painfully attractive, but leave the tie so the small dip at the base of your throat will cause her to think about very non-work-related things.

Tell her she's smart. Tell her she does a good job. Tell her she's the best.

Offer her money, success, the satisfaction of dreams.

Say her name.

"*Ugghhhhhhhh.*" The groan sounded in the small, tiled bathroom.

I moved to splash water on my face and glared into the mirror where little drops skated over my cheeks and dripped off my chin into the sparkling white basin beneath.

"You will get your act together. You will *not* be lulled into grateful passivity by this seemingly generous and ideal gesture of his. You will find his ulterior motive, then you'll find *his* manual, and you'll use it against him."

I wandered down Main Street, debating which new book I'd start after dinner. The workday had dribbled by like a summer stream in the desert, and I could have sworn I could sense Bauer wherever he moved in the building, even though that was ludicrous because I never left my small desk tucked in the staff room just before the childcare wing.

Despite it being Monday, and my policy not to eat out too often because it was more expensive than eating from home and I always felt sluggish the next day, I'd called in an order to *Guac*. I wished I could have called an emergency girls' meeting and vented my frustration, my disbelief, and my... *well, I probably wouldn't have vented* that.

But as I paced aimlessly in front of *Guac* and *Craic*, I was reminded just how far away Bel was. *Rise and Shine* was closed this time of day anyway, but the darkened storefront might as well have been shut down for good.

I mean no, not really. I loved the place, loved Sadie's bread and the coffee and the bright yellow walls, but my visits weren't as regular these last few weeks since Bel had moved. Why should they be? I no longer had the excuse to see my best friend every morning, and buying coffee really wasn't economical.

"Leo, order up," Luis called from the little takeout door next to the restaurant's main entrance.

"Thanks. See you soon."

I grabbed the bag and began my journey home. I didn't normally run around in my work clothes, which were nothing fancy—no *bespoke suits* or anything—but they weren't workout gear. But I also knew if I speed-walked home, I'd make it in approximately twenty minutes versus more like thirty if I walked normally. And having a bag full of piping hot Mexican comfort food paired with the prospect of beginning a new book in the quiet of my own space... that was worth some effort.

"Whoa Leo, where you heading?" Liam asked as I passed the Silverton Inn where he and Wells stood, wrapped around each other in a typically gushy display of newlywed bliss.

A pang of... something... shot through my chest as I slowed, wishing I could just keep moving. "Hey guys. Just grabbed some take out so I've got to get going so it doesn't grow cold."

Wells smiled wide and Liam pulled back a bit to track me as I passed on the sidewalk. "You going to be ready for the board meeting on Friday?"

"I'm always ready. Are you going to make it?"

"Of course. I'm not giving up my board position—I wouldn't."

His face had that disappointed, maybe even hurt, look

on it. The same one he got whenever I didn't show complete and utter faith in his perfect, heroic tendencies.

"Good. See you then. And Wells... girls' night soon?"

She agreed with a smile and wave as I picked up my pace, pushing up the hill toward the lodge, then past it, down the road toward Ma and Da's house, and finally turning down the long lane that led to the farmhouse and my miniscule little sanctuary.

I stomped up the stairs and shucked my shoes at the door, scampered to the bathroom to rinse off because, annoyingly, I'd worked up a sweat and refused to eat this meal all sweaty and disgusting. Plus, I wanted sweatpants.

My internal drive never steered me wrong, and right now, it told me I needed comfort on all fronts—comfort food, comfy clothes, and comfort entertainment in the form of a historical romance by my favorite author.

Once settled onto the couch to watch *Pride and Prejudice*—because one can't easily eat Mexican food one-handed so the reading would wait until I finished dinner—I let out a long, shuddering breath. I'd been doing that a lot lately.

And as I sat there, shoveling guacamole into my mouth with perfectly salted chips, Keira Knightley charming crusty old Darcy on my screen, and the peace of my little studio apartment surrounding me, I knew what was coming. I hated it, and yet I welcomed them, like I had so often and predictably in recent days.

The tears hit by my fifth chip.

In the weeks since Danny's engagement, I'd cried more tears than I had since Da's heart attack. Part of me wished I didn't feel like crying—that his engagement to Mia and the official signaling that everyone around me was moving on to the next phase of their lives didn't make me feel this consuming, aching, crushing sadness.

I didn't begrudge them their happiness. I was so happy for each of them—Liam and Wells, Jamie and Bel, Danny and Mia. But it left me at loose ends, unsure of what my life would look like, and honestly, a little scared. I didn't have any prospects. Everyone I'd considered in the past had turned out to be a bust—even the most promising of them, Wyatt Saint. He was a great guy, but I couldn't summon much more than acknowledgement of his overall perfection... there was nothing beyond that but friendship. My mind knew he would be amazing, but my heart and body couldn't get with the program.

So my nights turned to this more often than not. Me sitting in front of the TV or a book and letting out what felt a lot like grief for the life I used to have and a little like fear I'd never have what my brothers and friends had found.

A life not so different from what it was now, except I wasn't quite so alone in my singleness or the lack of clarity in my future.

CHAPTER FIVE
____

Jonas

The board meeting, which should have been straightforward, productive, and brief, crashed and burned like a forty car pile-up in a white-out snowstorm.

"Leo, calm down. He's just doing his job." Liam Morrison shook his head and pulled at his beard.

Looking at Liam's sister would tell me nothing I didn't already know. She'd arrived enraged, evidently finding something in the paperwork I'd set out to discuss during our meeting Monday entirely unacceptable, and our usual warring dynamic had snapped into place before the meeting ever began.

Nothing about her arrival, her mood, or her accusations shocked me, other than it'd taken her so long to identify my demands and deem them unacceptable, just as I'd imagined.

"You don't need to tell me to calm down, Liam. That's the best possible way to get me to be as opposite from calm as you can imagine. My point is valid—he came to me Monday saying I'd have free reign, he'd give me more money, blah blah blah. Then I sift through this agreement and tucked into the last few paragraphs are literally five different ways of saying he's in control, he can veto anything I plan, and he requires weekly check-ins." Her fiery gaze shifted to me. "Micromanage much?"

"I understand how you could think that. However, I only wish to cultivate a working relationship in the near term so that as we proceed, we have a foundation from which to work. We have not, historically, managed to cooperate effectively. I do not believe that will come organically. Therefore, I have created a plan to counteract our natural... antipathy."

Her bright, blazing blue eyes blinked back at me in shock, or maybe disbelief. Her mouth, which rarely deprived me of some clever, scathing assault, remained shut.

Liam cleared his throat as the shifting, uncomfortable sounds of Daniel Morrison, and the six other board members around the table, scraped into the air, and Bel Paxton and Jamie Morris on video conference awkwardly studied anything but the screen.

Had I said something untoward? *Oh, dear me.*

Liam broke the strain. "It's not a bad plan. And I should mention that we do need you to cooperate on something in the near term. I'd hoped to help out with the visiting prospective investors for Oktoberfest in a few weeks, but with the uptick in production for the brewery, and the opening night coming just a week later, I really can't be the point man on this."

"Say no more. Ms. Morrison and I will get it done—we understand everyone else is committed elsewhere."

I'd always intended to push the board in the direction of

multiple investors, but the resistance to the first investor had surprised me, plus we'd had a large initial sum with the first investment. I'd brought the vote back to the board this summer and everyone, even Leonie, had agreed pursuing another investor would only bolster our progress.

At my statement, Leonie simply nodded in agreement, but didn't meet my eye again, nor anyone else's for that matter. She might have been acting subdued, but I knew better.

By meeting's end, the irritated, restless feeling that climbed the rungs of my spine had reached the base of my skull.

Donnerwetter.

The German curse popped to mind like so many others, but no one brought out such expletives like her.

Something about her silence, far more than her tendency to argue, or even accuse me of being underhanded or controlling, drove me insane.

The woman was meant to fight, and if she wanted to fight with me... fine. Often, I welcomed it, provoked it, looked forward to it like a good meal. Small surrenders like this one, even if they were a purposefully icy freeze-out designed to elicit my own surrender, didn't sit well.

The meeting adjourned, everyone broke, some staying to chat, Jamie signing off and Bel confirming she'd check in with a marketing update next week. I pushed in my chair and nodded to Mr. Reiner, Mr. Sanchez, and Ms. Calloway, devoted and, might I add, helpfully cooperative members of the Silver Ridge board.

"Leonie." I spoke quietly enough from about ten feet behind her, but Liam and Daniel Morrison, who strolled together just in front of me, whirled around to stare at me.

"Gentlemen."

"Bauer," they both chimed, odd smiles on both their faces.

"Leonie." My steps ate the ground between us despite her acceleration. I almost reached out to grab her wrist and turn her to me, make her give me those eyes, but I hadn't touched her since the first time we met when we shook hands last November. Not a single time since then.

Not once.

Didn't mean my hand didn't nearly shake with the drive to wrap my fingers around her slim wrist and jerk her to face me.

Her skin would be smooth. Warm. The arm firm but soft, not unlike the rest of her... I had not forgotten anything of that very first—and only—touch of her.

"Ms. Morrison."

That got her. I nearly smiled.

"Mr. Bauer." Her voiced dripped disdain.

The Morrison brothers kept walking, though I could feel their occasional looks back at us.

"When can you meet next week?" I asked, hoping the question would quell some of the frustration wafting off her.

She cocked her head to the side. "Shouldn't you be the one to tell me that?"

"I don't know your schedule. You must tell me when you have time for me."

She crossed her arms. "Don't you? You've dictated weekly meetings, and now you've agreed, without my consent, might I add, to work together to get the prospective investor on board in a matter of weeks. I'm not sure I have time for anything *but* you."

I stepped closer, unwilling to raise my voice even

though I wanted to. *Heiliger Strohsack*, how I longed to tear into her and *make* her see all this indignation and anger didn't need to plague us. We did fine on Monday... why couldn't that last?

"I apologize for failing to consult you. There didn't seem to be an alternative as your brother is unable to assist. I hope you'll find it in yourself to overcome your frustration so we may move beyond this."

Her mouth opened, then she snapped it shut.

Fine.

I shoved my hands into the pockets of my suit pants, affecting a casual mien and resisting the urge to grind my molars to dust with frustration. People usually got along with me fine. Why did this woman test me so much? "If you refuse to assist me in scheduling our meeting, then I'll be forced to do it myself. See you Tuesday at nine. My office. At least two hours."

Her eyes remained hard, ice, and yes, I could see hate there. The creeping wave of red ire that swept up her neck, cheeks, and into her hairline signaled I should brace for a death blow. She'd parry, I'd block, we'd go at it a moment, and then she'd most likely storm off, leaving me to feel both shame and pleasure as she retreated.

But rather than yell or rage at me, her whole energy changed like she'd thrown a switch. Her brow smoothed, a placid, perplexingly sweet smile slid over her lips, and her voice didn't falter as she spoke in a smooth, slow tone. "Certainly, Mr. Bauer. See you at nine on Tuesday."

She turned and walked away, her stride unhurried and downright graceful. I didn't take in the lazy sway of her hips or the fact that her black slacks hugged her legs, nor could I appreciate the waterfall of wavy blond hair spilling almost to her lower back, the sides pulled behind and contained in a braid today.

I couldn't appreciate any of these things after she'd left in such an uncharacteristic way. I could only feel a confusing mixture of dread and disappointment, and a blistering anticipation for Tuesday morning.

CHAPTER SIX

Leo

L iam caught up with me on Sunday. And by *caught up with*, I mean he came banging on my door in the middle of my sob-fest after the self-flagellating exercise to punish myself into tears known as watching *The Notebook*.

"Whoa, what's wrong?" he asked, hovering at the threshold.

I turned and wandered back toward the couch where I slumped. He followed and sat on the other end.

"But really, what's going on?"

I pressed my lips together, feeling a sob gather in my chest. I had no desire to blubber to my oldest brother who I rarely actually got along with, but surprisingly, he was the first person to ask me anything I could answer honestly.

"This movie destroys me every time." I clicked the remote so the menu for the movie showed.

"Ah. Yeah. Brutal. Lovely, but totally brutal."

He gave me a kind smile, which was so like him, and I chuckled hopelessly. "Yeah. It really is."

We sat quietly, just the looped music from the movie's menu accompanying us. I wondered why he'd come, what criticism he might submit me to and how I'd respond. Normally, just being near him made my hackles rise, which was one of many mysteries about myself I hadn't solved. But today, I felt stripped, like a wooden chair left out all winter, all traces of varnish or paint or softness banished by the elements and leaving only a brittle frame in place.

I snorted softly. *Good grief,* I'd vaulted squarely into dramatic internal monologue.

Liam must've taken the small sound as clearance to speak. "So why are you sitting home on a Sunday afternoon torturing yourself with Ryan Gosling and Rachel McAdams as your chosen weapons?"

"Well, I often sit home on Sunday afternoons." I pressed my lips together, wondering what would happen if I told him. Would he use it against me?

"And?" He folded his hands in his lap like he'd wait patiently all day until I told him. Liam Morrison, resident psychologist.

"And what? Can't a girl watch a destructively beautiful romance with too-pretty people and sob uncontrollably for half an hour afterwards without being criticized by her older brother?" I curled my knees to my chest and hugged them to me.

Instead of taking my bait for argument, he smiled one of those sweet, concerned smiles. Distressingly, I couldn't find it in myself to hate it. No, I welcomed it—water from a well I hadn't encountered in miles.

"Sure she can. But this paired with... everything else? It tells me something's up, and I wanted to check on you." He surveyed my face, my hair, with his gaze, then a quick tour of the apartment, before landing back on me expectantly. "What's up, Leo?"

As soon as I decided to speak, my throat locked up. I tried to swallow but the muscles there tightened. I forced a gulp of water down, cleared my throat. Still no. I smoothed several wayward strands of hair out of my eyes, then pinched my mouth together until my insides settled and I knew I could form words without crying.

"I'm so lonely." And there came the tears. Tears, and crushing humiliation at the admission, especially to Liam, with whom I'd always been in a strange kind of competition even though it made no sense—or maybe it did, because he'd taken my mountain and lodge away from me first... or so it'd seemed to me for so long. I pulled my knees tighter to me.

"Aw, Leo. I'm sorry." His voice sounded genuinely tortured, and he scooted closer, then pulled me into a hug. He spoke into my hair. "You're not alone. I'm here, Danny's here. Wells loves you..."

"I know. And I'm... grateful. I don't want to take away from that. I don't *want* to feel this way."

I pulled back from him and wiped angrily at the tears in my eyes, then let my knees drop into a tailor sit so I could explain. I'd made it this far—the worst part was out there, and he hadn't laughed. Not that I'd *really* expected him to, but I'd trained myself to keep my guard up with him, and dropping it so completely left me feeling triply exposed. But the hug had bolstered the sense that I could tell him the truth.

"You don't want to feel lonely?" His head tilted to the side in question as he waited for my answer.

I pulled a slow inhale through my nose, begging my chest, heart, sad little soul, to calm.

"I don't want to feel envious of what you have. What Bel and Jamie or Danny and Mia have. I don't want to feel —" I cleared my throat hard. "Sorry for myself."

He sighed. "You're about the least pitiable person I've ever known, so I can understand your natural resistance toward self-pity. But tell me what you mean."

"I'm ashamed to feel this way... this jealousy over what you have. It's not that I begrudge any of you. That's what makes it so stupid—I am so freaking thrilled for all of you. I'm glad. I'm *happy*. But at the same time, I am so so sad for myself. And... *ughghg*." The groan encapsulated a myriad of feelings.

He patted my hand, a small frown hiding under his brown beard. "That all seems really normal. I know you're happy for all of us—we all do. Granted, you sometimes cause more trouble than any one person can handle, but I might not even be with Wells if it weren't for you, and Bel and Jamie can say the same. Wanting someone for yourself doesn't mean you're selfish."

I remembered running to Wells and telling her about Liam's supposed plan to talk her into selling her land last winter and cringed. I'd definitely caused more trouble than I'd meant. "For the record, I thought you were lying to her. You know I can't stand that. But I did apologize, and I'll say it again—I should have gone to you first."

"Yes, you should have. But that's done now, and it all worked out in the end." He raised his left fist in a cheesy display of the dark wedding band on his hand.

I summoned a chuckle, but it sounded hollow. "Why can't I just be happy, and leave it at that? I thought I'd made peace with being single and going on disappointing dates every few months. I thought I'd be okay with that. But ever since you and Wells came back and Bel left and Danny got engaged, I just feel... lost."

"I'm sorry. And I hope you aren't upset with Wells for not tell you about—"

I waved him off.

"No. *No.* You guys did what was right, and knowing her story, I can't be upset. You got married the way you and she wanted, and that's beautiful." My voice broke. "But everyone I love is moving on to this next phase. Not just one person, but *everyone.* And honestly, the few guys I thought might work for me around this ridiculously small town... let's just say, they haven't panned out."

"That sucks."

"Yeah."

"But I know the feeling. Moving back here was absolutely what I wanted, but my dating life tanked the day I set foot back here. If Wells hadn't come along, I'd be single, occasionally going into the city to have dinner with a friend or meet someone, wishing I could find the person I was meant to be with." He fiddled with the band on his ring finger.

"I didn't realize that. But I'm glad she came along." And I was. I'd had a front row seat to Liam and Wells' relationship, and as much as he and I fought, I'd felt privileged to help them along where I could. Granted, I'd had a mighty hand in potentially destroying them too, so I couldn't actually take credit. Point was, they were good together.

"Yep. So there's the crux of it, right? Don't give up. You're only twenty-four, for starters. That's *so* young, Leo. I don't mean it as an insult, I just mean... give it time. Who knows what interesting kinds of dudes are going to move into town? Maybe Jack McKean or one of Jamie's other fancy Hollywood friends will move to Silverton and sweep you off your feet."

We chuckled together, and a sliver of my sad little shell of a heart glimmered back to life. "Yeah, I won't hold my breath on that. Plus even if they did, sounds like Jonas Bauer will have me chained to the lodge, reporting my every move, so I can't imagine I'd have time to have a dating life anyway."

"It's not that bad, and you know it," he chided.

I rolled my eyes. "I know. I'm just... pissed. I'm a mess."

I slumped back into the cushions of the couch.

"In other news, we just had an entire conversation without arguing or criticizing each other." He flashed his eyebrows up and down.

I genuinely laughed at that. "True. Someone note the day and time."

"Already done." He pretended to tap a message into his phone. "But really, I know we don't talk like this unless one of us is having an emotional crisis, but I'd like to do it more often. Without having to come to the table with verbal battle axes at the ready."

"I'm up for it. I've got Jonas to contend with more regularly now, so I probably need to make sure my armies of wit and ire aren't spread too thin."

A laugh tripped out of him at that. "Fair enough. And just as an observation, that's the first time I've heard you refer to him by his first name. I heard him call you *Leonie* after the meeting Friday. Maybe the ice is thawing?"

Had I just used his given name? Good grief... What was happening to me?

I rolled my eyes. "No. Another weird form of professional chicken, or something. I don't know."

"Well, I'm impressed you got him to surrender his

formality. A chink in his armor, maybe. And you could let it inject a little congeniality into things... he made a strong case for getting rid of the *antipathy*, as he called it."

I shook my head. "Yeah. Didn't expect him to go for it that explicitly, but I can't deny it's an apt descriptor."

Something about him naming the dynamic between us had sent a cold flush through my lungs. I'd felt...embarrassed. I'd felt juvenile and like I could do better. Maybe that was what had me working so hard lately not to react the way I historically had with him.

"I wonder if you'll end up actually liking working with him if you can move past all the... negativity."

I smiled at that. "Here's hoping. Easier to comply with all those demands for now before I pursue my own agenda."

CHAPTER SEVEN

Leo

My placid demeanor knew no bounds. Call me Zen master, a woman ruled by the glacier inside me—only cool, calculating logic and agreeable, pliant cooperation at my disposal.

"Good morning, Jonas."

There, I'd said his name again. It meant nothing. Nothing at all. Just courtesy. Me being Miss Congeniality was all. Getting rid of the antipathy, as he'd called it. Yes. That.

His gray eyes tracked me as I entered his office, and he stood as I came in, then sat once I did. "Good morning."

He'd taken the official mountain manager's office which had most recently been occupied by my dad. For some reason, Liam had never moved in there; I guessed because he'd never intended to keep the job as long as he had.

Jonas seemed entirely at ease in the space, though not

because of any relaxed posture or demeanor. No, his face presented as severe as always, his jaw ready to slice anything that came in contact with it, his gaze ready to destroy cities at a glance.

I mean, obviously not really, but the man had an aura and it was intense.

The curved wall of windows behind him showcased a glorious view of Silver Ridge Peak and its sibling mountains —the range so familiar and lovely, sometimes even I neglected to enjoy it the way I should.

If I walked into the center of the curve and looked right, I would be able to see the plaza and the gondola station. Directly ahead would be the *kinderski* area when the snow came. I'd spent many afternoons as a kid sitting right here coloring or reading while my dad worked.

"Where shall we start?" I asked, feeling surprisingly plucky since I'd decided, after Liam left Sunday night, that I'd find a way to work with Jonas no matter what.

Discovering his plan to micromanage my work and essentially shackle me to him through weekly meetings, not to mention his volunteering us to head up the greeting party for the prospective investor... Normally, I would've lost it. I'd never felt more enraged by a single human being in my life.

But on Friday, just when I would've loved to blow my lid, I'd locked it down. I remembered my goals—to keep Silver Ridge in the family, to help it grow, and to eventually be at the helm of the whole operation.

I wouldn't be able to take it all away from him if I kept up walking in like a Valkyrie in battle. I'd switch gears and use strategy this time around.

Jonas hadn't looked away from me, but finally, his eyes

shifted to his computer screen for just a moment. "Would you like to update me on your department?"

Yelling at the current mountain manager and investor liaison would not lead me to success. This would be the mantra I'd chant every time he required me to do this check-in. Not that he wasn't entitled to the information—I managed the largest department, and he'd already said he wanted to increase the budget and let me grow the programs. What I resented was that he was my boss at all—that this man, an outsider, had any say in the future of my family's business.

"Not much has changed since last Monday when we originally met. You have an outline of all my childcare and instructional staffing needs, as well as my plans for the *kinderski* and adult lesson programming increases. I don't have much else to report, nor will I until November, at the earliest. I'm not sure what else I can tell you, unless you need help understanding my summaries." I folded my hands in my lap over the smooth fabric of my skirt and tilted my head, waiting for his response.

I'd dressed professionally today—black pencil skirt with a fitted, flattering pale blue button-down shirt tucked neatly into the waistband. Not that I wasn't typically dressed appropriately, but I wore what we called "mountain attire" which consisted of jeans or cargo pants and some kind of branded Silver Ridge Lodge shirt or sometimes a blouse, or in winter, ski-ready clothes. The job demanded hands-on interaction from November through April with kids, and being on the mountain itself teaching lessons. In the off-season, we'd always kept it fairly casual.

But Jonas wore a suit and tie at almost all times. I'd experienced a mild shock when I saw him in running shorts and a T-shirt at the triathlon in August because I had never seen him in shorts or a casual T. He'd worn branded polos and khakis or cargo pants the other days of the Sommerfest, presumably only because he did have to do some dirty work with barricades and fest tables and other equipment. I'd been shocked to see how muscular and fit he was, though it shouldn't have been a surprise.

But now, as usual, he sat across from me at the light wooden desk bedecked in a dark charcoal suit, crisp white shirt, and black tie. Even his wardrobe, undoubtedly crafted from the finest silks and wools or whatever fine suits were made of, was sharp. The desk itself featured no personal touches whatsoever, only a new computer and what I was fairly sure was his personal laptop, which sat closed in a thin silver clasp on the table in front of him.

"Very well."

His words shook me from my survey of the space. "Very well?"

He nodded. "Yes."

My chest tightened with irritation. Why have the meeting at all if he wasn't going to even talk to me? "Do you have any questions?"

His jaw ticked. I only saw the movement because nothing else in the whole room moved.

"I do not. Though it may surprise you, I am not a simpleton, nor do I require being spoken to as though I were one."

I stifled a gasp. Yes, a *gasp*. This man had no qualms about reading insults into every word I spoke. "I didn't mean to imply you're a—"

"I think perhaps you did, Leonie. You believe this is an unnecessary meeting foisted upon you by an egomaniacal dimwit. I hope, after we've spent a bit more time together, you'll discover I am neither of those things."

My heart thundered in my ears as his words sank in. Had I really made him think I believed that? No part of me would consider him anything but extremely, dangerously intelligent. "I'm sorry."

He shook his head to the left just once, and even though he didn't actually move, something about his demeanor softened. "No apology necessary. I fear our interactions haven't given you a very good impression of me. I hope to rectify that."

We'd never met one-on-one until last week. Every other interaction had been in passing, or in a larger meeting, or on the street when I'd done little more than glare at him. It was an embarrassing picture of my ability to adjust to something new. Even if I hated what he stood for... even if I hated the way he wielded his position. I could do better.

I would.

"I—okay. Let's do that."

His eyes captured mine, and though my heart should have slowed by now, it kept churning, his gaze like a touch across the desk. Then he dipped his head to his laptop and opened the lid, and just the corner of his mouth tilted, ever so slightly, into what must have been some version of a smile for Jonas Bauer.

So, with that warm invitation, I opened my own laptop, and we continued.

CHAPTER EIGHT

Jonas

How she tested me.

Every question I asked, she'd answer before I finished asking it. Every time I submitted a sense of concern or anything beyond utter praise, she pulled in a deep breath, took a moment, and then addressed the issue so thoroughly, I couldn't find anything to say in response but "Good." This woman had prepared for battle, and she wanted to leave me in no doubt about it.

She was easily the most maddening, inescapably compelling woman I'd ever met, and sitting across the desk from her for over an hour had done nothing to allay that opinion.

I'd spent the initial six months of our acquaintance feeling simultaneously repelled and drawn to her. Repelled, because she truly did assault me verbally the first few times we exchanged anything more than the one and only hand-shake when we met last November.

She'd viewed me as an interloper coming to destroy the Morrison family business. Some of that, her brother had explained amidst profuse apologies and embarrassed sighs after a particularly scathing video conference in January last year, was due to her concern that outside investments would eventually lead to the Morrison family having to sell, or not being the actual or technical owners of the resort.

She'd also resisted that—the terming of the place a *resort* rather than *lodge* like they'd called it for the first sixty years. But lodge made it sound like just a building—a big, beautiful, well-maintained one, yes, but it didn't suggest that what lay beyond the lodge was one of the most beautiful mountains I'd ever seen.

I'd won on the investor. I'd won on the renaming and calling it resort. And gradually, despite her inability to see me as a mere mortal working with and for her family, I'd come to see her as compelling rather than simply a juvenile, brash, rage-fueled temptation.

Because there was the other truth of the matter. Leonie Morrison was, without exception, the most beautiful woman I'd ever seen.

Then she'd open her mouth and murder any interest I might've had for her.

I didn't fully understand why she found me, in particu-lar, so entirely unacceptable. She'd been at least moderately polite to Karla, my partner at Bauer Group and long-time friend. But me? She'd frozen me out at first, then literally yelled at me and accused me of, what was it? Ah yes, she'd said, *"If you had any integrity at all, you wouldn't be trying to destroy what my family has built over nearly sixty years just for profit. You should be ashamed of yourself."*

My consolation was that she roundly misunderstood my purposes here. I had no desire to destroy a family-run business for pleasure. It wasn't that simple. I understood the value of the place *and* the people. My motives were my own, and all she need know was that all I did day in and day out here was work to grow the resort.

That said, if I had set out to buy and sell the place outright, which I could do any day of the week without breaking a sweat, I would never feel shame. It was business.

"Are you satisfied?" she asked, cutting through my wandering mind.

We'd each been reviewing a spreadsheet and some scheduling appointments on our computers as we sat across from each other, and my mind had roamed. But that phrase certainly bit through the ambling thoughts. Could she be angry with me again, already, for no reason yet again?

"Have I upset you again? I—"

"No. *No.* I didn't mean that to sound so... combative. I simply mean, do you feel we've done what you set out to do today? Are you satisfied with our time, and if so, I'd like to meet again this time next week before Oktoberfest kicks off the following week." She tugged at the end of her long braid, then dropped her hand.

Strange, her being nice, cooperating even. It left me flummoxed, but I pulled on years of business dealing experience and gathered my wits again.

"Of course. Yes. We'll meet again next week. I'll complete the presentation if you'll send me your slides by Monday. We can review Tuesday, and then we'll have another week to address any concerns before the all-staff meeting the following Wednesday and Oktoberfest the next day. Acceptable?"

I met her gaze—typically a perilous affair except today, when the usual frigid ice storm appeared to have calmed.

"Yes. Acceptable."

She gathered her things and left without another word, though she did nod cordially as a farewell. We hadn't graduated to verbalized greetings and departures, but gestures were new, and showed signs of progress.

My life in Silverton was a solitary one. Not immensely different from the life I'd led before moving here from New York, except for the drastic scene change. But the beauty of this place was not a passive kind of beauty—it demanded. It *took*. It stole one's soul if one let it. I suspected if I stayed long enough, it would own mine.

I'd let an apartment upon arrival here, but had recently moved into the mountain manager's cabin located just off the lodge's main building. Liam Morrison now lived with his new wife and had suggested I take the cabin since it had always been meant to accommodate the mountain manager. The cabin's proximity to the lodge proved optimal, so I complied. The home I'd recently purchased wouldn't be completed until early next year.

Small town life seemed far more routine in some ways, though as a creature of habit, I would call any given day no matter where I was routine. I'd moved here, created a new routine, and rarely deviated from it.

"Here you go, Mr. Bauer."

Garrett, an employee of the coffee shop where I took coffee every morning, set an espresso in front of me where I sat near the window of the bright yellow shop.

I arrived every morning at the same time to work a bit

over an espresso, and had done so since I'd relocated to Silverton months ago. Of course I could make my own coffee, but I liked the change of scene, liked the sense of community even if I stood on its fringes, and liked the predictable arrival of—

"Leo, what can I get you?" Garrett asked as he scuttled back to his post behind the counter, his pale cheeks flushed just from the sight of her.

She did look particularly appealing today—though I'd yet to get a glimpse of her when that couldn't be said. Fitted jeans, long-sleeved T-shirt in a blue that made her eyes seem to glow, hair in long twin braids. She didn't always come, and hadn't been in nearly as often in the last few weeks since Bel Paxton's departure, but when she did, the day began... differently than the rest of them.

"Bauer—er, Jonas, 'morning." She gave me a small smile which sent a pang through me and that I directly excused as hunger.

"Good morning, Leonie."

Her lashes fluttered twice, then she turned to the counter where Garrett spoke to her in an exhausting stream of consciousness I immediately tuned out. I shifted back to my computer, seeing a long list of e-mails waiting. Not many related to Silver Ridge management, but at least twenty relating to Bauer Group, my investment firms, and a few properties. Since Silverton was on mountain time and therefore two hours behind the east coast and a full eight hours behind many of my European colleagues, I usually woke to a full inbox.

"I'm glad you're here, actually. I wanted to talk to you about what to wear for the fest and make sure we're on the same page." She set a plate with a large slice of bread slathered with butter on the table next to me, but didn't sit.

My eyes flicked up to her, which she was clearly waiting for. "May I?"

"Of course." I would have reached for the back of the chair and pulled it out for her, or stood up, but she was so close, if I'd done that, we would have collided. A not-small part of me wondered what it might be like to physically collide with her, rather than just verbally do so regularly, but I slapped that thought away and gestured to the chair, which she promptly occupied.

She placed her coffee mug next to her plate and scooted in, then surveyed my set-up—computer, small leather-bound notebook, espresso cup and saucer. "Did you have something to eat?"

"I don't typically eat this early. I rarely feel hungry this time of day." I preferred to wait until lunch if I could, but would sometimes have a few boiled eggs or perhaps some granola and yogurt.

"Amazing. I think I'm always hungry."

She focused in on the bread and took a monstrous bite, then her eyes closed and perhaps I should have looked away because the face she made seemed like something only a lover should see. But I sat there, rapt, unable to do anything but watch her full lips close as her jaw moved to chew the bread, then swallow, then tilt up into a smile and loose a sigh so satisfied, I had to clear my throat or I might have mimicked it just to see if I'd ever made a sound so sweet.

Too soon, her eyes opened to find me watching. "Oh, sorry. I'm starving today after my run and I love their sunflower whole wheat."

"I believe you. Where do you like to run?" I asked as though I didn't know.

"Usually, I do the trails, but I'm thinking of running a half marathon in the spring and won't run much over the ski season so I figured I'd try to do some road running. I followed Elk River up the canyon a few miles." She sipped her coffee from a bright blue mug the same color as my espresso cup.

Everything in the shop was obnoxiously bright, but watching Leonie drink coffee from the mug, suddenly it all made sense. The robin's egg blue of the shop was almost exactly the color of her eyes.

She raised a light brown brow as she drank more coffee, her blue eyes flashing amusement over the rim of the mug. "Everything okay, Jonas?"

"Ah, yes." I smoothed down my tie. "What did you wish to discuss?"

Her face shuttered. "Oh, right. The family always wears traditional German clothing for Oktoberfest."

I nodded.

"Do you happen to have something that would work?"

I pressed my lips together, unwilling to smile at her question. "Are you assuming I have lederhosen because I have German heritage?"

She glanced at her lap, then sat taller in her seat and frowned at me. "I didn't mean to offend you. I—"

"I'm not offended. I'm simply wondering why you'd assume I own lederhosen."

"I— Well, I—" Her cheeks flushed. "In the spring when I came to show Bel my dirndl, and she asked you if you could advise and you said yes, and..." The blush deepened. "Maybe you don't remember."

I caught her gaze as my pulse jumped at the memory. "I definitely remember."

CHAPTER NINE

Leo

I'd thought his voice saying my name was something notable. Little did I know how my stomach would clench when he said that, his steel-gray eyes locking onto mine to make sure I heard him.

Oh, I hear you.

I choked a little, sputtered, and then, "Oh, good."

"I'll find something that will suffice." He blinked, then glanced at his screen before saying, "Thank you for letting me know."

I watched him tap away at his keyboard and registered that I'd been dismissed. Rather than stay there blushing like an idiot and sitting next to a man who clearly wanted nothing more than the table to himself, I popped the rest of the slice of bread into my mouth, stacked my mug on the plate, and left the table without a word.

~

With only a little over a week until Oktoberfest, the town brimmed with activity. Everyone was excited about holding the event again this year after having to cancel last year due to budget constraints. The *almabtrieb*, the cow festival, happened to some degree every year no matter what because Wyatt Saint's cows had to come down the mountain one way or another. Last year, the town had thrown more energy into that celebration due to the lack of a fest just before it.

In Europe, most Oktoberfests were actually held at the end of September into the beginning of October, but since our fest was usually just one long weekend, we held it the first weekend in October. Then the following weekend was usually the cow festival, so the town had plenty of activity to kick off the cooler fall months and give us all a little lift before the last six or so weeks until the ski season began and businesses finally picked up significantly.

I loved this time. I'd missed the fest last year and thus felt a ridiculous amount of anticipation for this year's event. Silver Ridge Brewing, Liam and John's brewery, would be providing all the beer for this event—a real first. They'd been working insane hours all summer, and especially the last six weeks since the Sommerfest, to prepare for this, and then in another few weeks, the official opening of their brewpub.

They'd have a limited offering food-wise, but the liquor laws required food to be served there, so they'd established a good-looking menu and hired a chef from out of town who I'd heard was amazing. I couldn't wait to meet her. Apparently, John had been working on this part of the deal along with continuing the brewing while Liam dealt with the lodge's crisis this last year.

John was another one of those guys I wished I could find a spark with. He was handsome, fit, super smart, devoted to his family. Wyatt, John… good guys, but I felt nothing. Warmth, happiness to be with them, sure. But no thrill. No intensity. No heat low in my belly at the thought of rough hands on smooth skin… just, nada.

And speak of the cowboy angel, Wyatt Saint waved at me from across the street. "Leo Morrison, how are you?"

His low, rich voice would do things to the right woman.

"I'm fine, Wyatt. Heading up to a committee meeting for the fest next week. I don't usually see you in town this early, do I?"

We hugged amicably, a new element to our friendship that had come about only after a miserable failure of a date a few months back.

"True. I just ran down here to grab a few things. I'll be back up the mountain until we make the trek."

The Trek referred to leading his cows the miles south from his pasture higher in the mountains to the one that rested just west, and at a lower elevation, from Silverton.

"Well it's good to see you. Let's grab lunch or something when you've got some free time." I patted his arm.

"Absolutely. I'll call you… before Thanksgiving." He flashed a half smile that, again, would devastate someone with the right genes.

"I'll look forward to it." I waved as he crossed back to the other side of the road.

Nice guy. Handsome, built, successful, friendly, kind of adorably shy until we realized we had zero chemistry… why couldn't it work with someone like him?

"Leonie."

From behind me, that unmistakable sound.

I turned, and of course there came Jonas down the path behind me, tall and almost menacing in his dark gray suit.

"Hello. Are you walking to the meeting?" I asked, continuing my walk once he reached me. Now we strolled side by side since the path had widened into an actual side-walk just before the Silverton Inn.

"Yes. I was in town for lunch." He wore sunglasses that shielded his eyes, making him even more opaque to my observations.

I didn't mind not having to look into his eyes. I'd decided, based on our last few encounters, that his eyes were supremely unnerving. The interchange at the coffee shop was an example of how bad it could be—I'd had such a physical reaction, much like that first time he'd said my name. It didn't sit well for hours after I'd left.

Thankfully, I'd made it through our meeting last week without issue. We'd checked up, reviewed the presentation, and now today, we'd meet with the committee and volun-teers working to put on the event. I felt surprisingly nervous considering I knew everyone involved, we'd prepared for all contingencies, and I was excited for it.

But...

This meeting represented the first time Jonas and I would be working *together*. Not in terms of normal lodge/resort activity, or in the way that his job as mountain manager meant we were constantly working together since *technically* I worked for him.

No. This was something we'd teamed up on, genuinely, and we'd made decisions and plans. The success or failure of our strategy to get the prospective investor on board was on us. Hopefully, the committee would like it, but they weren't the hard sell. The real test would come this weekend as we met with the investors, showed them around, and executed the plan.

Though part of me resented having to work on this together, and another large part of me couldn't ignore the flares of alarm constantly shooting up in my mind at the thought of *another* investor, I also knew that what Liam had said was true. Jonas had done good things for the resort and for Silverton. I wanted to see if maybe, just maybe, I could keep that in mind when he inevitably frustrated me.

"Are you ready?" he asked as we walked.

"I was born ready," I said, and raised one brow at him.

He *almost* smiled, but instead, the corners of his mouth pulled down. Something about that silly need of his to keep his smiles tucked away made me want to poke and prod until I got one out of him.

"Does it hurt?"

He tilted his head. "Does what hurt?"

"Frowning so much. Does it hurt? Is it kind of like when you smile too much and your cheeks hurt? Though I guess you probably haven't had much of that, huh?" I shrugged a shoulder like it was all the same to me. It was, although I couldn't imagine Jonas smiling full-out for longer than a flash.

I'd seen a rare smile from him once, and it was recent. He'd smiled with abandon as he crossed the finish line at the triathlon of the Sommerfest. I'd never seen him look like that... so happy, and unwrapped. If I'd let myself, I could've seen it as a thing of beauty. I could've noticed the wrinkles at his eyes that suggested he did, in fact, smile regularly. I could have admired his perfect teeth, or how his body radiated joy.

But I didn't notice those things because seeing Jonas in that way was not an option. I might not call him an enemy, exactly, but he was an opponent of a kind. We'd found a working rhythm, and that was necessary for moving things along. But at some point soon, I'd have to make clear I had plans, he wasn't in them, and if he did anything to cross me... *well*. I'd figure out how to make him pay.

A low chuckle came and shook me from my little rabbit trail.

"It doesn't hurt."

Nothing else. No effort to return the joke, but the chuckle was a surprise. I'd probably missed some version of a smile too. Sad, that.

We continued up the hill to the lodge in silence, though I had to admit it wasn't contentious or even uncomfortable. I might've even called it companionable if I didn't know for certain this man would never be my friend.

"Well, here we are," I said, feeling like something needed to be said before we launched into this presentation and the rest of the weekend.

"Indeed."

A generous conversationalist, he was not.

He extended a hand in front of him, inviting me to precede him into the lodge. *Okay then. Here we go.*

CHAPTER TEN

Jonas

It started behind my eye, as usual.

The migraine would be here in full force within an hour. If I didn't get out of this conference room, away from the fluorescent lights, and sleep, I'd be doomed and hardly functioning tomorrow, just when I needed to be at peak performance.

"Any concerns?" I asked, working to keep the pained edge from my voice, tucking my shaking hand into my pocket.

"Not from me. Anyone else?" Liam Morrison looked around the room, then stood. He likely had a list a mile long to address—I hadn't expected him to show for this meeting anyway, since it was really just a quick roundup of action for the long weekend's events.

The lodge wasn't solely responsible for the fest—the town council, convention and visitor's bureau, and several local businesses each had specific duties. But Silver Ridge Lodge—now Resort—had always been at the helm of the weekend, and so it continued.

Jagged punts of achiness punched at my temples, the area behind my left eye now a throbbing mess complete with blurring vision.

"We'll see everyone at noon tomorrow unless you're on setup crew today. Any questions, I'm point for communications, but Jonas is the man with the plan." Leonie dismissed everyone adeptly and conversation swirled through the room.

If it hadn't been for the impending agony, I might have been able to appreciate the energy and anticipation buzzing from everyone.

She turned to me from where she sat a few places away, gathering a notebook and other items I couldn't focus on. "Do you want to run through your presentation one more time? I can give you feedba—"

"No. I'm quite confident. I'll see you tomorrow at the keg tapping." I carried my belongings under my arm and quickly moved to my office where I turned off the light, powered down the ancient computer I used as minimally as possible, took the overcoat I'd worn since it'd been raining this morning, and left.

I stumbled into the cabin, thankful the walk took no more than a minute from the office to the front door. I tossed my keys and coat on the bar in the kitchen, loosening my tie with one hand while the other dragged down the wall of the dark hallway guiding me toward the bedroom, eyes shut.

In the bathroom, I searched in the medicine cabinet for the pain meds I took for migraines, thankful I hadn't needed them in months. I took a moment to rub an essential oil mix for headaches at my temples and the base of my skull, tore my suit jacket off and tossed it over a chair in the far corner of the room, and collapsed face first on the bed.

~

Hours later, the doorbell woke me. I squinted at my wristwatch to find I'd slept for three hours.

"Jonas?" Leonie's voice called from the front hallway.

No. That didn't make sense. She had to be outside.

"Jonas, are you here?"

Her voice carried down the hall and hit right between the eyes. The migraine glowed in my brain like a cluster of bioluminescent worms in a cave, but it was far from beautiful. I rolled to the edge of the bed and sat up slowly, bracing for the jackhammers in my mind to start. Mercifully, it was only that blaring glow of pain, and nothing sharper now. The medicine and sleep must have taken the worst of the blow.

I rose to standing, every effort feeling like a remarkable task, and moved slowly down the hallway leading to the front of the house.

"Oh, hi. I'm sorry I came in, but I was getting ready to leave and saw your door standing wide open. I—"

I braced myself on the wall as her image swam a little, then leaned full out on the cool painted surface and shut my eyes, but not before I saw her lunge the several feet between us to grasp my wrist.

Ah, not just the wrist. She set a hand at the center of my chest and pushed against it. *Odd thing to do to a person you'd only ever touched the one time.*

"Whoa, are you sick? What's wrong?"

Eyes closed, I could feel her sweet mint breath on my throat.

"Migraine," I managed, then cracked one eye to look at her.

Wide eyes looked me over from just a ruler's length away, alarm and concern bending her features. "What can I do? Do you need medicine? Caffeine? Or is that the opposite of what helps? Should you lay down?"

Her questions flew out, her voice likely a normal volume but each sound felt like a small hammer at the center of my mind, tempting the glowing orb to pulse until it broke.

"Why are you here?" I asked, sounding gruff, and frankly, like a jerk.

She stepped back, taking her cool hands with her. *Damn.*

"I told you, I was leaving and saw your door wide open. It seemed weird, so I just came by to make sure everything was okay." Her voice sounded farther away already.

I opened my unwilling eyes to see her nearly at the front door.

"Everything's fine," I ground out, the pain increasing with each word.

She stopped at the door, which still stood open, and if I didn't know better, I would have said the look on her face was hurt. Didn't make sense.

"See you tomorrow, then." And she was gone.

Another oblivious hour later, the doorbell woke me again, but no smooth, melodic voice chimed in to check on me. The headache had calmed another degree or two, so I managed to get out of bed and to the front in only a minute. Set at the threshold was a bag. I squatted to pick it up, careful to keep my head raised to avoid irritating the already fussy situation in my brain, and carried it to the counter in the kitchen.

Inside it was a still-warm tall jar of soup, a half loaf of fresh bread, two cookies, a bottle of pain medication, and dark chocolate. No note.

CHAPTER ELEVEN

Leo

The atmosphere in the fest tent was nothing short of elated.

Silverton residents and visitors alike were dressed in their best German traditional wear—men in lederhosen, women in dirndls, and plenty of people wearing cheap versions of them or T-shirts with images mimicking the styles.

Rows of thin fest tables lined the tent with benches on each side. A stage sat at the far end. The flaps of the tent were closed since the October day was surprisingly chilly, but inside was nearly roasting.

Liam was just starting his explanation of the traditions of keg tapping and opening ceremonies for a fest like this one. I couldn't pay attention, even though I loved seeing him so happy to command the tent in this role, finally representing his brewery and feeling right where he belonged.

But my mind circled the reality that for me, something had shifted.

Something essential had changed at the sight of Jonas yesterday, leaning against the wall of his house, clearly in agony. His refusal to accept my help had sent ice into my veins, all sense of concern that had clouded my mind when I saw his open front door fleeing. I'd wanted to take him by the shirt collar and shake him, ask him why help from me would be so repulsive.

At the same time, the human part of me whose mother had occasionally suffered from migraines understood he wasn't himself. He was likely in terrible pain, and we certainly hadn't had a relationship that included me caring for him, or doing anything at all for him, for that matter. How could he ask me for help, even if he knew what to ask for?

Seeing him so... human... shook something in me.

So I'd dropped off the little bag of soup, some delights from Sadie's arsenal I'd actually picked up for my own dinner, and a few other essentials. They may not have helped—he might not have opened the door until this morning, in which case all of the food would be bad, but the pain meds would be useful... or at least I hoped they would.

If I had to, I could handle the presentation on my own if he was still out of commission tomorrow. But I could admit that charming a prospective investor was not on the list of my most refined skills. I'd begrudgingly gotten on the investor train with the first one last winter, and I could see, even if I hated to admit it sometimes, the huge benefit coming from there. As Jonas had explained, the more investment funds, the more projects that had been sidelined as too expensive would become *current* instead of *future*, and then hopefully, more people would be drawn to the resort.

But when I didn't see him before the keg tapping, where the emcee of the Oktoberfest taps the first keg of the weekend, I got nervous. Of course, I was nervous about him not being there to do the presentation, which we'd planned to be mostly him. I was there as a representative of the board, of the founding family, and of the education department, which always looked great on paper.

He was a big man. Strong. Fit. I wasn't worried about him like... *worried.* I wasn't picturing him leaning against the wall, short hair sticking up on one side where he must have slept on it, shirt rumpled and tie hanging in a loose, knotted mess.

"Everything going well?"

Speak of the devil. I whipped around to see him standing just behind me, his eyes focused on where Liam and John had begun pouring their beer into giant steins for the pleasantly large crowd.

"Seems to be so far. Are you... feeling better?" I asked, refusing to admire the ornate leather work on the lederhosen suspenders. I definitely did not let my eyes dip down to see how the pants fit. No. No.

Don't do it.

"Yes. Fortunately." His eyes flickered to mine, then flashed over me from my hair braided into a crown at the top of my head, down to the bright white eyelet material making up the bust of my dirndl with the deep blue apron cinching my waist, down the skirt that ended just at the knee, to my brown-heeled feet, and back up.

Our gazes collided. Inexplicably, my throat grew dry. I forced a swallow, then remembered I was annoyed. Shouldn't he at least acknowledge the food I'd left? Of course I hadn't done it for acknowledgement, but as Mr. Manners, wouldn't he—

"Thank you, by the way. Your provisions aided my recovery significantly."

His voice came low and quiet to my ear as he spoke only for me. That was normal—he wouldn't want to interrupt the ceremonial portion of the evening, and Liam was chatting happily into the mic just ten feet from where we stood at the side of the tent.

Jonas didn't step away. Didn't say any more. He just... kept... looking.

Then his eyes did another head-to-toe sweep, and when he found me watching him, he didn't seem at all embarrassed I'd just observed him checking me out. Not just checking me out but taking a kind of languid, self-satisfying tour of my outfit. I arched a brow at him.

"You've seen what you look like." Absolutely no inflection to inform the statement.

"I did look in the mirror before I left, yes."

He lifted one of his own brows as if in answer.

"I'm wearing what many other women here are wearing." Was he accusing me of being inappropriate? He couldn't be. *Could he?* What was with him tonight, and why were his gray eyes making me feel like I'd forgotten my shirt?

"You may be. But you don't look like any of the other women."

Had his words dropped an octave, or was that all in my head?

"What does that mean?" I wondered aloud, hoping it didn't imply I looked poured into the dress. I could admit I was... busty in the thing. But that was how they were designed. When I got fitted for the dress after I graduated college, the woman in the store had literally forced me into wearing a push-up bra and then demanded I choose a lower-necked blouse. I'd filled out a bit since then, put on some weight, so I no longer needed the assistance of a push-up bra.

But it wasn't obscene or anything, I mean... come on. I'd shown Bel months ago, worried maybe it was too much. She'd assured me it'd be fine. In fact, *Jonas* had. And now he'd changed his mind?

"It means I have burned the image of you into my mind and I will thank God the day I die if only this picture of you never leaves me."

"I—" My mouth snapped closed as my stomach dropped through the floor and my breath left me.

Whoa.

"There he is, ladies and gentlemen, Jonas Bauer, Silver Ridge Resort's mountain manager—give him a round of applause!" Liam beckoned Jonas to come join him on the small stage.

Jonas set a hand on my waist as he slid by me, and before I knew it, his hand and its heat, and he, were gone.

In his wake, I stood reeling. Heart pounding, breath short, mouth still dry, mind stuck circling his words, wondering if he'd really said them. Wondering what they meant. Wondering what I wanted them to mean.

CHAPTER TWELVE

Leo

I didn't speak to him alone for what felt like hours.

Probably a mercy, because what would I have said? *Those were real nice words there, mister* and also *you have got to be kidding me* and also *could you please repeat that?*

The opening ceremonies for the fest completed, Jonas found the prospective investors, two fit, short men who looked like brothers and had donned lederhosen and Alpine hats complete with pheasant feathers. They introduced themselves as Jim and Carlos, owners of Piqued Peak Investments, and though I was surprised by their informality, it loosened some of the anxiety in my chest.

They seemed like MFs—mountainfolk, as Danny would call them. I hadn't expected that. In my mind, all investment types were pale little vampires chained to computer monitors who counted their money on weekends and harassed their children's nannies. Clearly, I hadn't actually *met* anyone in the field since Jonas was the mouthpiece and contact for the original investor.

Jim and Carlos had that laid-back feel to them, a lot like Danny. It worked out that we'd planned for Jonas and Danny to take them on a hike tomorrow during the day to show them some of the mountain. I'd happily opted out of spending even more time with Jonas when we'd planned that event, but suddenly, the thought of missing out on the hike made me feel restless.

Two hours later, we'd moved past any sense of formality and everyone was just enjoying the event, beers in hand. Our presentation would happen tomorrow after the hike and lunch, so tonight was about making them feel comfortable and welcomed.

This, it turned out, wasn't hard at all. By the end of the evening, Jim and Carlos felt like old friends. Danny had found new best friends, Liam had talked them into considering investing in his brewery for naming rights of a new beer, and I'd spent most of the time watching Jonas.

It'd become a problem. There were enough distractions that he probably didn't notice, especially since he didn't seem to notice me much at all except occasionally glancing my way, at which point I'd fidget, heart racing in my chest, and I'd suddenly lose the ability to remember what to do with my hands.

He was tall. *So* tall. I was a decent-sized woman at a little over five foot seven, and he still had inches and inches on me. He was taller than all of my brothers, which was saying something, and meant he was at least six foot three. I'd become obsessed with his height as we all mingled.

But Jonas' character wasn't completely altered. He didn't become a social butterfly flitting around the room. He mostly stood, interacting with non-verbal cues or short, specific comments indicating he was listening.

And then, he'd take a drink. The large beer mug looked almost normal-sized in his hand as he raised it to his lips. The action of his throat swallowing down the brew mesmerized me. And then there was the collar of his shirt, a blue just darker than navy checked with white, swirling dark blue stitched embroidery down the torso. I wondered what the stitching felt like. How would it feel to trace the pattern against his chest?

"So if I come back during the season, you're going to make me a better skier?" Carlos sidled up next to me and leaned on a high-top bistro table.

There was a little standing section here in the corner by the bar where we'd camped out, leaving the rows of fest tables to groups and families visiting.

"Absolutely," I said with a large smile.

The guy was charming. He and Jim both were. They looked like brothers linked by one parent. Carlos's dark hair, complexion, and full lips contrasted sharply with Jim's blond hair, angular face, and pale skin. And yet, they both had that same shorter, stocky, fit build, like cross-fitters.

"What about me? Do I get a lesson too?" Jim asked, sliding into place next to Carlos.

"Of course."

"If she's available, of course." Jonas' voice arrived over my shoulder, then he stepped to the table, filling in the remaining gap between Jim and Carlos, across from me.

"In high demand, are you?" Carlos asked, a flirty smile gracing his mouth.

I chuckled. "I have my own students, and I end up filling in when instructors are out sick, plus I run our children's skiing program. The season's pretty busy, but it is for everyone around here."

"Well that's what we like to hear," Jim said, and raised his beer to the center of the table. Carlos and I met it with a *clink* and we all took a drink—mine far more modest than theirs.

"Ms. Morrison is the most sought-after instructor by far. She has a waiting list for her private lessons and has some extremely high-dollar clients."

Jonas' insistence on my appeal wasn't surprising—it made us all look good if we could show we had capable ski instructors, and more so if the head of ski education was well-reputed.

"Oh, I bet she is," Carlos said over the brim of his mug, his eyes sparkling at me with heat.

"Do you?" Jonas inserted before I could respond, his voice edged with irritation.

Carlos' brows dipped and he blinked away from me, then eyed Jonas.

"Yes, I do. Seems like she must be hell on skis." He winked over at me.

"She is one of the most beautiful skiers I've ever seen, and her ability to teach students at all levels is, in my opinion, unparalleled. Aside from the mountain itself, Leonie Morrison is Silver Ridge Resort's greatest asset." He didn't look at me.

My mouth dropped open, but I quickly shut it as heat crawled from my torso up my neck all the way to my hairline. Jim and Carlos made faces at each other, impressed.

"That's high praise from Jonas Bauer. You must be doing something right." Jim tilted his mug at me in acknowledgement.

"Excuse me, gentlemen," I said, a customer service

smile shining at them as I left my beer, and found my way to the back entrance of the tent, suddenly desperate for space and air.

I stepped out and gulped in the cool evening air. The sun was setting earlier now, so at half past six, the sky glowed pink and orange. The mountains in front of me were shadowy purpled giants hunkering down 'til dawn. The sight of them settled me, just a bit, even as my blood pumped wildly through me.

Searching for something sturdy to rest against, I wound around the tent until I reached the lodge itself and where I let my back and head fall against the side of the building. I focused on breathing, finding my mind strangely empty while my chest felt too full. The picture of the peaks in front of me didn't quell the storm inside me any more than they had at first glance, so I shut my eyes and willed my pulse to calm.

What the hell was Jonas Bauer doing to me?

Why was I reacting to him this way?

For that matter, why was he even saying these things? The compliments about my work, my teaching, my skiing... I could potentially excuse them as part of the sales pitch. But all of that earlier, that... intensity. Sincerity? Hunger?

"I will thank God the day I die if only this picture of you never leaves me."

Could it be a way to manipulate me? Did I seem so desperate for male attention and he'd somehow figured out I'd never been talked to like that? Did he know of my failed efforts to date—could he tell how men found me attractive until I opened my mouth and shared an opinion? Had he sensed that the first thing out of most men's mouths when it came to me were words like *intimidating*?

If he'd figured that out, then he'd know that having

someone like him who knew full well how irascible and cold I could be saying things about me—first indicating he thought I was beautiful and then going on to praise me in front of others... he'd know how it'd slice me open and make me bleed a little.

"There you are."

I should have known I couldn't have a moment to myself. Of course he'd find me out here drowning in confusion over his words and my new and painful awareness of how attractive I found him.

"Here I am, sure enough."

He came to stand directly in front of me, blocking my view of the mountains if I'd been looking at them.

"Is something wrong?"

His low, resonant voice filled the air between us as his eyes skated over me, this time less a survey and more an assessment, checking for damage.

"No."

"You left abruptly." Though the words were accusatory, his tone sounded almost gentle.

"I needed some air. It's hot in the tent."

He stepped forward, now near enough that if I reached out my hand, I could grab him by the ridiculous leather suspenders and pull him closer.

"Did I upset you?"

There it was again, that perplexing suggestion that this big, infuriating, unflappable man could be gentle. How had I not noticed this before?

A flip remark on the tip of my tongue, I inhaled instead of speaking. My stomach clenched and my breath came up short, like the time I came home from a month in Europe and had to reacclimate to the altitude.

"Why would I be upset? You made me look good for the investors—that's not upsetting."

And yet, my voice sounded raw somehow. My eyes kept falling to the shadows under his chin, and I wanted so much to rise on my toes and press my lips to his skin and feel his pulse.

What is happening to me?

"Yes. I suppose that is what it looked like. I wondered if perhaps my earlier comment about your appearance was unwelcome." He inched closer as he as he spoke.

I swallowed, his proximity causing the small hairs on the back of my neck to rise in response and my stomach to tingle. "I—not entirely unwelcome. Just... unanticipated."

The world around us quieted when he reached out and ran one finger from the fabric on my shoulder down over the little puff of my sleeve, and further onto my arm. He watched the movement, like he was studying the way his hand moved over my skin, and I became nothing but awareness of his touch, the sensation of his knuckle brushing against my arm, then falling away.

His gaze returned to my eyes and pinned me there a moment, no longer touching me though I still felt the little explosions of perception along the path he'd taken.

He backed away, then spun on his heel and walked directly into the tent. I watched him go, staring after the place where he'd disappeared, my mind a jumble. I cursed the tightness of my dress as I nearly gasped for air and loosened the apron at my back a little, though that didn't make much of a difference.

What on earth did I do now?

CHAPTER THIRTEEN

Jonas

I hardly slept.

On the hike this morning, I struggled to keep my thoughts on the present. This was unusual as I rarely found my mind wandering. I was a man of purpose—if I chose to do something, there I was, doing it. If I became distracted, I stopped to deal with whatever problem had come to mind and then continued on my course.

Leonie Morrison had become far more than a distraction. I might have described her that way when I first met her—when her warm, soft hand had met mine last November and I'd looked at her face and felt the floor vanish from beneath me. If she hadn't made it abundantly clear she loathed me, I might have gotten confused.

But since the day I met her, I'd had nothing from her but disdain, frustration, and dislike. Until two days ago when she left me food.

That kindness, despite my rude response to her desire to help me, had broken through the caution tape I'd erected around all thoughts of her. Then, I saw her in the dress and, well, it addled my good sense. *She'd* scrambled any ability I had to conceal my interest in her, which had always been keen but had been switched decisively to the *off* setting until, apparently, forty-eight hours ago.

I'd been inches, literally, from taking her mouth with mine. *Meine Guete*, how I wanted to. But she'd seemed shaken, deeply, by my comments. I didn't know what had disturbed her more—my over-zealous suggestion that her appearance was what I considered to be close to divine beauty, or that I thought she was one of the best things about this place.

"Not entirely unwelcome."

I'd asked her directly, because I was a direct man. And her answer left plenty of room for doubt. Not *entirely* unwelcome, which meant it was unwelcome in some way.

And so, despite every instinct and physical impulse in me, I backed away after one foolish slide of the back of my index finger down her arm. She didn't recoil, but then she didn't seem to know what to do with me. I'd never seen her so unresponsive—not just verbally, but her face gave me nothing.

So today's meeting would be interesting. It'd be the first time I'd seen her since last night because, after excusing myself upon returning to the tent, I'd made rounds to the various town council and volunteer coordinator types and then retreated to my house. Not a particularly effective sanctuary when the fest tent was essentially in my back yard, and more than half of me wanted to bulldoze through the plaza, tent and crowds be damned, push Leonie up against the wall, and claim her.

But I didn't.

Carlos and Jim seemed no worse for the wear this morning—they must not have stayed too late last night. Reportedly, Thursday was the earliest night and Friday and Saturday saw the tent and band staying far later. I tried not to dread the night ahead.

"So, is your sister single?" Carlos asked Danny ahead on the trail.

Danny led the way, Carlos followed, then Jim, and I brought up the rear. Jim glanced back at me quickly, stretched his lips into a vague smile, then continued on.

"Why do you ask?" Danny spoke over his shoulder, but didn't actually look behind him. We'd entered a more challenging stretch of trail.

"I might be interested," Carlos said, keeping perfect pace with Danny.

We hiked the steep incline in silence for a few beats before Danny stopped as he summited a small hill that crested above the tree line, huffing more noisily than usual in the wake of his recovery from surgery a few months ago. Not quite the end of this trail but close, and a good stopping place to see the valley below.

"I'm fairly certain she is, but I'd ask her." Danny's eyes jumped to mine, then back to Carlos and an easy smile spread across his face. "I guess you're interested in more than the mountain, huh?"

Carlos chuckled and slapped Danny on the back. "The mountain is one of Silverton's many charms, I'm finding."

I grit my teeth and swallowed an audible groan of disgust. I liked this firm, and prior to this, I'd liked the reputation of these two, but I didn't like this man's approach to flirting or pursuing Leonie. It felt... smarmy. Wrong.

Granted, anyone flirting with Leonie, if it garnered her attention, unsettled me.

"You won't find a better mountain—I've skied every resort in the US and most of Europe. I can tell you that for the US, this is an exceptional mountain. There's so much untapped potential here, and with the right infusion, it'll explode."

I had no doubt. I'd seen the potential the moment we arrived in Silverton, and it'd been proving itself to me with each day. I couldn't wait to be in residence for the full ski season this year.

"All right, Bauer. No need for the sales pitch just yet," Carlos joked.

Jim and Danny chuckled good-naturedly and I nodded, then said nothing else. I'd have my time to give them the full display of my faith in the mountain, which was no small thing. I had a reputation for success, which was part of the reason I'd drawn the interest of another investor.

Another couple hours of mentally checking out as we hiked, enjoying the beauty of the mountain and all but blocking out the conversation around me, and I finally arrived home to an obnoxiously full inbox. I made the only phone call I had to before cleaning up and preparing for the meeting.

"Ah, finally. I'm beginning to think you've abandoned our partnership altogether." Karla Ritter's voice filled my ear.

"Of course not, but it has been a busy time."

"I know you're becoming invested there in more ways than one. At what point will you extract yourself and rejoin me in consulting?" she asked like she didn't know the answer.

We'd discussed this. "I'm not sure. At least another nine months here."

We sat on the line, quiet. Unlike us—neither of us relished wasting time like this.

"I'm not going to tell you what you already know." Her words were clipped with frustration.

"Then don't."

She sighed. "Jonas, you have lost sight of what you want. I honestly don't care what it is in the end, but I hope you figure it out and then embrace it. Continuing to pretend this acquisition will do anything for your portfolio—"

"I'll talk to you soon, Karla."

Another sigh, this time resigned. "Bis später, Jonas."

I set my phone face down and stared at it like it could give me answers. It failed me by being a phone. I gave myself a moment, just one to feel the full weight of conflict in my chest as I scrubbed my hands over my face and wished for clarity.

CHAPTER FOURTEEN

Jonas

Moving through the process of showering and dressing, my thoughts swirled. I'd set out to consult for Liam Morrison in November of last year and use it as an opportunity to decide whether I wanted the place for myself. Upon arriving here, I knew I'd take the job. I knew I'd want to take *everything*—take over, and probably could have due to the financial situation, but the family dynamic here was too strong. And that got to me.

I'd spent years rejecting my own family. As an extremely wealthy German family, they'd effectively disowned my mother when she fell for an American soldier and moved with him to the US not long after I was born. Though my father did have German ancestry, my mother's family found him lacking in this and many other areas. Throughout my father's career, he managed to be stationed in Germany several times so that my mother and I could be

close to her family as he didn't have any. Though they practically ignored my mother, my grandparents did attempt to
foster a relationship with me.

The moment at which I found one of my life's purposes
is still vivid in my mind. I sat around a gloriously filled table
on Christmas Eve at one of my grandparents' luxury homes,
the chairs filled with grandparents, my aunt and uncle and
their spouses, and several cousins, all of whom were a
decade older than me.

"Jonas, will you be attending university here?" my aunt
Marie asked in perfect German.

Fortunately, I'd learned the language well—something
my mother had insisted on and had cemented effectively
when my father spent four long years stationed at an army
base in Wiesbaden in my early elementary years. Each trip
back had further solidified my grasp on the language, along
with my mother's use of it in our home whenever possible.

"I have been accepted to several universities in the US,
so I will attend there," I responded, my German equally
perfect.

A scoff from down the table where my uncle sat, then a
sneer. "No surprises. Angela's taste in poverty and compromise has been handed down quite deftly."

I sat straighter, expecting someone to defend my
mother, but I should have known better.

My grandmother, who died not long after, said with a
kind of regretful smile, "I do wish you could understand
how it hurts us, to see her with your father. To see her give
up a good life."

It became clear that day, and in almost every other small
interaction I had with that family, that they only wanted me
if I wanted a life like theirs. If I chose the lesser version, in

their views, like my mother had, then I was of little worth to them.

And it was that day I planned to amass more wealth and assets than all of them combined, particularly my aunt and uncle and the cousins. My grandparents had passed, and they hadn't been nearly as overtly insulting when they were still alive. When my father was killed during deployment to Afghanistan a decade ago, only one of my cousins managed to make it to the funeral. While I never expected them to all come, the very minimal effort my aunt and uncle made at offering even the barest of condolences to their own sister confirmed what I'd always known.

I'd spent the last decade gaining education and building wealth. I went to the best schools, not because I had connections, but because I earned it. I got jobs, worked hard, advanced, and channeled my father's heart for service into my heart for success.

I'd become a consultant for ski resorts and other luxury travel destinations and had amassed an insane portfolio. I'd hungered for more and more until I knew I out-owned and out-performed my family. My primary victory had come at twenty-seven when I'd bought out a fairly large resort in Austria my cousin had taken over and then utterly failed at keeping afloat. I'd made a point not to speak to my cousin, but only his lawyers, when I acquired the place in person.

Call me a cold bastard. I could admit it.

But meeting Liam Morrison had shaken me. Though his sense of duty grated at times, he held clear convictions about his desire to keep his family's business. He'd nearly pushed himself into a collapse of stress and anxiety with the way he'd taken everything on himself. Ridiculous, perhaps, but admirable. We were about the same age, and his polar opposite view regarding family, his drive to do more and more for them, had made me pause.

At thirty-two, I was keenly aware I'd done nothing for anyone but myself. Yes, I'd purchased a home for my mother, supported her, and visited her every few months. But that was no stretch—spending money on her was easy. I didn't have a drive for anything but an odd kind of vengeance against my extended family which they probably didn't care a bit about. The older I got, the less satisfying each acquisition had been.

Silverton had charmed me immediately. Silver Ridge Lodge felt alarmingly like a place I might want to call home, and I'd become accustomed to the sense that I'd never truly be at home again once my father passed. He'd always been our anchor—each move, each change, it was him who made everything right.

So meeting Liam, and seeing the way he fought for his family, his town, and even his own dream of making beer... it'd cut the legs out from under me.

And then, there was Leonie Morrison.

Until a few days ago, I'd been able to keep my distance. I'd observed her to what might be an unhealthy degree, all in the name of research and observation about the health of the resort. If she hadn't been so clearly opposed to my very existence from the start, I might have pursued her upon moving to Silverton last spring.

So the change in her—it shook me. And somehow, she was mixed up in all of my plans, which didn't make sense. She, more than Liam, had thrown my takeover of Silver Ridge off course. Granted, I effectively had. I'd invested several million dollars in revitalizing the resort, not that any of them knew it was me. I'd taken over as mountain manager. And if these Piqued Peak idiots decided to invest,

I'd buy into their investment group and work to gain control there too.

But the thought of taking it—really moving against the family and taking the lodge, the mountain... it didn't sit right. It wouldn't do much of anything for my portfolio considering the size of the place, nor would it impact my family because they couldn't care less what happened in the US, which was both maddening, and why I'd made my permanent home and much of my business here.

I slid the knot of my tie into place, settled the ends neatly together, flattened a wrinkle in the shirt where it tucked into my belted waist.

If Karla asked me again, I knew what I'd say. Liam Morrison had what I'd never realized I wanted. I wanted to stop the travel, stop bouncing around. I wanted a home. And if I could manage to convince a specific woman I was better than *not entirely unwelcome*, I wanted Leonie Morrison too.

With that thought in mind, I pulled on my suit jacket, forgoing a top layer since the day was cool but bright, and jogged across the plaza to the lodge where Carlos and Jim waited for me to sell them on Silver Ridge Resort.

CHAPTER FIFTEEN

Leo

Watching Jonas present to the investors was the strangest experience I'd ever had.

Here was a man I'd viewed, for most of the eleven months I'd known him, as opposition. I'd questioned his motives, loathed his demeanor, resented his replacing Liam, and undermined his authority. I'd avoided him, ignored him, at times despised him.

But during this presentation, even though I'd known what he would say in advance, he entranced me.

I couldn't look away as he stood in front of the men we meant to woo and extolled the qualities of my mountain, my lodge, my community, even my state. He presented the overwhelmingly positive side to the resort as an investment such that the objections we'd anticipated—location, barriers to access, historical data on low numbers in the season, etc. —were never voiced.

I suspected, like I always did, that Carlos and Jim were won not by anything we said, but by simply arriving and standing at the base of the peaks that surrounded Silverton and were part of Silver Ridge Resort. The mountains spoke for themselves, and the first investor had taken the largest risk. Now that the infrastructure was already improving, secondary investments had a kind of cushion, and also the guarantee that someone else had seen value too.

My concerns about more outside money, however strong they'd been at times, were fleeting ever since Jonas had outlined the potential changes in budgets for lifts, refurbishing, building out a midmountain lodge, opening another face of Silver Ridge Peak, and eventually a hotel space if we could get the land.

Even a month ago, I would've resisted his vision. I would have assumed he had malignant motives and would somehow turn all of this to his benefit. But something had shifted in me these last few weeks. Working closer to him, seeing him take responsibility for errors, even small, perceived errors like when he thought he made me uncomfortable with his comments last night, had forced me to soften my harsh judgement of him.

And now that that'd happened, now that he'd forced me to see him as a human man and not just a hulking nemesis, I couldn't *unsee* him.

Now all I saw was the man. The smooth, carefully shaved jawline. The ridiculous curve of his lower lip, the strong chin, the nose that suited him perfectly, how his eyebrows were a shade darker than his hair, the nearly invisible glasses he only sometimes wore... I saw it all.

And that voice. A voice that had sent a chill through me whenever I'd heard it, that I now may have to admit was not from dislike. Perhaps my body had recognized then what I was fast discovering now—that Jonas Bauer's voice was a danger to me. The low timbre, the cool quality to it, the slightest difference in his pronunciation of certain words that hinted at his heritage and time spent out of the US.

And that—the reality that I knew absolutely *nothing* about him personally. The things I knew about him were a sum total of what I'd observed in the previous months and they were minimal because I'd been so busy being angry.

I slowly exhaled, unwilling to venture down the path of thinking of how often my tendency to react with anger had caused me problems.

Too often.

Before I knew it, I was delivering Carlos and Jim back to the Silverton Inn before heading home to change without a moment to speak with Jonas privately. I wanted to tell him how well he'd done.

I wanted to tell him he could touch me again, look at me, if he wanted.

No idea how I'd do that, but suddenly, all I wanted was the moment from last night back so I could tell him his attention was not at all unwanted. It *was* wanted.

I wanted it.

Of course, a not-small part of me knew what a fool it made me to want anything from him but what I'd always wanted—the job. I knew this, and yet I found myself thinking about the many things I might want other than just the job.

At home, I grabbed a snack, devouring it. Probably good I didn't speak to him while hungry as doing anything while hungry was nearly as bad as doing things while angry.

To prepare for the fest tonight, I fixed my hair into two long braids and tied them with ribbons that matched the blue detailing stitched into my lederhosen. Yes, I had my own lederhosen and loved them—the shorts were a bit on the *whoa baby* short side, but they were broken in and the leather had softened. Tonight, I wore a white blouse, similar to the kind that topped my dress last night, but it ended in a cinched ruffle an inch or so above the waist of my shorts. The suspenders tipped over my shoulders which were bare as the blouse sleeves rested at the caps of my shoulders and left my décolletage and neck free.

The shirt was a calculated choice. It was a bit sexy, I could admit. But I'd decided perhaps I'd... do something tonight. I'd communicate, in some way, that Jonas had changed my mind about him. I might not be certain of what I wanted, but I knew I couldn't pretend to view him as entirely opposite me. I couldn't go back to seeing him as an enemy.

And so, me and my suspendered short leather pants and navel-grazing top headed out to find the man... and I'd probably have to chat with Carlos and Jim as well, but that'd be fine.

"I'd like to make a toast to whoever decided women can wear lederhosen too." Carlos cheerily raised his beer mug amidst chuckles.

I might have blushed since the comment seemed to be directed at me and my leather pants, which I knew were flattering and kind of strangely appealing, but instead I was annoyed. "The twentieth century?"

Carlos looked at me, mouth open, plainly delighted by my surly response. "Sure. Whoever. I'm just generally going on record and thanking the universe for it."

His eyes warmed as they looked at me, but didn't leer.

He wasn't being creepy or gross; he was being flirty and funny, and it made me want to punch him in the face.

Okay, maybe nothing that extreme, but I was over it. Particularly because each time he said anything to me —*anything*—Jonas settled into a glower so refined, he should win a prize for it. And then said nothing.

Why any of this should make me salty, I didn't know. The fest tent was packed to the gills and people spilled out the side flaps and onto the plaza. Quinn Darling's band had taken the stage and as always, they were excellent. The night was starry and clear with crisp air cooling the tent through the open doorways.

I'd been here several hours already. I'd eaten half a roast chicken and a giant pretzel and a decent version of spätzle—German noodles—and I'd had exactly one and a half of Liam's Avalanche Pale Ales, all of which should have put me in a perfect mood.

But like it had almost every time I'd interacted with him over the last eleven months, Jonas' presence pressed against me in a way I couldn't ignore. I should have been prepared to face him—I'd thought I was. But instead of greeting me and accepting my congratulations for a job well done on the presentation when I saw him upon arrival, he glared at me. Something happened behind his eyes, behind those glasses he was wearing again today for some reason despite not wearing them for at least the last week, and then he nodded curtly once, mumbled a thank you, and walked away.

Um...

At that moment, I felt the pull toward anger, the most familiar emotion that ran through my encounters with Jonas. But it wasn't pure and simple—it was tinged with disappointment and maybe, if I forced myself to admit it, a little hurt.

Rather than sit down in that, I searched out Carlos and Jim who were chatting away with Mia and Danny. I sat with them to eat dinner and smiled along with Mia, who sported a new and very flattering dirndl, as she told the story of Danny proposing, then laughed with everyone as Jim told a tall tale of his own engagement to his now-fiancée that involved a botched hidden ring and a trip to the ER for him.

We raised our glasses in traditional German fest toasts led by Liam and John. I wandered around and thanked people for coming, putting on my friendliest teacher demeanor. I tracked Jonas wherever he went, which was always at opposite ends of the tent.

But then I joined the high-top table with Jonas, Carlos, Jim, Wyatt, and Liam, just in time to hear them talking about Jamie and Bel's plans to return next weekend for a long-weekend visit. So I stuck around, listened, interjected here or there, and then came Carlos' toast.

Followed by Jonas' expert-level glower.

His normally gray eyes seemed darker, stormy. He stood stiffly, towering over even Wyatt and Liam, stony face grim, his lips pressed together except when he took a drink of his beer.

"Well, I'll thank the universe for the invention of them to begin with, because you all look fantastic," I said, laying on the charm, working to salvage my mood, my evening, my ability not to be controlled by Jonas Bauer's glares.

My eyes though, they flickered to him, and found his gaze on me. I swallowed.

Carlos chimed in again. "Do you have plans the rest of the weekend, Leo?"

Jonas stiffened, cleared his throat. "She's busy."

CHAPTER SIXTEEN

Jonas

Why? Why did I speak? Why did my idiot mouth choose that moment to find Carlos Arroyo's shameless flirting unbearable?

All eyes turned to me. Not surprising considering it was the first time I'd spoken in what felt like hours, but realistically more like ten minutes. Still.

"I am?" Leonie asked, her eyes squinting just a touch.

I slowly raised my beer stein to my lips, took a long drink, urging my mind to come up with something—anything. "Of course. It's one of the busiest weekends we have all year."

Her brows dipped, and she stared at the table while the men surrounding us chimed in with "oh, I'm sure it's crazy" and "yes, that makes sense."

Then came Liam's, "She can always find time for important visitors."

I felt the frown pull at my lips before I ever gave it permission. "Yes, but we'll be... working... so..."

Donnerwetter. Where had my sense gone?

Then she looked up, pasted on a fake-looking smile, and said with a snarl in her voice, "Whatever you say, boss."

Ouch.

"I'll be back in a bit," she said, addressing everyone with notable eye contact except me.

And then she walked out onto the plaza, and I knew I'd follow her. But someone was speaking to me.

"Damn, Bauer. You seem to bring out the ice queen in Leo faster than anyone I've ever seen." Warrick Saint, a man I knew only by his association to his brother Wyatt, took Leonie's spot at the table and widened his eyes at his brother, clearly having heard and seen everything.

No response from me. What could I say? I did bring out this side of her, though I wouldn't call it ice. That cold calculation she seemed to wield wasn't at all frigid like some people I'd met. It was pure, raging flame. Dangerous, volatile, and completely attractive to me now that I'd become a stupid, weak-willed moth.

"Pardon me," I said, not waiting to hear what any of them said, my mind already jumping ahead to where she might have gone. Would she be leaning against the wall like last night? Would she have gone all the way home? Would I have to wait until tomorrow to hunt her down and—

"Bauer."

Bad sign. Back to the last name. My misstep inside the tent had been larger than I'd realized.

"Ms. Morrison," I responded in kind.

The moon shone on her, increasing the glow of her golden braids and casting a shadow where her eyes would be. She crossed her arms, jerked her head to the side, and walked away. I followed, recognizing the gesture and admitting whatever conversation we were about to have shouldn't be had in front of the crowd still milling around the plaza, chatting happily and enjoying the evening.

She stomped more than walked along the sidewalk skirting the lodge until she came to the far side, stopped, and whipped around to face me, arms still crossed. I came to a halt a few feet from her, not wanting to seem like I was towering over her now that we were alone and in a fairly isolated location.

She looked at me as if waiting for something. She faced the mountain so the moonlight lit her face and I could thus see when she raised an eyebrow.

"Yes?" My pulse hammered in my neck.

She huffed. "Why are you being an ass?"

I rocked back on my heels. "Am I?"

Her jaw hardened and she exhaled out her nose. "You know you are."

"Perhaps you should enlighten me." I tilted my head to one side.

"You—" She grabbed each of her braids, pulled at them, then paced around in a circle, then her voice softened. "I don't understand you."

Something about the way she said it made my chest ache. "What don't you understand?"

She looked out at the mountains for a minute, then longer. I wondered if she'd speak at all or if this was one of those times she'd simply wish me away. The beautiful night pulsed with a base beat floating from the tent in the distance.

Eventually, she broke the silence between us. "I tried to tell you what a good job you did. I wanted to congratulate you, shake your hand, something. And what did you do?"

I had no idea if she could see the shock on my face, but it was there thanks to the tone of her voice—real hurt laced the now almost sultry sound of it, no doubt from talking loudly for hours inside the tent.

"What did I do?" *Mein Gott*, would I spend the whole night parroting questions back to her?

"Are you really asking me? What did you do? You *ignored* me." Her hand fisted at her side now.

"Not true. I said thank you." I'd barely scraped it out.

"*Barely.*"

I chuckled low. Could she read my mind?

"This isn't funny! I don't understand you, and I have to work with you for who knows how much longer. I don't— I can't—" Her face smoothed into a neutral expression and she blew out a breath slowly.

"We needn't be adversaries," I offered.

Her mouth dropped open a touch before she slammed it shut. "Oh, needn't we? What a relief."

"*Weibsbild*," I muttered under my breath.

"What?" Her voice was razor sharp.

"Nothing. I simply mean... I should have—thank you for your congratulations," I ground out.

I meant it. She'd come into the tent, found me immediately, and offered a downright effusive, joy-filled congratulations I didn't know what to do with. Particularly because I'd been enjoying the sight of her in lederhosen, an event I hadn't realized would impact me so viscerally and yet, in that moment, I'd been unable to do anything but say thank you and flee. Otherwise I might've grabbed her and satisfied my now-constant need to feel her lips on mine.

She observed me, her gaze sliding over me in all directions.

"You're welcome." She hesitated a moment, then took a large step toward me. "Why do you do that?"

"Do what?"

She shook her head a little, then huffed. "One moment you're sincere, and then the next you're looking right through me."

I reared back a bit, surprised. "I didn't realize..."

"The things you said yesterday... and then we talked, and today you're all stoic, evasive, even. I don't know what to think." She fiddled with a braid with one hand, the other at her side.

"What do you want to think?" My voice emerged low and solemn, certain her next words would be something about leaving her alone or never seeing my face again.

Her quiet laugh surprised me. I inspected her face in an attempt to make sense of it, but found only a frustrated smile there.

"I think I should ask you that."

Her eyes glittered back at me. The full effect of their depth and color was ruined by the low light of the moon, but they still cut through me. The theme of the day was being questioned and required to provide specific answers.

I didn't like that.

The frustration found its way into my voice. "No."

Her brows jumped. "*No?*"

"No, you shouldn't ask me that. I told you I think you are incomprehensibly beautiful and you, in turn, told me that was *not entirely unwelcome.* In this instance, I am bound *not* to say more in order to avoid becoming *entirely unwelcome.*"

And I'd mentally chastised myself for the events of the evening—the words, the touch, the white-hot wanting that came with seeing her now. Any ability to stay away from her, to reason myself into avoiding the attraction I'd felt from the moment I first saw her, had been stomped into oblivion with that little bag of food on my porch. The fact that she seemed even mildly responsive to me only served to further trash my will to avoid her.

Her lips parted and she seemed to be holding her breath, her words a whisper. "You didn't say it that way. You wouldn't—"

"How else shall I say it? You are magnificent. When I look at you, even when you're berating me or ignoring me, I am assaulted by the vision of you. When you give me your full attention, it feels a little like I'm dying. I can't—"

She didn't let me continue. Instead, she stopped me in the best possible way. She stepped to me as I ranted, pulled me down to her by the leather suspenders at my chest, and kissed me.

CHAPTER SEVENTEEN

Leo

I pressed into his lips with mine, then eased back, releasing him.

There. That's what I think.

I moved to step back, but before I could, his arm wrapped around me and tugged me back to him. And then he took my mouth.

I say *took* because it was nothing like the gentle, if sudden, kiss I'd given him. Not at all.

The man had come to play, and he'd come to win.

His lips slid over mine, teasing, pressing, until I opened just enough for him to deepen the connection and steal my breath.

Somehow, I'd never thought about whether Jonas would be a good kisser. I'd known instinctively he would be, just like he seemed to be annoyingly good at everything else he did. And if I put even partial stock in what he'd said about me—how he found me attractive—the combination of his words and his mouth, and the way his arms forcefully pressed me to his tall, muscular frame... it proved a heady cocktail.

One of his hands slid up my back and around my neck to cup my cheek in a touch so gentle, I became breathless. My heart galloped in my chest and little thrills sparked in my belly. The movements of his mouth, the delicate, almost reverent way he held my face... I'd never felt so confused, exhilarated, or scared.

Yes, scared. That was the feeling creeping up from my stomach amidst the molten lava his kisses had heated to boiling point. What did this mean? What was happening?

I pushed against his chest where my hands rested, and he released me immediately, though the way his palms smoothed down my arms before he let go completely told me he was reluctant.

"I should go." I sounded shaken, small.

"Should you?" His voice rumbled in a chest I had now felt just a little.

And what a chest it had been...

I nodded profusely. When a half smile twitched at the corner of his mouth, I returned to myself, a flash of irritation giving me strength.

"Yes. I should. Good night, Jonas."

And I left. Didn't look back.

The drive home passed quickly—it was only a few miles, after all, and even going slow on the road to the farm since this was the time all the little creatures liked to explore the path, I made it back in minutes.

I stripped out of my hosen and sought the comfort of sweatpants and a T-shirt. Then, I dialed Bel, hoping she wouldn't be asleep.

Probably not since she was an hour earlier on Pacific Time, plus normal people didn't go to bed this early. Though she always had, but that had been because of her job opening *Rise and Shine*. Now that she didn't work there, it occurred to me I had no idea if she still got up early. This realization made me feel mildly wretched since, until this moment, I'd felt I could envision her life in LA fairly well, which made me feel closer to her.

"Leo! How's the fest going?"

Bel's sweet voice immediately eased a bit of the tension roiling in me.

"Uh... I kissed Jonas." Right to it. No point in pretending there was any other reason I'd called.

"Ohhh. Okay. Tell me."

I loved her. No surprise, or judgement, just... readiness to talk. Though, a bit annoying she wasn't at least a little surprised. "Why do you sound like this isn't a total shock to you?"

A little laugh, then, "I've wondered when it would happen."

"*What?*"

"He's been watching you like you're a meal for months, my friend. And though I know you've had legitimate reasons to mistrust him, I think your overly-strong reaction and dislike of him come from something else."

I twisted a braid around my fingers, then inspected the ends. "You say that like it's so obvious."

She laughed louder. "Don't get surly with me. It's not

like I knew all along or something, but I won't pretend to be shocked by this. He's an extremely attractive and capable man who is definitely attracted to you and isn't scared away by your personality."

I scrunched up my face, letting myself wince at the statement. If only she hadn't hit the problem I'd had with so many others head on.

In high school, Aaron Ackers had lied to me about why he had to break up with me just before prom—he said his parents decided he couldn't date anyone, and he couldn't go to prom. Inevitably, he *did* go to prom with pretty, sweet, vanilla pudding Jessica Tillman. He must've expected me to stay home, but instead I went, determined to have fun with my friends. I cornered him in the hallway and asked why he'd ditched me, and he'd said, "Because of *this*, Leo. It's too much. You're too much."

You'd think men would come up with some other way to say it, but I'd heard "*you're too much*" three times, and variations of it more than that. "We're better as friends," was a favorite, but that could mean anything.

Blind dates never worked. I couldn't maintain a sweet, simple personality for long, and I never tried—even though I'd been hurt and hurt again by the idea that I was *too much*, I had positive influences who never made me feel that way. My parents, for one, and my brothers most of the time, though they could be jerks just like any brothers.

And in books, I could find women like me accepted fully by men. Fiction, yes, but a source of hope. Reading those wild west historical romances always left me with a bittersweet feeling, because I identified with those women— strong, independent cowgirls and intrepid females breaching new frontiers, never afraid to speak their minds and get their hands dirty, and the men of the time loved them for that, for not being simpering little misses and fully taking the reins to their lives in their own hands. It's what I needed, too... except, I lived in the now and not in the wild west.

In high school, I'd focused on the lies Aaron had told, and that began my utter intolerance for deceit. It was one reason why, when Liam lied and said he had access to Wells' land, I'd lost my cool. I could see the lie, could see he knew it was a lie, and my ability to think clearly about the situation and see it wasn't my job to tell Wells about the situation fled. I messed up, but in retrospect it was no surprise. The particular betrayal of lying in a romantic relationship flipped a switch in me and I'd come to terms with that. It didn't make what I'd done okay, but it helped me understand why I'd done it, and thankfully Liam and I had made peace. Maybe better than that, he'd proven to be the man I knew he was and owned the lie, the consequences, and did everything to make it right.

So... lies were a problem for me, and it all started with stupid Aaron Ackers. But as the years ticked by and I kept having the same feeling—one of disappointment, hurt, sadness, and especially the sense that none of these men had taken a chance to know me before they decided I didn't fit what they wanted, I accepted the truth.

I was too much for most men. For whatever reason, the combination of my looks and my "big personality" were intimidating, and most men really hated to be intimidated by a woman they might date. I was too strong—physically and emotionally. I was too direct. I was too confident. I was too certain of who I was and where I was going.

Wyatt was the first guy I'd dated who hadn't made me feel like too much. Before we dated, he was shy and sweet, but never *scared*. That was just him—polite, thoughtful, almost soft-spoken. An insane contrast to the hulking cowboy babe image, and whoever ended up with him would be a truly lucky woman. If only we'd had the spark.

"Did I lose you? You know I don't mean *I* think you're too much, dear friend." Bel's voice came through the line soft, apologetic.

I let out a breath.

"I know. And you're right. I just had a little mental pity party as I reviewed all the men who *were* intimidated or repelled by all that is me." I forced a laugh.

"Oh Leo. You know you're a lot, but those of us who love you know how amazing you are. If people are too dumb to give you time and see that, it's their loss."

I rolled my eyes, but was glad she couldn't see. "Yeah yeah, I'm super amazing once you get past all the rage."

She laughed loudly again. "We probably do need to talk about you and Jonas, speaking of rage. Do you like him?"

I covered my face in my hands, the phone pinned between my ear and my shoulder. "I don't know."

"You do."

"Fine. I do. I like him, even though I still don't understand why, and I definitely shouldn't."

She giggled then. Gee, I must've been just hilarious.

"I can understand why you like him."

"Then you tell me, oh wise, engaged one." I flopped to one side and kicked my legs up onto the couch so I lay on my side.

"Well, he's a gorgeous broody half-German ski-loving introvert."

I sighed. "He is kind of gorgeous, right? I've been in denial but... *yeah*. And he's got stealth soul. That's what pushed me over the edge."

"Stealth soul?"

I pressed a hand to my chest as my heart tripped at the memory of his eyes when he said those things... *ugh*. Those things people just didn't say out loud in real life. "Yeah. Like, you know Jamie's going to be soulful—he's a musician and he's just always been like that. But Jonas looks like a well-dressed ice cube and uses words only when required. The idea that he'd say some of the things he's said..."

"Tell me. You have to tell me!"

I wanted to hoard his words. I would definitely write them down and read them over to myself. But I could share a bit with her, because if I didn't share with her, I'd never tell anyone. "He said I was exquisite. He said when I look at him directly it makes him feel like he's dying."

"*Oh.*"

"Yeah." Then a thought occurred. "That's good, right?"

I could hear the smile in her voice. "I'd say so. It's all kinds of dramatic and descriptive. You're right... that's stealth soul."

I groaned, frustration and exasperation in the sound. "I don't want this. I don't want any of this."

The knot in my stomach twisted.

"Not much you can do about it other than ignore it, if you really don't want it. But... you should consider being open to it, if you don't mind my saying."

I did mind it, but on the other hand I didn't. I'd warred internally over the same thought all night, and I knew I would for days to come. I didn't want this mess, to feel these things, to see him this way... but then, part of me really really did.

We switched gears then as I turned our chat to her life there, if she was excited to come back to Silverton next week, and how wedding planning was going. Before we hung up, she circled back to me and Jonas.

"You never told me how it was."

"How what was?" I asked.

"How was the kiss?"

I huffed a laugh. "Oh… I guess to use his own phraseology, it felt a little like dying."

CHAPTER EIGHTEEN

Leo

Our obligations kept us apart the rest of the weekend. I didn't know if that was good or not. Clearly, he felt I should be the one to come to him if I... well, honestly, I didn't know. I thought about him nonstop and couldn't escape that, though it was a tangled mess, I wanted more.

More of his time. More of his attention. More of us talking without fighting. More of his hands pulling me to him, and more of his kisses.

Yes. More of all of it.

But that left me in the precarious position of pursuing him. Don't get me wrong—I had no problem being the one to pursue someone if I'd ascertained they were interested. Long ago, I'd decided I wouldn't put myself out there unless I knew it was worth it.

And Jonas... some intrepid, private part of me suspected he was really worth it. But that scared me, and it was precisely why I'd fled the scene of the most delectable kiss I'd ever had, bar none.

There were many problems with being with Jonas, but the biggest, aside from him being my boss and his holding my family's business and my dream job in the palm of his hand, was the fact that I still didn't know if he was a decent guy. I didn't know him, and I'd spent so much time crafting a version of him I could easily dismiss, that I'd opposed at every turn, that it turned me inside out to try seeing him in a new way.

Granted, he'd forced my hand there, with his sensual, surprising words and his compliments and his aggressive support of me, my programs, my skill, my family's legacy...

So why hesitate?

The hope.

The hope had me hesitating. I'd felt it when he had pulled me back to him and kissed me. I'd thought, "This is it," and then immediately, the fear had set in.

The part of me that had relaxed into the kiss, both enthralled and at peace, was the part that needed care. It needed the defense of the hardened part of me that had been hurt and hurt and hurt again by men who couldn't "handle me." And I could admit, I *was* a lot to handle. I was trying to learn how to calm my quick jumps to anger when I felt out of control. I'd made real progress in the last six months, even, but I'd never be a docile, sweet girl.

I'd always been sure, confident, a little pushy and a lot mouthy. I'd always been *me*. And Jonas had said he liked the way I looked... *a lot*... and he thought I was a great skier and teacher and that whole thing about my being the best thing about Silver Ridge other than the mountain... *yeah, that was a good one.*

But we didn't get along. Even our talk before the kiss

had been mildly confrontational, not tender. Not like potential lovers.

Did that mean we wouldn't work? Did it mean I should just avoid him long enough for both of us to forget about the whole thing and move on? That would probably be best, and yet I knew it'd be years... ages... before I forgot.

The week following the event was packed because the town's *almabtrieb*, the festival for Wyatt's parade of fancied-up cows, took place the next Saturday. We squeezed in a post-event review, plus for some inane reason, I'd chosen that week to schedule childcare staffing interviews.

By the time the last cow ambled down Main Street, flowered head dress adorning her like a crown and the bell ringing, I slumped against the brick wall next to *Rise and Shine* and vaguely daydreamed about buying myself a latte and also snapping my fingers and landing in my apartment where I could fall into bed and nap.

Only one of those things was possible, so after high-fiving Kai, who'd stood by me during the whole parade while Mia and Danny snuggled together against the chilly October day and were generally adorable and disgusting, I pushed the bright yellow door of *Rise and Shine* to satisfy at least one of my dreams.

And *oh, look*, there was another object of my dreams—not the day kind—ahead of me in line. I'd worked hard not to spend mental energy on him while awake, but he'd snuck in without permission while I slept, and the dreams were doing nothing to strengthen the flimsy resolve I had when it came to resisting him.

I hadn't noticed him walk by, but I'd been in a kind of hypnotized state brought on by only a smattering of fitful sleeps and clinking cowbells.

"Hey, Jonas." No point in pretending my heart hadn't jumped the minute I saw him.

He turned, and *oh. Dear.*

No suit today. He wore a close-fitting sweatshirt in charcoal gray and dark jeans. No glasses. Just him and his gray eyes and a smile. An actual, white-teeth-baring smile I could hardly handle.

"Leonie. Lovely to see you."

What was I supposed to do with this person? This couldn't possibly be the Jonas Bauer I'd come to know. He was... taciturn. Unsmiling. Begrudging of words and certainly not prone to small talk. Even the man I'd kissed wasn't like this...

"Are you well?" he asked, a concerned tilt to his head as he reached out and gently took hold of my arm at my wrist.

"Uh..."

He'd shut me up like this the first time I saw him. That first meeting last year, I'd never forget it. I'd been so angry with Liam for bringing in consultants, something I could now concede was short-sighted. I'd been stewing in my frustration with Liam so hadn't really looked closely at Jonas and his partner, Karla Ritter, and then came my turn to shake his hand.

It was one of those moments—the kind like in a movie when the heroine feels a *zap!* and she's essentially thunderstruck by the touch. It's the moment we understand these two people must be meant for each other.

And then I'd looked at him. Tall, well-built but not hulking or too big, piercing gray eyes behind nearly invisible glasses, blond hair graying at the temples and which I recalled very specifically made my stomach cramp.

And just like now, I didn't have words. *Me.* Leo Morrison. I couldn't come up with a single response besides, "Um..."

Jonas squared himself to me. "Is something wrong?"

Snap out of it, crazy!

I shook my head, hoping to clear away the fog the sight of him in a hoodie apparently caused. "Yes. No. Sorry. I'm just exhausted."

His brow furrowed and he stepped closer. "What can I do?"

Melting. He'd melted my cold, ice-hardened insides with that one phrase, and I loosed a rough breath at the feel of it. "What can you do?"

There came another smile, this time soft.

Guh.

"Is there anything? I could drive you home—did you walk today?" His offer, his concern... my exhaustion-addled brain couldn't take it. I didn't have it in me to pretend like it didn't matter to me.

"Uh, yes, actually, I did. And, if you don't mind, a ride home would be perfect. I'm supposed to meet Bel and Jamie for dinner later, and I'd love to have some time to rest before I need to be back."

We would have stood there smiling at each other if someone behind me hadn't interrupted with an unnecessarily aggressive, "Are you guys in line?"

The spell broken, we shuffled forward. Jonas attempted to buy my coffee, but I refused and insisted I buy his since he was giving me a ride, which he flatly rejected. So we each bought our own coffees, accepting the détente.

With our to-go cups in hand, we wandered down Main

side by side. I waved to Mia and Danny who'd crossed the street. Danny's brows lifted when he saw the man at my side, and then he gave me his blazing *oh I can't wait to hear about this* smile. I rolled my eyes dramatically, and we kept walking, quietly following the path up to the lot where Jonas had parked his car.

"Did you ever go to an *almabtrieb* in Europe?" I asked him as I buckled into the passenger side of his black Audi sedan.

"Only once. My father wanted to go, so we attended one in Mittenwald. It's a small town with murals on the buildings and a long thoroughfare for the cows. It was raining when they came through, and I spent more time jumping in puddles than anything else." His eyes didn't stray from the road as he spoke.

"Is it your father who's German, or your mother?" If he was willing to share details, I'd continue to pry.

He raised a brow and glanced at me. "How do you know either one of them is?"

"Oh come on. You have an accent, and your business partner does too. Your last name is German and you're just... *German.*"

He chuckled low. "My mother is German. My father was American—his family had German roots somewhere way back, so Bauer is, in fact, a German name, even though he was born and raised in Virginia."

My breathing hitched. *My father* was *American.* "Was?"

He nodded, swallowed. "He was killed while deployed to Afghanistan eleven years ago."

"Oh Jonas, I'm so sorry." My throat tightened.

"Thank you. He was a great man. I will never stop missing him."

I wished he'd stop driving so I could... I didn't know—look him in the eye, or something. This man had known pain, and that knowledge tore at some part of my heart that had been clinging to the notion that I couldn't—shouldn't—get involved with him.

Just as the thought came, the car stopped, and I looked up to find us parked in front of my place. How did he know where I lived?

CHAPTER NINETEEN

Jonas

Seeing Leonie Morrison flustered was a delight I'd never tire of. Even when angry, she seemed composed in a kind of steely, purposeful meanness. But lately, I'd gotten glimpses of this other side—the softer one, the more open version of her.

And now, her mouth dropped open. I wondered what words warred for speaking rights.

She turned sideways in the seat, her back to the door.

"First, I wanted to say..." She reached out and placed her hand on mine where it rested on the gear shift. "I'm so sorry about your dad. Mine had a heart attack not long ago and it terrified me. I can only imagine actually losing him."

"You father is a good man," I offered. I'd met him on several occasions and had always been impressed by the combination of easy, congenial demeanor and confidence. It was something each of his children had pieces of.

"He is."

"The other thing?" I prompted. Not that I wanted her to leave, per se, but I couldn't guarantee maintaining a respectable distance if she continued to sit there looking sleepy and sincere and talking in her quiet, exhaustion-roughened voice.

"How did you know where I live?" A glimmer of something like suspicion shone in her eye.

Of course she'd ask. Of course she'd consider something mildly sinister from me. I shook my head. "Are you concerned?"

She narrowed her eyes. "Should I be concerned?"

My smile split open, unable to maintain the façade. "Not unless my running habits concern you. I run all over this area and more than once, I've seen you turn up this way. Add to that the fact that I've seen your address on the employee profile paperwork when I took over from Liam, and it wasn't hard to figure out."

"Ah." She looked around the car a moment like she expected to find a clue as to what to say next, then seemed to register her hand still rested on mine. She pulled away abruptly and pushed open the car door.

I got out and walked with her, a step or two behind because she moved quickly and I didn't think jogging to keep up with her would be the right call. She glanced over her shoulder and her eyes widened as she saw me next to her.

"Uh, what are you doing?"

"Walking you to your door," I said, like it was that simple. I left off the *to see how much it'll take to provoke you.*

"But... why?" She seemed genuinely perplexed.

"I'm a gentleman."

"But this isn't— We're not— You don't—" She stomped her foot in a little gush of frustration. "That's kind of you, but I'm just here." She nodded to the door up the flight of stairs. "I'll see you Monday. Thanks for the ride."

Knowing when I'd been dismissed, I dipped my head in a gesture showing I understood and walked slowly back to my car, certain I could feel her eyes on me as I went, and heard a door slam just as I turned to face her again. No trace of her.

She made me want to pester and provoke her. Now that we'd managed to talk congenially and not rip each other's heads off with actual disagreements, I missed it a bit. I wanted her energy and her competitiveness, her quick wit and that flash of irritation that blazed in her eyes. Most of all, I liked that half the time, instead of frustration, she became flustered and a stain rose to her cheeks and her eyes got a little hazy, like she wasn't sure what was happening.

Leonie Morrison made me come alive in a way I had never felt before, and I was starting to like this feeling. Maybe not more than riling her, though. And I would admit it: yes. I liked that, too.

I didn't plan it out. I just... did it.

Unlike me, indeed. But she'd presented the information so deftly, and I'd become addicted to the sight of her. Even weeks like this last one when we didn't interact much beyond large group meetings, I found I wanted to see her, and the weekends when I wasn't guaranteed interaction with her dragged on.

So I shouldn't have been surprised when I found myself wandering into town that evening, deciding to dine out. Not

Mexican, not bar food, not *The Elk... Basta.* Perfect. I shuffled across the street, wishing I'd worn another layer over my light sweater as the fall wind cut through my clothes.

"Hi, Jonas." Bel Paxton offered a thin smile when I wandered up to the door of the restaurant next to which she and Jamie stood.

"Hello, Ms. Paxton. I hope you're well."

"We're fine. Good to be back for a bit." Her anger with me had cooled, and now I could have sworn I detected a glimmer of mischief in her eye.

We'd had a slightly better working relationship until I pushed her to reveal information about her now-fiancé's property development plans. I may have been slightly deceptive in my approach, but no one was harmed in the process, and really, there had been no need for the secrecy to begin with.

This event was something Leonie had berated me for and it had added a significant dose of lighter fluid to her already burning dislike of me this past summer. Fortunately, time marched on, Bel and Jamie forgave me, and it seemed Leonie had, perhaps despite herself, managed to overcome the issue.

"Have you seen your house?" Jamie asked, referring to the property I'd purchased in his new neighborhood.

Only a few homes were finished including his, Julian Grenier's, and one or two others. Mine had begun construction late in the summer and the structure was complete, but the interior had a long way to go. I wouldn't live in it for a while yet which was fine considering I had the mountain manager's cabin and appreciated the proximity to the office.

"I drove by not a week ago. I'm very happy with the progress. I'll look forward to moving in the spring."

"You're moving?" Leonie's voice came from behind me.

"Not for a while yet." I turned to see her wrapped in dark blue coat, a braid starting at one side of her head and arching over to the other side and behind her ear. How did she do these things?

"Are you meeting someone for dinner, Jonas?" Jamie asked, pulling Bel to him and wrapping an arm around her shoulders.

"Just picking up."

"Why don't you join us?" Bel asked.

A cough sounded next to me. "I'm sure Jonas has things to do."

Ah, so it was like that. I had no intention of barging in on their dinner, but I wouldn't miss the chance to mess with Leonie just a bit.

"I'm actually fairly wide open this evening," I said, turning to her with brows raised.

Her lips parted, then disappeared as she pressed them together and looked at Bel. Her eyes widened meaningfully, and I suppressed a chuckle.

Bel, apparently, didn't intend to rescue her. I wondered if she knew about the kiss.

"Oh, that's great! That'll make us an even four," she said, smile beaming at Leo with intent.

She had to know. That must've been the reason she kept looking so pleased with herself.

Leonie paled next to me. Was it so horrific to imagine a night with me? It'd all been in good fun—I wouldn't impose on their dinner, but something dropped in my gut. She genuinely didn't want me to join them.

I snapped my fingers. "Ah, you know? I've just remembered a conference call."

"This late?" Bel asked.

"It's with a client in Hawaii." *Lies.*

"You still have clients?" Leonie asked, the color returning to her cheeks now that she wouldn't have to face a whole evening with me.

"Of course. Bauer Group continues to function, even as I'm here full time. Karla does most of the in-person assessments, though I will likely be traveling for a consultation before the season begins."

"Oh," she said, the sound full of some emotion I couldn't identify. Most likely a veiled disdain, based on the way the conversation was going.

"I'll be off. Enjoy your evening. Good to see you, Ms. Paxton. Mr. Morris."

CHAPTER TWENTY

Leo

T he need to go after him and say something—anything —crawled up my back and over my scalp as I followed Bel and Jamie to the table.

"So..." Bel smiled, obviously proud of herself.

"You made him super uncomfortable," I grumbled, unfolding the menu only to close it back since I already knew what I'd order.

Jamie didn't say a thing, the jerk. He just watched us with his hand resting on the back of Bel's chair.

"I did not. *You* made him uncomfortable by making an excuse for why he couldn't come after I invited him to join us." She primly sipped her water to punctuate her point.

"I just... it would have been awkward. I mean, you guys don't get along with him, and—"

"I get along fine with him now that we cleared the air

about the development. He's going to be our neighbor eventually." Jamie looked at Bel, then swooped in to kiss her cheek like he couldn't help it.

God save me from these precious couples who were genuinely adorable but made me want to pull my hair out. "How special for you."

"Seriously though, why didn't you let him join us?" No more teasing inflection.

I swiped a hand over my braid, finding the little ripples of twined hair soothing.

"I haven't spent much time with him outside of work. I don't think I want to do that for the first time with my beloved brother and you." I tucked the napkin in my lap. "Plus, I want to see *you*. I miss you guys. I mean, Jamie, I love you, but I mostly miss Bel, but still..."

Jamie chuckled.

"I'm old news. I know. I can't blame you." He ran a hand over Bel's shoulder, letting his fingers slide through the long caramel strands of her hair.

Ugh.

"We're coming back at Christmas, and actually it might even work out to be here for Thanksgiving and opening day." Bel said this to me, but she was looking at Jamie all doe-eyed and ridiculous.

I let them have their moment, craning my neck to see around the restaurant. Only about half of the diners were people I knew in one way or another which meant plenty of people had lingered after the cows had paraded through to stay for dinner. *Excellent.*

Hoping it'd been enough time, I turned back to the table to find them sitting close, Jamie's hand obviously resting on Bel's leg under the table, and her cheeks notably flushed.

"You done?" I said, deadpan.

"Never."

Jamie's vehemence made me smile through my false impatience. "So when's the wedding?"

Bel perked up, but looked to Jamie.

"Hoping spring. Here, of course. We're firming up some scheduling issues, and then we'll know for sure."

Spring. They'd be married in spring. Danny and Mia wouldn't last through the end of the year to have their big day. Liam and Wells had been married coming up on two months.

And me? I'd gone from no prospects, being surrounded by lovesick couples on all sides, and feeling the acute *lack* of Bel in my daily life, to... what? Crushing on my hard case half-German professionally questionable and extremely good-looking boss who'd stolen my dream job?

Yikes, Leo. Yikes.

My chest pinched, just a little. I was genuinely so happy for all of them, and maybe especially Bel and Jamie since they'd been such a long time coming, but the more time I spent with these beloved people, the more sharply I could feel the harsh reality that I was not someone's beloved. I never had been. I'd never had someone look at me the way Jamie was looking at Bel even now—like he didn't want to look away, like she was too good to be true.

Then it came. The memory of Jonas' words low in my ear. *I will thank God the day I die if only this picture of you never leaves me.*

Jonas might look at me like that. He really might. If he wasn't joking that night, and if all his incredible, intense statements were true, then...

I shook off the thought as the waiter arrived, and

resolved to stay present and soak up the little bit of time I'd have with them. Tomorrow morning, they had a meeting with a decorator for their house, and then the afternoon would be swept up into preparing for the brewery opening that night. It was a soft opening before their first full weekend next weekend, though I suspected Liam had scheduled it when Jamie could be here without concern for the soft or hard of it.

And Jonas would be there. Based on my reaction to the thought of being in a non-work setting with him for longer than a few minutes, I should probably just ask him out. His problematic role at the lodge, my suspicion of him... it hadn't disappeared. But he was handsome, successful, and the more I learned about him, shockingly enough, the more I liked—if I could ignore that whole area of suspicion. And maybe I couldn't... but I'd never know unless I tried, and the more I thought about it, the more I wanted to try.

In the face of these two lovebirds, the small, shy part of my heart admitted it wanted to see... to ignore the huge, obvious problems with Jonas and just see what might develop.

If I ever wanted to have a conversation *not* on Silver Ridge property or in front of family or colleagues, which I could admit now, I did, then I'd have to make it happen.

Mountain chic was the dress code for Liam's brewery opening. Technically, it was a brewery and restaurant, but the restaurant wouldn't be fully open for another month. The first four weeks would be a limited menu and limited hours as they got going.

I interpreted mountain chic to mean dark fitted jeans,

nice black short boots with as much heel as I ever wore—about two inches—and a tight navy V-neck sweater. Nothing fancy, but all of it flattering. I felt good, comfortable, and I'd actually styled my long hair in waves with just a small braid to hold the strands near my forehead in check.

It was a crystal-clear night, so I walked. About five minutes in, I wished I'd decided to drive, but too late now. I had the fleeting thought that if I had Jonas' cell number, I might've called him earlier in the day to see if he would give me a ride.

Lame excuse to get him alone, yes. But I still would have. Maybe the first step in all of this was just to get his number... it was weird I didn't have it anyway. I had his office number, but for events, we used walkie talkies, so I'd never really needed it.

Except now, as I shuffled along past the lodge, the little butterflies in my belly, so active these days, flitted around at even the thought of seeing Jonas.

"Leonie."

I smiled to myself before adopting a neutral face and turning. "Oh, hey Jonas."

See how calm?

"May I walk with you?" he asked as he drew even with where I stood on the sidewalk.

He stopped next to me and I gazed up at him. The sun lit just the farthest reaches of the sky to our west but it was enough to see his brutally handsome face, no glasses tonight, fresh shave...

"I'd love it. In fact, I was just thinking about you as I walked by." *Oh.* Okay. So, subtle was not going to be my approach. Thank you floppy little bugs in my belly, no luck with being the cool one tonight.

"Were you?" His brow arched.

I turned and began to walk, and so did he.

"I was. I thought how weird it is I don't have your phone number." I glanced at him, but his face told me nothing.

After a few steps, he spoke. "What would you do with it?"

Times like this right here felt like flirting. We *were* flirting. But his face could be so opaque, and his tone was just normal and straight with no hint of teasing or that little oomph you'd get with someone who was interested in you.

"Text you? Only when necessary. Nothing silly. No bad poetry or jokes or memes," I assured.

"Well if it's nothing silly, I suppose I could give it to you."

Then he made a sound, kind of like a regretful sound.

"What?"

"Well it's just that if I give you my number, then I'll have yours."

He eyed me as we walked, and my nerves pinged around in my chest. Somehow, the idea of him having my number, even though he knew where I lived and clearly could have gotten my cell number from the same place, made me feel floaty with anticipation.

"Is that a problem?"

"Well, it might be. What if I want to send you bad poetry or jokes or memes?"

I chuckled and shoved his arm. He caught my gloved hand in his and tucked it under his arm into his elbow. *Okay then.*

I had to bite my lip to keep from laughing, needing some way to break the thrill that raced through me at his move. It wasn't particularly forward or even intimate, but it was very definitely something that made heat burst where the sleeves of our jackets touched, where he placed his hand on mine at the crook of his arm.

Maybe I'd been reading too much historical romance, but walking into town on Jonas' arm had me positively lightheaded.

"If you must send one of those, make it bad poetry."

CHAPTER TWENTY-ONE

Jonas

Before we walked into the old mill building straddling the Silver River, Leonie released my arm.

I could understand not wanting to walk into the party for her brother's business paired up with me. We weren't paired. We'd simply walked together, and though I'd relished the feel of her close to me, her hand tucked into my arm and her body canted toward me as we went, I wouldn't read anything into it.

Better not to show everyone my hand here anyway—as helpless as I was against her charms, it demonstrated a weakness I instinctively disliked. Not that I had some antiquated idea of masculinity or felt the need to remain emotionless or without attachment—quite the opposite, in fact. But if anyone had an inkling of just how ridiculous I felt over Leonie, they'd never take me seriously again. I'd have to expedite the sale of my stock and get out of town fast.

And the biggest problem with that, of course, was then I'd have to leave a place, and a person, I suspected I might never want to leave, however imbecilic that made me.

The October night held a new chill, like the weather would turn to winter any minute and soon frost would cover windows and meadows. I hadn't been here this time last year but anticipated the change in season—the fall to winter transition heralded my favorite part of the year.

"Thanks for walking with me," she said as we ascended the sagging wooden steps to the main door of the large brick building.

"My pleasure."

"Maybe we could walk back together—just to the lodge. If you want. If we leave on time." She twisted toward the door, then whipped back. "You know what? Never m—"

"I'd like to walk back with you."

She bit her lip like she wasn't sure she believed me. Honestly, I wasn't entirely sure I believed her. I thought we'd gotten somewhere with the kiss last weekend, but last night, she'd seemed overcome with awkwardness and dread at the thought of me joining her party for dinner. I'd left confused, and resolved to give her space and take the cue. I'd determined to refocus on business and get my head out of the fog she put me in.

Then she came trotting down the road, and just like every other time I'd been alone with her outside of a strictly professional capacity in the last month, I couldn't keep my distance.

It should be noted for the record that when I said *I couldn't keep my distance*, it wasn't an excuse. Obviously, I *chose* not to. Nothing in this life is so tempting and powerful we have *no choice* and therefore escape responsibility for our actions. I loathed the idea that people were so overcome, so in love, so attracted, so *whatever* they just couldn't help themselves and... what? Cheated? Assaulted someone? Said the thing that was entirely inappropriate and offensive?

No. Unacceptable.

Each move I'd made with Leonie had been, at least on some level, calculated. The first night of Oktoberfest when I'd commented on her appearance, it'd come from an overwhelming desire for her, but it also wasn't crossing the line. I'd decided, after her kindness to me, that it was time to determine if there might be something else between us beyond enmity.

With all that said, being near her did cast me into a new place. As an extremely controlled, methodical person, I found myself responding to her in surprising ways. This behavior stemmed from the root cause: I'd admitted to myself that underneath all that wild, blazing beauty and passion, she was also a genuinely lovely person.

I'd seen it from a distance for months—her skill at teaching children, helping them when they fell or failed, communicating with parents, assisting various staff or jumping in to solve a problem whether it be a broken zipper on Jiff's winter jacket or a purchase order for the cafeteria gone missing.

I'd seen her care for her brothers and Bel, for the town, and especially for her family and its legacy in Silver Ridge.

But the moment she set that little bag of soup and bread on my porch, that did it. It flipped the switch a not-small part of me had been *waiting* to flip. I'd been looking for an excuse to give myself permission to see what she was like—really like. And now I had it.

Because of this, I had no desire to pretend my interest in

her was professional or brotherly or anything but what it was—utter fascination with a healthy dose of wariness. And I was wary, because the woman was formidable and intense, but also possibly directly at odds with what I'd been working toward here. She wanted to keep Silver Ridge Resort in the family. I'd expressly planned to take it from them.

Though admittedly, that plan had changed the more time I spent here, and she'd played a role in that.

"Are you coming?" she asked from the doorway. She must have walked ahead while I mentally meandered.

"Yes." I jogged up the steps and through the doorway, moving to set my hand at her lower back, but thinking better of it before I made contact. If she didn't want to hold my arm, she might not welcome that gesture. Better to be sure, especially in a room full of everyone we both knew and then some.

"Wow," she said, stopping abruptly enough that I nearly rammed into her.

"Impressive."

Liam Morrison was a capable manager, and it came as no surprise his brewery would be stylish yet comfortable, welcoming and appealing. I'd met his business partner John Wallace in my early days here, and he seemed capable as well. He certainly knew how to brew a decent beer.

"Leo. Jonas? Welcome!"

Liam waved to us as we wandered farther into the large room. The main mill building featured brick walls and stone flooring. At the far end, glass encased what must be the actual brewing operation, and the space leading up to that area was full of wood-carved tables and inviting chairs. Despite the dark brick and the evening outside, the room shone brightly thanks to the modernized lighting.

The space was packed despite this being a supposed *soft* opening.

"Hang jackets over there, if you like," he said, then pointed to a long row of hooks just inside the entrance. "Did you guys come together?"

His gaze shifted between us as he extended a hand to me after kissing his sister's cheek.

"We were walking down at the same time," Leonie explained, but then she did it again—bit her lip, just before she turned to hang her coat.

That action struck me as both strange and wonderful. If I didn't know her better, I'd almost say it was a shy movement, something indicating a bit of embarrassment or lack of surety, but that couldn't possibly be the case because Leonie Morrison didn't have a shy bone in her body.

My stomach clenched at the thought. I didn't know if she was shy—I only knew she wasn't around me. Maybe this lip-biting, occasionally blushing, hidden-smiling woman was another version of her.

I wanted this one too.

"Oh, that's nice. Well come on in, grab a beer, grab some food, look around." He patted my shoulder, and then moved to greet the next small group of people who'd entered.

Leonie looked at me, then tipped her head to one side. "Shall we?"

I followed her to the bar and took a pint of the Black Diamond Stout. The chill in the air made me anticipate winter, and I loved nothing more than a nice stout with the cold. It was a bit early, but I wanted to see how they'd done with it. After a sip, "Ah. Well done."

"It's good beer, isn't it?" she said, beaming before she

took a drink of her own, something lighter, and set it gently on a coaster at the counter.

"Well hello there, Leo."

The mountain of a man sauntered up to her, his eyes sliding over her body.

She raised her glass a bit to him in a toast. "Warrick, good to see you."

He stepped up to the bar next to her, handed his empty glass to the bartender, then focused all his attention on her.

My gaze shifted around the room, taking in the small groups of people talking, the stylish details I hadn't noticed before like large black and white photographs of what looked like old photos of the mountains, resort, and town.

"You look good."

Warrick Saint's voice caught my attention, but I denied myself a glance at Leonie. The way he said it though... the words were filled with warmth, familiarity... was this a past lover?

The thought sank like a rock in my gut.

"You do too, War. How's farm life treating you? Missing the city?"

"Not much. I like the fresh air, the view of the stars, and all the pretty girls."

If I was the type, I'd roll my eyes.

A voice I knew a bit better interjected. "Is this giant pestering you, Leo?"

"Hey, Wy." Now it was her voice that sounded warm, familiar.

Jealousy clutched my chest, hot and sharp. I turned to the bar and gave Wyatt Saint a nod.

"Jonas, good to see you," Wyatt said, offering his hand. "Have you ever met my brother Warrick?"

Apparently, all the Saint boys were huge, but this one

had really been eating his Wheaties. I'd seen him at the fest but hadn't officially met him. "No. Pleasure."

Warrick, who had to be six foot six and probably close to three hundred pounds though guessing weight wasn't my forte, clasped my hand in his. I was a large man, but his hands swallowed mine like I'd put on a pair of my dad's gloves. This person was genuinely huge.

"Nice to meet you man. You're manager up at the lodge, right?" He flashed a smile, and his face was open and friendly.

"Yes."

He nodded, brows raised like he was impressed, then hooked an arm around Leonie's waist and pulled her to him. "Great place. And is that how you know our girl here?"

CHAPTER TWENTY-TWO

Leo

I elbowed Warrick in the ribs. Not gently.

The little *oof* gave me extreme satisfaction and I cut him a glare. "*Our girl*, really Warrick?"

He chuckled, then patted my head. Heat flamed in my chest, and the urge to knee him in the nuts danced in my mind before his older, wiser, *better* brother intervened.

"Warrick used to play with Leo when they were kids. He was only a year ahead of her in school. He's also a former NFL player and is still trying to find himself." Wyatt clapped his brother on the back and Warrick shot him a glare.

I gave Wyatt a genuine smile. What a nice guy. I braced for that familiar drop of disappointment that I couldn't manage to like him *that* way to hit, but it didn't come... especially not with Jonas standing there, watching the scene.

"Have you been back in Silverton long?" Jonas asked, keeping his focus on Warrick.

I hid a smile in my glass as I took a drink. He looked so severe standing next to smiley, energetic Warrick and even Wyatt, who didn't perma-grin like his brother who was always flirting with someone, but who had a face that just seemed... kind.

Bel came and grabbed me just then.

"I'll see you guys later," I said, and made sure to catch Jonas' eye. I hoped he understood that I particularly meant him. His only response was to spear me with his gray eyes before Bel dragged me away.

"Where have you been?" Wells asked, a hand on her hip.

"Uh, at the bar?" I held up my beer as evidence.

"No, I mean like, in life. You've disappeared off the planet. We haven't had a girls' dinner in over a month."

Her frown and furrowed brow spoke of more than disappointment. I could see, or maybe hear in her voice, she was hurt.

"I figured you were busy, and Mia was too, plus all the events the last two weeks, I've just been..." I shrugged.

I couldn't defend my choice not to initiate a girls' night because I now felt lonely even when I was with them. I couldn't come right out and say, "*Sorry, but I'm having an extended pity party for myself and being around you guys makes me feel ashamed.*"

Wells didn't let me off the hook. "You figured Mia and I were too busy to have dinner like we have every other week in recent memory?"

I shifted my weight between my feet, wishing I hadn't worn these boots. "No, I just figured with Bel gone and—"

Bel stopped that. "Don't blame me. I told you I'd video conference in if I had to."

I shot her a frown. "I'm sorry. I am. And I don't want to make excuses. Let's plan something for next week."

Wells' face dropped. "I can't next week."

I chuckled and looked to the ceiling. "Okay. The week after?"

She smiled wide, then pulled out her phone and began searching for days. I slowly inhaled, calming the jumble of emotion the exchange had caused, and gave Bel a spare, close-lipped smile as she squeezed my hand.

The brewery opening was a hit as far as I could tell, but I was glad to leave the room that still brimmed with people. I found Jonas waiting by the stairs.

"Ready?"

"Very," I said.

I loved a good social event, but lately they'd exhausted me. Likely because they were stacked on top of each other. I felt the relief flood in as I realized the next big event I had would be Thanksgiving with my family. My parents had decided to fly in for it this year, so we'd make it a big deal and enjoy the calm before the true madness of the season set in.

"Did you enjoy yourself?" he asked as we strolled along the sidewalk that led past Elk Street, then around the back side of the building at the end of Main, and up the path toward the Silverton Inn.

"Of course." I tossed it out there before thinking. Did I really?

Yes. I did. I got to see Bel and Wells and see the pride in

Liam's face, and the brewery and restaurant themselves looked fantastic. But somehow, I was happier to be out here in the crisp night with Jonas. That thought should've bothered me more than it did.

We walked in silence until he spoke.

"Did you notice how the Saint men can't keep their eyes off you?"

I guffawed. "They're good friends."

"Friends?" Pure skepticism in the word.

"At this point, yes. Wyatt and I tried dating last summer, but we had no chemistry."

"Hmm." Not quite a harrumph, but... an odd sound. Who knew what it meant, and I wasn't about to ask.

"Poor fool," he mumbled.

"What?"

His eyes cut to mine, then bounced back to the path ahead, lit occasionally by streetlights. "I said *poor fool* because he is clearly still enamored of you but you've placed him on the sideline. I feel for him."

I sputtered. "What? No. He's not interested. It was totally mutual."

"No."

"It was!"

"Sure it was."

I sigh-groaned dramatically. "Not that it's any of your business, but I'm pretty sure he's already moved on. He and I were friends, and we are again. We kissed, it was weird, we *both* thought so, and now—"

He halted his progress and whipped around. "You kissed?"

I stopped before I ran into him.

"Yeahhh..." I drew out the word, not sure where this was going.

Without answering, he turned on his heel and stalked up the hill toward the lodge.

"Um, hello? What is happening right now?" I called as I jogged after him, frustration lighting into a little ball of irritation and the desire to push him—verbally for certain, and maybe even physically. Being six foot four or whatever he was meant his legs covered ground like it was their job and also meant I had to work to catch up with him. Handy for me, I never wore a pair of shoes I couldn't walk a mile or run at least a little ways in.

When I reached him, I grabbed his arm to slow his progress. "Seriously, what's up?"

He faced me, hands shoved in his jacket pockets. "Is that where they all end up?"

I looked around, waiting for a clue. "Who? What?"

"Anyone you kiss—they all end up relegated to the friendzone?" Frustration and judgement edged his voice.

My jaw clamped shut, teeth grinding. I skipped the calming breath I might have attempted if I wasn't cold, tired, and full of unmet expectations. "You say it like I'm running around town gathering up the men of Silverton, sampling them, and casting them aside. Which, by the way, is none of your business. I can't believe I'm even acknowledging this conversation, much less that I feel some bizarre need to defend myself."

I waited for a response, but got nothing but steely gray eyes studying me. Another beat, then I nodded and took off, lengthening my strides so I could get as far away from him as quickly as possible. The footsteps behind me told me he followed, but I didn't want to talk to him.

Funny how all evening, I'd been itching to get back here alone with him, wandering up the star-lit street, chill nipping at us but maybe holding his arm again. *Never mind then.*

I shouldn't have been surprised. Why would I expect the nature of our relationship, which had always been contentious, to change so quickly? Or for us to be able to talk things like this through calmly, when neither one of us seemed to know what we wanted or how to get it?

His hand, shockingly warm on my cold one, stopped me with a gentle tug. "Leonie."

I gave him time, hoping whatever he'd say would make this better.

He pushed an exhale out his nose, his mouth frowning. "You don't need to defend yourself."

Not enough. I jerked away from him and started walking, but he caught up, grabbed my hand again, shaking his.

"Sorry. Damn. I should say I'm sorry. I'm jealous of every man you've ever kissed, and I have no right to be. I dread the thought that our kiss might put me in the same place those other poor saps ended up."

His hand gripped mine more firmly as he studied me. Meanwhile, my mind circled around what he'd said, then a laugh escaped me. "Why didn't you just say that?"

His eyes shifted to the side. "I just did."

"But why'd you worry about anyone else? They have no bearing on our relationship..." I coughed, trying to cover my use of the word, which was clearly premature. "Or whatever this is."

A half-smile. "I don't know. Being confronted with your stable of admirers threw me."

I scoffed.

"I can't say I blame them. I count myself among them in that regard," he said with a quiet smile.

My chest heated and I couldn't hide the smile. He was

such a strange mix of intense and somber and then persistently complimentary. Not even that... it was more than just compliments. It was... *forward*.

It shouldn't surprise me though. In everything else, whether in disagreement with me, or suggesting a new course of action, or praising something about the mountain, he said what he meant.

And he'd said he was an admirer of mine.

He insisted on this idea, always offering me verbal praise despite whatever disagreement we found ourselves in. And really, the last few weeks, there hadn't been much. I might have felt like I was wandering around blindfolded when it came to him, but he didn't leave me any room to wonder if he was interested. Now that he'd decided to let me know, he *really* let me know.

I'd confused him yesterday. I knew I had. I'd been confused myself. But I could set the record straight and make clear what I wanted, even if I knew better than to want it. That's what I did, right? I went after what I wanted.

I cleared my throat and ignored the fizzing nervousness and anticipation flashing through me. "You know how to set yourself apart from the rest of them?"

His eyes narrowed and he shook his head.

"Kiss me again."

CHAPTER TWENTY-THREE

Jonas

"Forgive me if I'm wrong, but I believe you kissed me first."

Her mouth dropped open in that disbelieving way she had, then her lips slid into a smile. "Seriously?"

"Am I wrong?" I stepped closer. I might be making a point here, but I had no intention of missing the chance to take her up on her suggestion.

Her eyes narrowed on me, but I could see the faint pull of a smile at the corners of her mouth. Then a low, "No."

Mein Gott, this woman and her voice and that look in her eye. "So?"

"So, your turn."

She didn't need to tell me twice. I crowded into her space and took her face in my hands, her cool cheeks soft against the pads of my fingers. She tipped her head up just as I leaned down and captured her mouth.

I intended to keep it simple, particularly since the temperature was dropping and I could feel her shivering, but she pulled me closer, her hands sliding up around my neck and into my hair, then rose on her toes to deepen the kiss.

I may have moaned.

A car drove by and flashed its lights at us, and we broke apart at the sound of the engine and the interruption.

She dropped her hands by her side, then grinned so widely, the street brightened with her. "Well. Okay then."

And then off she went, moving again, evidently unperturbed by the kiss that had just changed all my plans. No way could I deny any longer that I had this woman in my blood. And though this proved problematic, well, to hell with it right now. Nothing mattered but whatever this was developing between us.

We walked up the crest of the hill and onto the plaza where she stopped right in front of the door of my house and turned to me. "Thanks for walking with me."

"My pleasure, truly."

"Any chance you'd give me a ride the rest of the way?"

I retrieved my keys from my coat pocket. "Of course."

The walk to her house would only take her a few minutes, but it was full dark now and even though she'd done it a million times before and there was likely nothing to fear, I wanted to take her home, see her to her door.

I did just that, and then risked parking the car, getting out, and following her up the stairs to her place. She turned and leaned in, looked at me with hooded eyes.

"We should probably spend some more time together," she said in that quiet, textured voice that hit me between the ribs.

"Yes." I stepped closer, hoping to close the distance and

steal one more kiss—might as well since we were here at the doorstep scene and all.

"Soon."

With one hand at her side, I leaned down. "Yes."

She tilted her head and spoke not an inch from my lips, the warm air of her breath reaching me with her words.

"Goodnight, Jonas." Then a soft, translucent kiss.

The next week plodded along, slow-moving like a calm before the storm. I didn't take Leonie out. I hardly saw her. She conducted interviews and when she wasn't doing that, I had various meetings and responsibilities. I'd decided I wouldn't seek her out at work, particularly because we'd decided we'd see each other outside of our professional lives and I wanted that. Somehow, seeing her at work seemed like *less* if I couldn't touch her and speak to her the way I wanted, and I certainly couldn't and maintain appropriate boss-employee boundaries.

Julian Grenier called warning of his arrival the following week. We had what I'd call a positive adversarial relationship. I suspected anyone other than Jamie Morris and the man's own mother had a somewhat adversarial connection with Grenier. He was... odd. Stiff, almost uncomfortable with human interaction that wasn't precise and direct, and yet he'd already proven to be incredibly generous with the town and useful to me.

The week finished with a spectacularly terrible meeting.

"What are you suggesting?" Leonie asked, no edge to her voice yet, but I could see the tightness in her jaw.

"The proposal I presented months ago included plans

for a hotel. With Julian Grenier's help, I've arranged for an architect and builder to come out in early November after we get the land surveys in. I've submitted to the county about zoning and it's all but approved." I smoothed a hand down the front of my suit.

"Wait. You're moving ahead with this? What's the timeline?"

No one else at the table spoke, which included two of her brothers and the rest of the board.

"Assuming Piqued Peak invest, which by all accounts they'll do by week's end, we'll be looking at breaking ground this coming summer." I clicked to a new slide on the screen, ready to move on.

"This is... wrong. This doesn't sound like what you proposed. Forty rooms? That's... where is this going to go?"

Though her words were flustered, her voice came out clear, firm, demanding.

I clicked a few slides ahead and used the laser pointer to show her where the hotel would be. "We'll have to clear this area, which can be done late spring depending on the thaw. I've told the architect we want to keep as many of the mature trees as possible, of course. This will allow for ski-in, ski-out, and shouldn't—"

"Where did this land come from? That wasn't lodge land, was it?" Pink tinged her cheeks now, and she leaned on one elbow as she studied the map.

"No, in fact. We've acquired it."

"Whose land?" she persisted.

"Most recently, Julian Grenier held the land."

She swallowed. "And before that?"

She wouldn't like this. I didn't need to tell her this, not *here*. We could have this conversation elsewhere, but in the end, everyone here already knew, or should know. "William and Alice Morrison."

Her lashes shuttered, then those blue eyes cut to Liam, then Danny, then me. The two Morrison brothers straightened, but Liam spoke first. "What? When?"

No doubt he was considering how much toil the ownership of this land might have saved him during the original consulting process when I'd found an investor who insisted on land to build out a hotel. They didn't have it, and that's when Liam had foolishly mentioned Wells Bryant's land, which he had no claim on. I knew as much, and in the end, I stepped in to invest after seeing the family pull together and Liam own his error. As the unnamed investor, I could afford and happily fund the clearing of this newly acquired land.

That their parents had sold land associated with their family legacy was not my problem. I said as much.

"I suspect you should discuss the particulars with your family." The three Morrisons, and each other person on the board, regarded me with wide eyes. Perhaps my tone was a bit sharp. "If there's nothing else, I'd like to get to the fourth quarter budget review before we dismiss."

I should have known Leonie would find me after, but some foolish part of me thought perhaps she wouldn't take out her frustration on me. I'd been the bad guy in her eyes so many times over the last year, I supposed it was default.

"How could you keep this from me?" Her eyes blazed, her mouth shut tight as she stood in the doorway to my office minutes after we'd left the conference room.

"I didn't keep it from you. I proposed the plan this summer and it was approved." I shuffled papers on my desk to keep from having to look at her with that storm cloud face.

"You presented it in the five-year plan. You insinuated it

would be toward the end of that time, and said nothing about having the land in hand. You—"

"If you review the meeting notes, you'll see I did indicate a potential for the land. I hadn't yet found a way in with Grenier, but thanks to your brother and their development partnership, after securing property of my own in their neighborhood, Grenier was open to my putting him in touch with my lawyer to discuss—"

"Are you telling me you bought a house in that neighborhood to make the connection?" This, based on the look on her face, was horrific news.

And that visage made me straighten and drop the papers. "Yes. It's business."

"When you said 'we acquired the land,' who is *we?*"

"I did." Her eyes grew wide, and I rushed to speak. "Again, it's business. It was a good move for the resort."

Pink rose to her cheeks, but I knew better than to call it a blush. A *flush*, likely rage-induced.

"It isn't *just* business. It's my family's legacy. And you plopping some garish hotel that blocks the view of the mountain for half of the resort and anyone sitting in the plaza, much less taking land that was part of my family—" She cut herself off, cleared her throat. "Wells Bryant is breaking ground on her hotel in the spring."

"Excellent."

Her hands fisted at her sides. "That's two hotels in one small town. Neither will succeed. We don't need two hotels."

"Leonie, with all due respect, we do. If this resort succeeds in any way, more than one hotel will be a necessity."

"Did you actually just *with all due respect* me?" Her voice rose in tenor and volume.

I cleared my throat, my mind casting out for a response. "Yes."

She stood there a moment, laser beams shooting from her eyes, then whipped around and disappeared down the hallway as though rocket-propelled.

CHAPTER TWENTY-FOUR

Leo

The family meeting that weekend was contentious, right up until my parents came on the screen.

My brothers and I had initiated a video meeting with our parents. My gut response was to blame Liam for this, but then I found he had nothing to do with any of it. That made more sense considering his desperation about not having land last year—if he'd known my parents owned or even *had* owned a parcel that would work so well, I would've heard about it.

"What happened? Why did you sell the land?" Liam spoke for all of us, though he and I were likely the ones who cared the most.

Ma sighed. "Your father's heart attack happened."

"What?"

This didn't make sense. They had great health insurance—that was always a priority for them and for all the employees at the lodge. It was one of the ways I lured child-care workers to us.

"Not the medical bills, but the decision to move. You know we live in a nice area here. We haven't sold the home there, so we had to sell something. We weren't even considering it but Mr. Grenier came to us with an unusually generous offer and we saw it for what it was—a chance to retire somewhere without the toil, without having to sell our family home, without—"

"You don't need to justify it, Ma. It's great." Danny's voice cut in, full of sincerity.

My chest felt a little like it was caving in. I didn't want them to feel bad about this choice. Of course it made sense. And good for them. Why shouldn't they take the offer. But why didn't they—

"Why didn't you tell us?" Liam sounded resigned, and we could all hear it there—*Why didn't you tell me?*

"Honestly honey, it was a crazy time. We were all running in different directions, your father was recovering, and we just took it. We didn't mean to keep it from you, but it's also not land we had plans for. We own other land in the valley and up the canyon but it's not useful."

"I'm glad you sold it," I chimed in, not wanting to seem bitter, as I was so often accused of being. *As I often am,* I admitted to myself.

"Yeah, it's great. It just sort of blindsided us today," Liam added.

Da chimed in then with a typically silly comment. "A parent's first job is to raise his children well. His second job is to do everything he can to torment them when they're grown. Consider this a small effort at tormenting you with surprise."

We all laughed, and the tightness in my chest eased

some. They deserved rest and peace and warmth and the absence of financial stress. I wished I could feel glad about the sale—I shut my eyes and genuinely prayed I could get on board with a hotel on that land.

The call ended with promises to talk soon and plans to visit for Thanksgiving—even Jamie said he was trying to make it work for him and Bel. I went to bed that night feeling conflicted—glad, relieved, and happy for my parents. Grateful to the enigmatic Julian Grenier. And yet, sad for the way the lodge—*resort*—would change.

And if I let down my guard and spoke truth to myself, there it was—if there was a hotel too, I didn't know much about that world. This scenario would decrease my chances of a smooth transition to managing the whole resort. Managing a hotel wasn't something I'd trained for. I knew every inch of the mountain and the business otherwise— that would make me a compelling choice. But a hotel... that changed things. I didn't want it... we didn't need it. If Jonas maneuvered it in here so soon, I couldn't make a very good case that I was the best woman for the job.

The thought of losing that life-long dream pressed in on me, and I fought the whole night without sleep.

~

Wells and Mia met me at *Guac* a few days later. I'd avoided Jonas thanks to the weekend, then my own busy schedule, and presumably his too.

"So, when's the wedding?" I asked, feeling both trepidation and anticipation.

Mia blushed deep, which wasn't entirely unusual but told me just the thought of marrying my sweet, dorky, mountain-loving brother thrilled her.

"December. We're thinking the twenty-third so your parents would be here anyway, Kai's off school, and it's not exactly the busiest days of the season, though it is getting there. We'll wait for a honeymoon, if we even take one..." She trailed off.

"Of course you're going to take a honeymoon!" I said, just as Wells said, "Liam and I will take Kai!"

Mia tucked her lips into her teeth and smiled, all surprised joy. "Well. We'll figure out when then. But we'll just do an evening ceremony... if it works for everyone."

"You keep hedging like we might be too busy to show up for your wedding. We'll definitely be there. It's going to be amazing, and I just need to know what to do to help." I patted her hand across the table and Wells pulled her in for a quick hug.

The conversation from then on was largely wedding-focused—colors, dresses, venues, flowers, reception plans... but eventually they asked what was going on in my life and I filled them in on the hotel news. I left out the developments between me and Jonas because at that moment, they didn't feel like anything but ancient history.

"Wow... a hotel. That's great." Wells' voice emerged strained.

I sighed. "I know. *I know*. I'm fighting it. He made it sound like it was years away, and now it's breaking ground this summer. That's just insane. You've been developing your plan for a year, and you've already got the architectural design and permits. I'm just sorry you can't start building for another few months."

"It's good though, right? Ultimately, we want to get to a place where Silverton needs far more than just two small-ish hotels. This is a good start, and will only help the economy and everyone's business." Mia's words were gentle, but wise.

"It's true. I can't help but feel a little competition at the outset, but in the end it really is good. For everyone. What I'm offering at my hotel won't be the same as what your resort hotel offers. They'll be different, and that's good. We need more space, more rooms, and people to fill them."

We continued chatting, eating, catching up, but the uneasy feeling in my chest didn't go away. I felt... unmoored. Like I was waving about. Too much change was coming—brothers and friends married, my family's legacy landscape changed entirely, and my whole vision of myself and my future seemed opaque.

And not that this was a concern of mine, but who was Jonas that he could buy out the property from Julian Grenier and only mention it as an afterthought?

CHAPTER TWENTY-FIVE

Jonas

Grenier's visit proceeded as expected—moderately uncomfortable, but with excellent results.

I showed him and his contact around the space. Grenier had intimated he would be interested in investing in the project, but I'd told him we were all set. Piqued Peak had signed on the dotted line. I'd make them an offer through my other channels in a few weeks and based on what I'd learned, they'd at the very least be willing to make me a silent partner, if not owner of their firm. This would get me the majority of Silver Ridge, which I'd always planned on having, without rocking the boat too much and showing my hand that I was, in fact, the initial investor. If I could keep *that* quiet, all the better.

All was going to plan.

Except the part where Leonie had avoided me since the meeting more than ten days ago. She'd had a full plate last week, but this week she'd canceled our weekly check-in, begging off with the excuse of an appointment and to avoid any rescheduling, provided an insanely thorough review of her staffing progress, the schedules she'd developed, the education plan for a new group progression... more than we would've covered in our regular meeting.

I finally tracked her down on Wednesday, twelve days after the meeting in which she found out the hotel would break ground this summer, and that her parents had sold land once belonging to them... land I now owned. I did this because I could no longer tolerate the distance between us, the very idea of which grated against my logical side that knew I should use this opportunity to get a hold of myself and let her grip on me loosen, and yet...

"Hello, Leonie," I said as I came to stand next to the table where she sat eating with Danny.

Her eyes raised to me, then refocused on her sandwich. "Jonas."

Um Himmelswillen. I braced against the desire to roll my eyes.

At least she hadn't reverted to using my last name, but then perhaps that was only because I'd used her first name —she seemed to take the lead on naming conventions from me.

"I would like to speak to you privately when you have a moment." My jaw clenched.

"Danny and I are—"

"I'm finished. I'll catch you later, Leo. Jonas." Danny hopped up from his seat, grabbed his tray, gave me a friendly smile, and wandered off in the direction of the cafeteria tray deposit.

I couldn't be sure, but I thought I heard Leonie sigh.

"May I sit?"

She flicked out a hand toward the chair across from her. I took the seat and watched her, waiting for her to acknowledge me. After swallowing her food, taking a drink, and wiping her mouth in what felt like slow motion, she spoke.

"How can I help you today, Jonas?"

Her neutral expression caused a flare of concern. This wasn't the warm, kissable Leonie from the brewery opening. This wasn't even the combative spitfire. This was the boxed-up version, and I had no interest in *her*.

"I would like to take you out." There. Done.

"Oh?"

"Yes. You know this. We agreed we should go out, but I haven't seen you."

She picked up her utensils and piled them on her plate, then balled the napkin and tossed it on the tray. "You have my phone number."

"I prefer to initiate such interactions in person rather than via text message. We had several meetings on the schedule in the last ten days, all of which you've missed for one reason or another. That led me to believe, all the more, I should ask you in person."

She studied me and inhaled a deep breath. As maddening as she was in the moment, her sparkling blue eyes still made me feel I'd lost my footing in the best way.

"I thought we said we'd go out."

"We did. But that was before."

My self-control flexed, mercifully, and I did not curse her stubbornness. "Before what?"

Her lips pursed then she said, "Before the hotel issue."

"That's business."

The tension between us grew, and not in the teasing, chemistry-filled way it had in days past. It made the air stuffy and thick. Her gaze didn't waver, but she kept looking, waiting for... something. Then she stood, grabbed her tray, and said, "Business is always personal to me."

"That's absurd."

She blinked pointedly. "Is it?"

The phone rang several times before she answered.

"To what do I owe this pleasure, son?" my mother's alto voice asked in German.

I answered in kind, glad to speak the language with her. Sometimes, a part of me ached from the disuse of it. "I'm overdue to check in. Forgive me."

"And how is my boy?"

"Folded up."

"Ah." The smile in her voice was clear, even through the single syllable.

Folded up was my father's way of saying he was confused or stressed. He'd say it as though he were folded up and he needed someone to flatten him out, turn him to rights.

"Ja."

"So?"

"It's a woman, I think."

"You think?"

"Ja."

Her low chuckle made me frown, even as I smiled. As much as I didn't feel like talking, I did need to catch up with her, and she might have insight. I hadn't spoken to my mother about a woman in years—the first time I'd done so was after my father died. I'd made an effort to include her in my life, to knit us back together after we'd both been ripped to shreds by his death.

"Tell me."

"She's... infuriatingly intelligent. She challenges me about everything—we've agreed on less than a handful of things I've ever said. She's..."

I could hear my mother shifting around, likely sitting in my father's old leather chair that still had a sound that reminded me of him. A pang of missing him snaked through my chest and made slow, coiling laps around my heart.

"Does she care for you?"

"I don't think so. I—" I ran a hand over my head, then back and rested my elbow on the table, my head in my hand where I massaged my temple. "I don't know. Sometimes, yes. But other times, she truly loathes me."

"That is a problem for you."

"How helpful."

The chuckle sounded again. "Ah, my son. I don't know if this woman cares for you. But since you are so folded up over her, you must find out. Find out if she can flatten you out."

CHAPTER TWENTY-SIX

Leo

Avoiding Jonas had been fairly easy.

Last week, I'd made a point to work out of the office as much as possible, plus I'd had interviews and meetings. This week, after he confronted me at lunch and set my pulse racing in a maddening combination of fury and anticipation, I hid out.

All my righteous indignation over his scheming about the hotel fueled me. I organized file cabinets and ate lunch at my desk. I re-sanitized the toy bins and every surface of all our childcare rooms. I cleaned out my e-mail inbox, a task I'd been avoiding for years.

But by Friday afternoon, I decided it wasn't my job to avoid him. *He* should avoid *me*. He should be the one to alter his lunch routine and come in a different door. He should be ashamed of himself for thinking he could spring something like this on me and then assume we'd still go out on a date.

What? Like I'd still find him unbearably attractive? Like his stupid gray suits would still set my heart to a different pace, or the distinctive sound of his fancy shoes on the stone floors would make me breathe a little faster?

And sure, maybe part of me recognized we'd have to continue working together. We would move beyond the plan to date each other, move far beyond his expert kisses and my foolish willingness to be kissed, and in the meantime, I'd figure out a plan to deal with this hotel business.

Inevitably, my decision to stop avoiding him meant that the minute I stepped out of my part of the lodge building, I saw him. I embraced that I should confront him and get the first encounter out of the way.

He stood just outside his office doorway, hand on the frame, looking down at the carpet.

"Jonas," I said, my voice raised just a bit to make sure it'd carry down the hallway.

No change. He just stood there. I tried again.

"Jonas."

His head lifted and he stepped forward, then stumbled and caught himself on the wall.

What on earth? I jogged to him just as he raised his eyes to meet mine. They were hazy instead of that clear, breathtaking steel I'd never gotten used to. Panic flooded me, my heart at a sprint now, my mind sharpening with a jolt of adrenaline.

"Are you sick?"

I ran a hand up his arm, keeping him steady as I searched for clues.

"Migraine."

He sounded *anguished*. Absolutely in torment. The

tightness of his mouth, the drawn, dull look in his eyes, the pale quality to his normally healthy-looking skin... it made sense. And it all hit me straight in the gut—this man needed help. I pulled his arm around my shoulder and moved to place mine around his back so I could walk with him.

"Let's get you home."

He made a sound of consent, at least I interpreted it that way, until we exited the lodge and I realized maybe he needed to see a doctor.

"Should I take you to the clinic before it closes?"

"No, thank you."

A smile tugged at my mouth while I pulled at him, surprised by how heavy he felt even though he was still walking on his own two feet. He'd slumped against me, letting me take some of his weight, and his head hung close to my shoulder despite him having what must be at least eight or nine inches on me in height.

He handed me his keys as we reached his door and I opened it, then helped him shuffle through.

"Bed."

He pulled at his tie with his free hand as we walked. I revisited the strange sensation of being in his house which had been Liam's place just a few months ago. I knew it well, had been there any number of times in the last few years, and yet this felt different. The home smelled clean, a little like peppermint and... orange? Something. Not Liam's house scent.

Once he cleared the doorway to his bedroom and shrugged off my support, I took in the space, which revealed a large bed, one night table with one book set at a perfect right angle to the edge, a lamp, a chair in the far corner, and nothing else despite fairly ample room for more—Liam's version had featured an overstuffed chair and ottoman in the corner and a bookshelf or two.

"What can I do?"

After whipping off his tie and suit jacket, he looked at me with one eye closed, the other squinting. "You've done enough. I'll be fine."

"Don't be an idiot. Tell me what to do."

He exhaled, though it had no dramatic effect because all of his actions were designed to cause him the least amount of movement, and therefore pain. "Could you get me some water from the kitchen?"

I nodded and moved quickly to fill a tall glass with cool water. By the time I rejoined him in the bedroom, ignoring the odd twinge in my belly as I approached the door, I found him sitting on the side of the mattress eyeing his shoes. They were laced boot-style leather, unlikely to be easily removable.

I set the water on his bedside table and dropped to a knee, then bent to untie his shoes. I looked up at the sound of his sharp inhale, the question in my eyes.

"You shouldn't be doing this." His normally lovely, smooth, almost tantalizing voice sounded ragged.

"It's done. Lay down." I rose and pushed at his shoulder until he scooted back just a bit and then lowered himself gingerly to the bed. I started to pick up his legs, but perhaps he anticipated this because he kicked them up before I could grab them.

"Do you need medicine? What can I get you?"

"I took some. I'll try to sleep now. Thank you."

He dragged the fluffy gray comforter over his shoulder as he rolled over. I tucked it in toward his back and squeezed his shoulder before I left the room.

We hadn't turned any lights on when we entered the

house, so I flipped on the entryway lamp. It was nearing five o'clock and the sun would slip away soon enough. If he slept a few hours, he'd wake to a completely dark house.

I made a mental checklist, took a quick peek in his fridge to see what food he had, and then set out to get my car. I'd run home, gather what I needed, and then head to the store. Try as I might to avoid him, I'd learned Jonas' schedule in the last few months. He always went to the grocery store on Fridays. He might've gone other days too, but I knew he went Fridays after work because I did too. I'd had to rearrange my shopping schedule and go Saturday mornings the last few weeks just to avoid him.

But the man was in crazy pain. He'd need food, more medicine, and maybe... my throat constricted at the thought. Maybe he'd need someone to care for him.

I could do that. In fact, for the last half-hour, taking care of him—helping him to his house, getting him settled—it had felt completely natural. Leaving now felt unnatural, and that was why I planned to come back.

The moment I saw him stumble in the hallway, all thoughts of frustration, the hotel, my ridiculous anger, the suspicion over his sneaky way of doing things... it evaporated like so much steam into the desert air. All of it simply didn't matter anymore.

At nine that night, I heard bumping around in the bedroom. I'd made myself comfortable on his couch in the living room, e-reader in hand. I popped up, eager to set eyes on him and figure out if he'd returned to the land of the living.

"Leonie?"

I wouldn't have thought just looking at a person could

make my heart break, but that's what happened in that moment. Something about seeing Jonas with a creased undershirt and disheveled hair, glasses slightly askew and slacks wrinkled, shocked to find me sitting on his couch... it made him unbearably human, and it broke my heart.

For him?

For me?

I couldn't tell. The only thing I knew?

I didn't want to be anywhere else.

CHAPTER TWENTY-SEVEN

Jonas

Not for the first time, I cursed the evil devil trolls hammering away in my head. Their persistence had flagged—the migraine seemed like it might recede by morning—but they maintained their grip on my vision and on my brain itself.

What would I give to discover Leonie Morrison in my house, looking quite at home, at a time when I could do something about it?

Alas, I wouldn't know, for in this instance, I had little to no control over my body. Plus I knew I looked a ridiculous mess. Not a compelling picture when trying to win someone over to one's charms.

"I let myself back in—you needed food, and I didn't want you to wake up and find you had an empty fridge. I know you shop on Fridays and thought I could get at least a few things in case this sticks around."

I leaned an elbow on the bar, feeling weak and shaky after the pain meds and failing to eat lunch or dinner.

"Thank you. It's marginally better. Hopefully by midday tomorrow I'll be better."

She watched me a moment, then moved to the kitchen. "Do you like grilled cheese?"

"Yes."

"If I make you one, will you eat it?"

"Yes."

Then she moved into the kitchen with a familiarity that struck me until I remembered she'd likely been in the house many times since her brother had lived there for years before I'd moved in. I could tell she tried to minimize the noise she made, which I appreciated. More than pain, hearing her clinking around in the kitchen as I took a seat on the couch a few feet away gave me comfort. Not being alone, though I loathed presenting her with this version of me, was welcome.

"Do you get them a lot?" she asked as I startled awake and adjusted my glasses—no chance of wearing contacts mid-migraine.

She set a plate with a perfectly golden-brown grilled cheese in the middle, cut on the diagonal, and a glass of water on the coffee table in front of me.

"I've had them more often in the last month or so. But normally it's only a few each year. I can usually tell when one's coming and take preventative measures but these last two have been unavoidable." Troubling thought I couldn't escape. I'd need to call my doctor and confirm this increase in frequency wasn't cause for concern.

"Is it a coincidence that in the last month or so you've had to work with me more?"

An airy chuckle escaped before I took a bite of the sandwich and chewed, the crisped bread satisfying under my teeth. I took a few more bites, savoring the melted cheese and the curbing of hunger. I devoured the last bite, chugged the rest of the water, and finally looked up to find her watching me, her lips twisted to one side in an alluring, smug smile.

"Are you suggesting you're the cause of my migraines?"

She shrugged, one shoulder raising and dropping. She collected my plate and glass, then returned and held out a hand. "Come on. Back to bed."

Even my broken brain recognized the opportunity to feel that softness again without being a creep. I took her hand and kept hold of it as she led me to my bed. She pulled back the fluffy duvet and I slid in and rested back against a pile of pillows—laying flat still felt like someone hacking into my brain with a dull axe.

In a dreamlike sequence, she tucked the covers up over my chest, then gently removed my glasses, folded them, and set them on the nightstand. Then she smoothed a cool hand from my temple to my jaw, kissed my forehead, and left.

Heaven might feel something like that.

I sipped coffee from a small mug, hoping the caffeine would continue the work that sleep and pain medication had done overnight. I'd slept from the moment she'd left my room until six this morning, and when I gingerly opened my eyes, it didn't feel like anyone was trying to gouge out part of my brain. *Progress.*

"Knock knock, Jonas?"

I perked up in my seat, but didn't stand, since I could tell she spoke from inside the door. At some point, I'd need to remember to lock it, though the failure to do so yielded Leonie in my space so I wouldn't complain.

"I'm here."

She shuffled into view, canvas bag from *Rise and Shine* in tow. "Oh, good. I was afraid I was too early, but didn't want to miss feeding you if you were up."

She said it like feeding me fell under her purview. I liked that. Maybe too much, in fact. I'd been independent for as long as I could remember, no one getting close enough to matter. But then again, before, I hadn't known Leonie Morrison existed.

My headache had receded enough that I could appreciate her black running tights, long-sleeved white shirt, and her hair in one long braid emerging from the back of her white hat. I knew this to be her running hat, and so far any time I'd seen her exercising, she'd been wearing it.

"Did you just run?"

One side of her mouth jumped up in a half-smile. "No. Not yet. Thought I'd check on you first."

I nodded, swallowed, savoring the sensation of her willing attention. It was almost enough to make me grateful to the migraine, but I wouldn't go quite that far.

She moved from the kitchen to stand in front of me where I sat on the couch, her energy bouncing and restless like I'd seen at a distance. Never with me though. Not 'til this moment.

"Well, have you eaten? Are you hungry?"

"I should eat." Not much of an appetite, but I could take more medicine and put the lid on this episode of migraine madness if I did.

"Give me a sec, I'll bring it over."

She rustled around in the kitchen, opening and closing cabinets, then returned with two plates. "I hope this is okay.

I read that sugar can exacerbate the problem, so I tried to get something low-sugar that would still taste good."

I raised a brow. "You read?"

She narrowed her eyes quickly before picking up what looked like a breakfast burrito from her plate. "I figured if I'm going to feed you, I might as well aim for something that's not going to make things worse. Since you were largely incapacitated last night, I had to turn to my own devices."

The grin on my face grew without my permission, though I made no attempt to stifle it. "Does this mean you've forgiven me?"

Her eyes dropped to her plate, and with them, my stomach plummeted as worry that I'd pushed the issue too soon flooded in. But before I despaired too much, she lifted her face and I saw the mischievous glint in her lovely eyes.

"Not forgiven, no. But perhaps we'll call it a détente."

"Should I be concerned you've referred to our cooperation in terms of war?"

When she erupted in a laugh so unexpected, I had to laugh with her. My heart swelled and I felt dizzy in a way I hadn't before.

"Maybe that's a little extreme."

I nodded, then took a bite of my own breakfast, relieved to find it appetizing. The grilled cheese last night had tasted good, but it was small, and waking after a long night of hard sleep often left me feeling queasy, especially with migraine meds on board. It would have been an hour before I could have summoned the will to peel myself off the couch and shove something in my face so I could medicate again.

But Leonie had solved that problem.

"How do you feel today?" She scooted forward on the

couch so she could lean closer and inspect me. She reached up and placed a hand on my forehead.

"I don't have a fever. It was a migraine, not a virus."

She pursed her lips together for a moment before letting her hand glide over my hair and stop at the base of my neck. I closed my eyes at the cascade of pleasure the touch created.

"I'm glad you're feeling a bit better, Jonas."

Her voice, soft and intimate, made me want to pull her into my lap and press my face into the soft place under her jaw. I wanted to hug her, to kiss her cheeks, to lie back on the couch and thread our fingers together and sip coffee in silence.

My eyes opened to find her studying my face, a look so tender on hers, my chest constricted. Could the last twenty-four hours have changed her mind about me? Could my ridiculous migraine problem be the galvanizing force Leonie had needed to see me as a man, not an adversary?

I placed a hand on her wrist and stroked the smooth skin there. "Thank you, Leonie, for caring for me. You've been very kind."

Her eyes burned into me, her face so serious, and I wished I didn't still feel the cruel pull of exhaustion and lingering pain. I wished I could kiss her, claim her, keep her.

"I'm glad I could help."

We sat close, our faces closer, and even through the fog of the last eighteen hours, I could feel the tension and attraction, and especially, my own ridiculous longing for her.

"I don't know how I'll repay you."

A half-smile again. "You won't. You'll owe me. It'll drive you insane."

I chuckled. "No, no. I'll be happy to owe you. Then I'll

have an excuse to ask you repeatedly what I can do for you. How I can help you. What I can give you."

Her mouth opened just a touch, like she'd speak.

I wanted her words. I wanted her response to me, my offer. I wanted to know if she could read the meaning I'd packed into my sentences.

"If you insist."

CHAPTER TWENTY-EIGHT

Leo

Before I left Jonas for my run, I made him promise he'd use the number I'd given him weeks ago to contact me if the migraine returned.

The lack of expression on his face when I extracted the promise might've been caused by the lingering effects of pain, or it indicated his unwillingness to reveal what he thought about me bossing him around, repeatedly walking into his home uninvited, and feeding him.

He may not have known how he felt about it, but I could say I'd enjoyed it quite a bit. Well, I'd enjoyed feeding him and walking into his house, and catching him all disheveled and helpless, so human and vulnerable, not so much the in-control ice cube any longer. But I didn't like that he'd been in such pain he didn't even balk at my helping him—not really. His weak protests the night before had been just that, and likely because he knew he could use the help.

I'd never had a migraine, but based on seeing him and Ma's experience with them, I prayed I never would. I'd wanted to ask him why he thought he'd been getting them more often, and what his doctors said. I fleetingly thought maybe the migraines were signs of something worse—something terrible—but refused to give that little anxiety-ridden trail a foothold in my imagination.

Even mind-numbed by pain and meds, he seared me with his intensity. *I'll be happy to owe you... I'll ask you repeatedly what I can give you.* I coughed out a harsh breath as I worked my way up the winding canyon, pleased with my pace despite going to bed later than I usually would have the night before.

What would I want from Jonas? What would I say if he asked me?

No idea. Not yet, anyway.

I had several messages waiting for me on my phone—I'd check them when I got home. My watch had buzzed to notify me, but I refused to read them while running—if I needed to clear my head on a run, I couldn't be fielding new messages and reacting to them. It didn't work.

But denying my interest and the little flutter of anticipation I'd felt when I saw *Jonas Bauer* pop up on my little watch screen indicating he'd messaged... well, that'd be a lie. I wanted to hear from him. He'd promised to call if the migraine returned, so the message must've been something else.

An hour later, I inhaled slowly through my nose and exhaled out my mouth as I circled the driveaway in front of my apartment. My run had gone well, and I'd finished just in time because dark clouds were gathering to the south and it looked like rain—might even snow up here, and definitely would on the mountain overnight.

That thought, and not the excitement of reading Jonas' texts, had me racing up the steps to my door.

Jonas: *How can I repay you?*

I rolled my eyes while I smiled, the thrill of his immediate communication bubbling up. I didn't even have to pretend to be aloof and wait to respond because he'd sent the message well over an hour ago.

Me: *You can't.*

Jonas: *Why not?*

I grinned at his immediate response.

Me: *There is nothing to repay.*

By the time I showered, braided my hair, changed into sweatpants and a T-shirt that had Matthew MacFadyen's Mr. Darcy face in a shadowy black and white print that looked a little like a Rorschach test, Jonas had replied.

Jonas: *What can I do for you?*

Me: *Nothing. I'm fine.*

Jonas: *How can I help you, then?*

Me: *I'm fine. I told you.*

Jonas: *What can I give you?*

So he planned to literally ask me those questions repeatedly? I should've known he'd speak specifically and purposefully and deviate not an inch from his word, even in his compromised state.

I could keep putting him off, but I'd let go of my anger about the hotel. I didn't agree with him on timing, and we had a lot to talk about, but it wasn't his fault he now owned land my parents had sold—he hadn't coerced them or treated them unfairly... fortunately, Julian Grenier hadn't either. As for how I'd manage a hotel *and* the resort... I hadn't worked that out. Yet. But I'd spent a lot of time fighting inevitabilities in the last year, and I'd resolved not to continue those futile efforts.

Me: *Why don't you let me bring you dinner tomorrow night, if you're feeling better?*

Jonas: *You bringing me dinner is hardly an effective method of repayment for me.*

I searched the room for someone to bear witness to this man's nonsense. Who texted like that?

Me: *I've already clarified that you owe me nothing. You can give me the opportunity to bring you dinner. You can help me by agreeing. You can do this for me, so I can eat in your company, despite my better judgement.*

Jonas: *You are extremely stubborn.*

Me: *This is not news.*

~

I arrived at his house with a bag of take-out from *Basta* and in jeans, a fitted sweater, and cozy boots since the cold drizzle hadn't stopped since starting yesterday. I tricked myself out of feeling nervous by telling myself I was helping him again—that he'd still be recovering from his migraine. Though I didn't attempt to deny the chemistry between us and my very real attraction to him, thinking of him as the disheveled, mildly disoriented, in-need-of-help Jonas helped it all feel like I was showing up on the doorstep of a good bud.

When he opened the door, I pushed air out my nose slowly in a futile attempt to calm my immediately rioting heart, and I knew the jig was up.

He stood with one hand on the door, unsmiling, but not unwelcoming. He was tall—had he gotten taller? Was it unusual for a thirty-something man to sprout inches in days?

His hair had a different style than it did at work—more casual by spiking up in places while still looking orderly without the rigidity of his work hair which tended to be styled close and parted to the side. He wore his glasses, those nearly invisible lenses held up by wire-thin silver-looking rims that tucked behind his ears, right where his hair showed off just a touch of salt and pepper—if pepper was dark blond. He wore jeans and a soft-looking shirt, probably cotton, in a cobalt blue with four buttons, the top one undone in a sign of casual ease that made my stomach clench.

"Hello, Leonie."

And then there was that. Still, his voice and my name were a lethal combo—though he hardly had an accent, he said my name with one and it made my toes curl in my boots.

"Please come in."

I stretched a close-lipped smile on my face, hoping he couldn't see the jump in my nerves. He stepped back, one hand still on the door, and waited until I crossed out of the way and stopped just past him before he shut it. Then he turned to me and I discovered how close to him I'd halted my movements—we were inches apart. He looked down at me from the same distance he might kiss me. Index finger and thumb rose to trace along the collar of my jacket, and for some dumb reason, this made my pulse spike even though he was only touching the outer layer of my clothing.

"Can I take your coat?"

His deep voice pressed against my ears, my chest, my lips, and I opened my mouth in response. "Yes."

He guided the coat from my shoulders slowly, and try as

I might, there was no escaping thinking of him removing other layers. No help for it. He moved with such measured purpose, like he was perfectly at ease taking a full minute to remove the garment. Frankly, I didn't mind because it put him right in my space and the clean, citrus and mint scent of him was rapidly becoming my favorite fragrance.

He tucked my jacket in the hall closet, then held his hand out, palm up. My first impulse would normally have been to tell a joke, but nothing about this was funny. Nothing about it was uncomfortable either—it wasn't *dis*comfort. It was anticipation and nerves and the heightened awareness of being with someone you desperately wanted to know and you passionately hoped would like you as much as you did them.

And just a little flag of guilt I immediately buried when it reared its head. I couldn't worry about how things would work out, or how I knew they *couldn't* work out between us, given the fact that he still had what I wanted, and I still planned to take it from him, whether we kissed and connected more or not. I pushed those thoughts down, down, down.

Instead of joking, I set my hand in his warm, large one. He laced our fingers together and then murdered my resolve to stay calm with a quick little flash of teeth in a smile that disappeared when he turned to lead me farther into his house.

I followed him, my hand in his, my heart in my throat and my brain all but shut down to anything but the grip of his fingers, and I knew. This wasn't helping out a friend. He wasn't feeling sick anymore. I'd come knowing these things, and I'd come denying all the reasons I shouldn't be here.

And I was doomed.

CHAPTER TWENTY-NINE

Jonas

Everything about this felt different from the times she'd been in the house before.

Good.

I wanted different results from this visit. I wanted her to see me as a man, a possibility, and not a charity case. Not that she'd treated me as such, but having failed handily when I asked her out last week, I'd been working through a plan to convince her she needn't hold the business aspect of our relationship against me. In fact, I'd clung to the idea that separating our business dealings from this personal attachment eliminated the problems being with her created—I just had to clarify a few things for her. I'd present the positive progress of the resort and like she had before, when she wasn't blindsided about her family's land, she'd see the truth. Or, if she didn't, at least I would have made a case for it not being paramount to our private interactions.

Somehow, the migraine had worked for me, and now, no looking back. I thought I would have preferred to take her out somewhere, go on a real, traditional date with a doorstep scene and everything. But she'd insisted on this, and now that I held her hand in mine, now that I'd seen the look in her eye as she took me in just as eagerly as I did her... *well.*

If she'd planned on this being anything other than a date, I'd made clear that though she brought dinner, I'd bring *mood.* A fire lit the hearth in the living room, low music played unobtrusively in the background. I'd poured two glasses of red wine and set the table by the windows looking out at the mountains.

The house was tiny and nothing like the one I was currently building a few miles away in material or style, but the view was similar and the builder had wisely showcased that. Knowing Leonie loved the mountains more than anyone I'd ever met, it seemed an appropriate background for my plan to push us well past the back and forth, the uncertainty, or even the possibility that a work disagreement could derail us.

I wanted her to unfold me, but that couldn't happen until she knew she could.

Her steps stuttered as we came into the open kitchen and living room, her eyes stuck on the set table, complete with flowers in the middle and already-poured wine.

"I hope you like red."

She turned to me, cheeks flushed. "I do."

I waited for her to set the bag of food down, but she stood as though transfixed, taking in the room. I released the hand I held and grasped the handles of the takeout sack, carefully pulling it toward me until she let go. I took it to the kitchen and unpacked the containers, smiling inwardly at her stunned demeanor.

"Are you well, Leonie?"

She blinked out of her daze, and her eyes found mine. "Uh, yes. I am. Sorry. I just..."

I waited, watching as she searched the room again before returning her attention to me.

"I didn't expect this."

"What did you expect?"

"I don't know."

"You don't?"

She stayed standing there, her posture almost rigid except that wasn't quite right. She looked coiled, ready to spring, but in a different way than her usual energetic reserve overflowing.

"What's happening, Jonas?"

"We're going to have dinner."

She frowned.

"I view this as our first date. I'd like to think the late-night grilled cheese didn't count considering I was only partially functioning."

She didn't speak again, and I wondered if perhaps she wasn't well. I'd rarely seen her at a loss for words, and the way she'd insisted on having dinner together made me think she'd be right here with me, ready for this step.

I paused in my movements. "Leonie, have I done something to disturb you?"

She startled out of her state, whatever had caused it. "No... I don't think so?"

I chuckled, because... who was this person? "Is that really a question?"

She squinted at me, looking genuinely perplexed. "Can I sit down?"

I rushed over to her, worried she might truly be feeling

ill. I pulled out a chair at the bar facing the kitchen and guided her to it. "Yes, sit right here."

She ran her hand over the countertop. I kept a hand on her shoulder, making sure she was steady, then rounded the island to continue unloading our dinner which also gave me a perfect view of her. After doling out servings of each of the dishes—she'd chosen very well—I delivered our plates to the table and returned to her side.

"Will you join me at the table?"

Once she was settled, I held up my glass of wine. "To beginnings."

She raised hers to touch mine, and we each took a drink.

"Uh, so... can I ask you a question?"

"Of course."

She twirled pasta around her fork, then, "Why am I here?"

I smiled behind my glass as I took another drink before responding. "You demanded to be here."

She rolled her eyes and shook her head ever so slightly. "No. I mean... why, after the last few weeks, do you want me here, like this?"

She held my gaze, and as they always did, those blue-flame eyes lit my lungs on fire.

"I want you any way I can get you."

Her mouth dropped open for a beat, then she clamped it shut. "That's not actually helpful."

I watched as she ducked her head and took a bite, chewed, swallowed, repeated this several times. This person was so unlike the Leonie I'd come to know, I didn't know what to think. What had changed from the time she was here yesterday, or later in the day when she arranged this evening together, to now?

"Tell me how I can help, then."

Her eyes popped up and she finished a bite of food before speaking. "Tell me why I'm here. Why are you interested in me?"

Not what I expected. This woman was all confidence, and now she needed reassurances? "I'm not sure what you mean."

Her lips pressed into a thin line but didn't speak, so I attempted to guess. "You're here because I like you. You're interesting. You're challenging. You're stunningly, mind-meltingly beautiful."

"You like me."

"Is that such a shock?"

"No." She inhaled, then shook her head like she was trying to clear it. "I'm not used to people liking me."

"That's a lie."

"It's really not."

"Leonie, everyone who knows you likes you. Women adore you, your brothers admire you, and just about every unattached man in town is wondering if he's got a shot with you."

Her eyebrows rose slowly, and she burst out laughing. "Thanks. I guess you really do have a high opinion of me."

"I do." A tad earnest, but fact.

She took a few more bites, then, seemingly warmed up, spoke again. "People don't usually like me. I mean, my students, the people I manage, yes. But adults my age? Rarely. And men..."

Finish that thought.

"They've never really liked me."

"Nonsense."

"No, it's true. They find me attractive, sure. Usually, yes. But *like* me? No. Or they like me at first, when they see me and think I'm pretty and sweet. Then they get to know me and figure out I have a backbone, an opinion about everything, and I clutch my convictions with an iron fist. I know I'm a lot, and I've found, historically, that men don't find that appealing. So if you—"

My hand on hers stopped her. "Leonie, I know you. Not everything about you, but I certainly know you're not sweet."

Her mouth opened in a wide smile and she giggled. "Thanks."

"You're not. You're strong, confident, infuriating, generous, thoughtful, stubborn... not sweet. And that's fine for me. I don't look for *sweet* in a woman." I leveled her with a look so she'd know I meant it.

"I guess that's good."

"I think so."

CHAPTER THIRTY

Leo

Between opening the door and sitting down at the table, something had happened to my brain.

Seeing him, it became clear this was a date. And then, I walked into the home to find the fire blazing, music low, the table set beautifully... it was all so... *romantic*.

Something I'd never had, but longed for. I'd never been on a date like this, never had someone want to do anything like this for me, and it was so small.

Then I started to doubt. My confidence wavered in these moments—the romantic ones where, if I opened myself to someone else, I would definitely be hurt.

Especially this man, with his glasses and his soft eyes looking at me like I shouldn't be surprised he liked me. Did he realize he was essentially Mark Darcy-ing me? If the next words out of his mouth were that he liked me *just the way that I am*, well. There'd be no going back.

I shouldn't want this with him. How was it possible that of all the people in Silverton—or, you know, the world—it was *him* doing this? And how could I look myself in the eye after this—after falling all over myself about this evening and hoping for more?

But I couldn't stop it. And the moment he said my name like he did—that tone that said he *knew* me and he liked me and he wanted to know me more... well. I turned my back on the knowledge that I shouldn't be getting close with this man and gave into the experience.

The food, predictably, was delicious. *Basta* was both fine dining and comfort food. Well, maybe not *fine dining* but it was delicious and mildly fancy, and since we lived in Silverton, it remained affordable. I dreaded the influx of Jamie's fancy friends into the neighborhood and the likelihood that they, the expanding resort, and a hotel would inevitably drive up prices.

Speaking of the hotel...

"About the hotel."

He froze, fork halfway to his mouth, then set it down. "No."

"That's not—"

"I appreciate that we will need to discuss the hotel. But we work together five days a week and that is reasonably something we can expect to discuss, even fight about, during those five days. Right now while I have you to myself in a situation that very much resembles a date, in which we're getting along pretty well, I do not wish to begin discussing something that will only anger you."

"Of course. I can... wait." Against my nature, perhaps, but I could. If I had to. Especially because I did like the point about it being a date, and us getting along. I wanted that to continue. I wanted him to keep liking me. If we avoided discussing work, I could more easily ignore the part of me that knew this was all a mistake.

His low laugh sent a thrill racing up my spine. Serious Jonas, who I never would have guessed had a deliciously sinister kind of laugh, was proving to be a man who actually *did* have a sense of humor.

How many times had I looked at him across the conference table to see him stone-faced and stern, not giving any sign he was anything other than a business-minded cyborg? That Danny liked him and Liam nearly worshipped him had always been proof that my brothers were idiots and not that Jonas had something likeable about him.

But here I sat, finding his company engaging, appealing, and downright pleasurable. He'd always been ruthlessly handsome and attractive to me on a troublingly primal level I didn't know existed until he walked in the room, shook my hand, and ruined my plans. But I'd easily found him abhorrent personally, especially after he'd signed on and clearly had an agenda that didn't match up with my vision for the lodge, and that'd pushed him far from my list of eligible bachelors.

But these last few weeks, he'd worked his way into my mind as a viable option before I even realized it. And now, here I sat, hoping he liked me enough to kiss me again, or more. Part of me wanted to roll my eyes at myself or storm out and lecture myself on being an independent woman, the wild west woman, but the other part of me recognized what I'd always known—Jonas was a good guy. He was prickly and strict and formal and a little odd, but somehow those qualities were becoming more attractive and less infuriating to me by the second.

Maybe those qualities weren't less infuriating per se, but I was seeing more of the full man. I couldn't pretend he was some maniacal businessman sent to ruin my life. I couldn't ignore the thoughtfulness with which he'd treated me on more than one occasion now. I certainly couldn't disregard his willingness to support me professionally, even if it came through his own twisted way of doing things.

And though it would've killed me to say so months ago, the fact that he'd already impacted the business in incredible ways could not be ignored.

If Leo of last December could see me now...

"What *can* we talk about, if we can't talk about work?" A bit petulant, but part of our relationship had always been combative, and there was no reason it couldn't be a little fun.

"By all means, you decide."

"How about I ask you questions, and you answer them."

A half-smile cracked that stern, beautiful face. "Fine."

"Good. So..." I folded my hands in front of me and tilted my head to the side. "Tell me about your childhood."

He took a slow drink. "My father was active duty Army. He married my mother while living in Germany. I arrived not long after. My mother's family was wealthy and they were very disappointed she married an American."

"Really?"

His smile was small and regretful. "Yes. Perhaps they would've accepted his nationality, but they could not abide that he was a soldier. He didn't come from money, and he planned to retire with the military."

"Soldiers make decent money, though."

"True enough. But my family's money is old and their wealth is... vast."

Vast. Wow.

"Eventually, once they saw she had no intention of leaving my father and was quite happy, they effectively disowned her—cut her off and such. She didn't care, or she never showed that to me. I was livid when I found out as a teen, which only happened because I'd wanted to go visit the family because we were living back in Europe. I arrived and heard nothing but vitriolic tirades about my mother's ungratefulness. I was praised for favoring my mother and looking nothing like my father..."

I had no words. I couldn't imagine being a teenager and walking into that, much less having family like that at all. My extended family was lovely, and I missed them and wished I could spend more time with them.

"In the end, I left and never looked back, but vowed I'd succeed despite their hatred."

"Well, you've certainly done that."

He twirled the last few strands of pasta against his spoon, then set the utensils to the side. "I suppose."

I swirled the wine in my glass. "You don't think?"

"In some ways, I know. But my father is gone, and it is hard to feel I've succeeded at much without him."

I inhaled a shaky breath. His love for his father came at my heart like a battering ram. It was lovely and tragic and made me feel so much for him. "I'm so sorry he's gone, Jonas."

"Thank you. He was a truly great man. He served his country, loved his family, treated everyone well. He understood what was important, and I wish..."

His gray eyes found mine, a slight glint from the lights flashing across his glasses.

"You wish?"

He touched his napkin to his lips, then placed it on his plate and stood. He held out a hand to me. "Come with me."

The command would've raised my hackles in other

circumstances, but his soft voice instead sent delicious curls of anticipation through my belly.

I took his hand and stood, then walked with him to the couch. He sat and pulled me to sit next to him—*right* next to him.

We hadn't been this close since our last kiss. It'd been weeks, and we'd walked a hundred miles since then. I'd been attracted to him then, but now I *liked* him. He wasn't completely terrible all the time—in fact, he had a really lovely, kind side. And that politeness wasn't always a shield like I'd thought—I'd begun to suspect it was one way he showed respect to people.

I was invested in him now that I knew about his family, his migraines, all these small things that made him a flesh and blood man instead of a laptop-loving robot, and even though I knew we'd fight as soon as he flipped on the light to his office in the morning, I wanted him to know me.

Thinking about the kiss must have sent my mind toward his mouth, his beautiful curved lips, and I—

"Leonie..."

Heat rose to my cheeks. The small smile playing on his face told me he'd seen the object of my gaze. "I—"

His lips met mine before I could speak, and before my mind could build the moment up anymore, I kissed him back.

CHAPTER THIRTY-ONE

Jonas

More than once, I'd overheard men refer to Leonie as the ice queen. Not her brothers, but men who were undoubtedly attracted to her. I'd heard Warrick Saint say it, though that was before I knew him. I'd heard several men agree.

Aside from wanting to dump their beers over their heads, I'd wanted to tell them they were idiots. Clearly, Leonie was one of the most passionate people on Earth. She was *a lot*, as she put it, but it wasn't ice cold.

I could now confirm. Leonie Morrison was all heat, all flame, all adept touches meant to build an inescapable inferno.

Any wavering or insecurity she might have felt before now had fled. Her hands helped themselves to a tour of my arms and chest, alternately smoothing over the fabric separating our skin and then grabbing, or holding my arms.

I kissing a line from her mouth along her jaw to her ear. "You are maddeningly beautiful."

A breathy laugh. "You are maddeningly good at using words to drive me insane."

I leaned away and found her eyes. "Just words?"

The smile that graced her face then sliced through my chest, and I pulled her to me, practically crushing myself against her.

In most things, I prided myself on being in control. In fact, in basically all things. But being able to touch and kiss Leonie had sent my logical brain running. And after teasing and kissing her perfect lips, after sliding my hands over the silk of her hair, I wanted to do nothing but get closer, have more of her.

And it was that notion that had me pulling back, taking her face in my hands, relishing the desire there, a perfect imitation of my own.

"Dessert."

My voice emerged roughened, and deep. Her answer was a slow inhale as her sapphire eyes bore into mine, then dropped to caress my lips. My stomach tightened, and I clenched my jaw.

She pressed her lips together, but I didn't miss the smile. She liked what she saw, and her feeble attempts to hide it wouldn't keep me from enjoying the same.

"I didn't actually bring dessert."

"Oh... right. That's fine." Adrenaline coursed through me and I knew precisely what I wanted for dessert—more of her—but something told me, particularly after our conversation moments ago during dinner, that she needed to know I wanted more than just her body.

But to be clear, I definitely wanted that too.

She leaned close and pressed kisses into my neck. I

swallowed and tilted my head away, giving her access, my hands coasting along the denim on one of her thighs and the other at her back, urging her toward me.

"I have questions for you," I said, though it came out in a whispery breath.

"Ask them," she said, before covering my mouth with hers.

She kissed like she functioned—certain, demanding, and with a kind of swagger you wouldn't expect from an angelic-looking woman with her hair constantly in braids. And just like a conversation with her, though exponentially more potent, her kiss sent my heart racing and gave me the curious sensation that my mind had both scattered and sharpened.

"*Mein Gott,* you are delicious."

She stopped, her face only inches from mine, a delighted little grin breaking through the heat. "I've heard you say a few things in German... mostly swearing, I think."

I straightened a bit, used the moment of clarity to create a bit of space between us and suck in a breath. "Not swearing like Americans swear."

"No? It sounds... aggressive."

I shot her an exaggerated frown. "Don't tell me you're someone who hears German as a *harsh* language."

Her eyes grew large. "No. I think it's beautiful. I don't know much of it, but I love it. But tell me some of your words and maybe I'll tell you which one I'm thinking of."

I chuckled, looking side to side. "The one you've probably heard is *Donnerwetter.* It literally means 'thunderstorms.'"

She clapped and let out a whoop of joy. "See? That's just so completely perfect. You are this serious, giant man and you walk around saying *thunderstorms*. That's something Mr. Rogers would say as a curse."

Heat rose to my cheeks. "It's not that tame. It's... I don't know. I don't get to speak German all that often, but I still speak it to my mother when I call her. Those kinds of things come automatically even though sometimes I feel very disconnected from the language."

She pressed her palm to my chest, over my heart. "Makes sense. I don't mean to make fun. I genuinely love that your form of exclamation comes out in German. I wish I could hear more of it."

"More German?"

"Yes. You can speak to me in German whenever you feel like it. Just translate for me afterwards since I'll have no idea what you're saying."

I palmed the back of her head and brought her close so I could kiss her forehead. "*Suesser*."

She tilted her chin up so she could see me, her head resting against my shoulder. A raised brow told me she was waiting for my explanation.

"You won't like it."

"I might."

"Literally it means *sweetie*."

All traces of amusement, happiness, intensity—gone.

"I'm not sweet. I'm not your sweetie."

I studied her—the frown of her mouth and furrowed brow. "Alright."

She pushed off of me slowly, then stood. "Don't placate me."

I grabbed her hand. "Leonie, I'm not. Please, sit down."

Her mouth a flat line, her body rigid, she stood there, not moving, not giving in to my plea.

"Please. Please sit down."

She looked out the window and inhaled slowly, as if gathering courage from the view of the mountain. Then she sat.

I waited, because there was no chance I would push her on this. What I thought was an endearment, a joke, was something very different for her.

"I am not sweet." Her voice trembled—whether from rage or simply adrenaline, I couldn't tell.

"Why does it bother you so much to be thought of that way?"

"Because I'm not. So if you're calling me sweet, then you don't know me. Being sweet is great, but I know who I am and I'm simply not a particularly sweet woman. And if you don't know that, then this is all pointless, and I'm not doing it again."

"Again?"

She ran her hands over her face. "I asked you why you liked me. You seemed to get it. But this makes me wonder if—"

"I understand. I won't say it again. I don't need you to be sweet—who gives a damn for sweetness? Give me your salty."

She started shaking, then finally openly laughing, then pressed her hands to her eyes for a moment. When she looked up at me, she looked tired, but no longer distressed, and at least a little amused.

"I'm sorry. I'm not great at trusting men. I've been lied to, and I hate it."

I nodded in understanding.

"Just don't lie to me, okay?"

CHAPTER THIRTY-TWO

Leo

I slept hard after leaving Jonas' house and woke feeling hopeful.

This week, I'd get to the bottom of his hotel plans. We'd work through that and I'd help him see it should wait. It *could* wait, and so it really should. We had connected last night, and his persistence with me—both generally, and with specifically accepting who I am without shying away from the fact that I'm not a retiring, sweet girl like so many men in my past had apparently wished for.

A few things nagged at me as I moved through the day, eager to find Jonas but occupied with a long list of tasks before I could hunt him down. First, I'd forgotten to pin him down on the whole super wealthy thing. He'd mentioned his family's fortune was *vast*, but then hinted his mother hadn't had the benefit of that resource. Where had his money come from? He must have had a leg up at some point, but it didn't sound like it'd come from his father's family.

He'd purchased a huge, expensive parcel of land like it was no big deal. At least, that's how he spoke about it. I didn't know him well enough to know if perhaps it *had* been, but I wanted to know everything. Talking about money wasn't exactly sexy first date discussion, and we'd committed not to focus on the hotel, so it was better that I hadn't pried into that part of the issue, but I would. I'd have to.

The other thing niggling was something altogether unfamiliar. It was the low-grade pressure in my chest driving me to find him, see him, be near him. He compelled me in a way I'd never felt, and it forced me to forget all the reasons I knew I should be cautious.

I wanted to hear his voice, see him straighten his glasses, maybe give me a mildly disapproving frown that I would happily interpret to mean he couldn't wait to be alone with me either.

By four o'clock, I thought I'd crawl out of my skin if I didn't set eyes on him, so I shut down my computer and decided to find him. I'd long since surrendered to the reality that I should not feel this way, and that this was very likely going to end in flames when I tried to have what I wanted from him *and* take what I felt I was destined for. Inevitable, all of it.

I moved quietly through the hallway and found him typing furiously, glasses in place, brow furrowed as he focused. I stood in his doorway and watched for a moment, enjoying the fluttery, light sensation floating through me as I did.

At length, he dramatically clicked and tapped, then

shut the laptop and hit me with a heart-bendingly beautiful smile. "Hello."

"What were you working on?"

He pushed back from the desk and approached me with purpose—an action that sent my belly dropping. He glanced behind me, craning his neck this way and that, then set his hand on my hip, tugged me a bit, and touched his lips to mine with such delectable familiarity and sweetness... ugh.

He stepped back and shook his head, looking stern. My arched brow communicated my question, and he answered. "Dangerous."

I chuckled. "You think?"

He looked at me, his eyes hooding in a way I'd savored the night before, shook his head just once, and swiped a thumb over my cheek before stepping away. "I know."

He rounded the desk and took his seat, gesturing for me to sit across from him, so I did.

"So? What were you typing so furiously?"

"That's how I always type."

I pressed my lips together to stay my grin. "Ah. I guess I've seen that before. I shouldn't be surprised your typing is just as intense as the rest of you."

He opened the lid of the computer, then shut it again, crossed his arms and leveled me with his gray eyes. "The surveyor needs to come again before it snows next week, but claims he doesn't have time."

My heart jumped a bit at this news. "What does it mean if the surveyor can't come?"

He exhaled with a frown. "It'd mean delaying the hotel timeline."

"Oh." I stifled the desire to say *that's great* because obviously on this point, we disagreed.

"I do not want to delay."

"Will it push things off by much?" I crossed one leg over the other and leaned my elbows on the edge of his desk.

"Potentially."

"Would it be such a bad thing? Maybe a delay allows everyone—everything to adjust to the changes and expand at a more measured pace."

His eyes narrowed as he studied me, then his phone rang. He quickly disposed of the call, and returned his full attention to me. "Would you like to spend the day with me Saturday?"

"Yes."

"Good."

"Good," I agreed.

"I have to make a call, but I'll see you tomorrow at the operations meeting, yes?"

I left him at his desk in a cloudy mood, something far more familiar to the months before we'd struck up this... whatever this was. My own mood had lifted, though. We had plans for a date, and perhaps better than that, or just in a different category, the hotel project sounded like it might be delayed without me having to do anything at all.

Maybe my interest in him didn't have to be such a problem—if things naturally worked out professionally, I could explore my interest in him without guilt. The hotel would be delayed, and maybe he'd figure out he wanted to take some other job and... well, I had no idea how it might work out, but for now, I could pretend.

The bright late October day beamed at me as I took a step out onto the plaza. I pulled in a slow breath, luxuriating in the chilly air and puff of white as I exhaled. In less than a month, this same empty space would be flooded with skiers eager to make tracks in what I was determined would be our best season ever.

I couldn't wait.

~

Grandpa Will sat in his cushy chair in the corner of his suite at Silverton Springs and grinned at me like an alligator.

"Don't give me that look, Grandpa."

"Why not? You're my last little duckling and you've found yourself a mate."

I snorted and rolled my eyes. "Isn't that something my ma should be saying?"

"Maybe, but that doesn't mean I can't share the sentiment."

I loosed a small sigh, and he clucked.

"Oh Leo, don't get sour with me. Forgive me if I feel a speck of triumph at seeing you aflutter over a man like Jonas Bauer."

My mouth dropped open. "I am *not* aflutter."

His eyebrows flashed. "Mmhmm. Okay, child."

"And what does that mean, *a man like Jonas Bauer?*"

"He's a real man. Not in a brawny, irritating way. But he's sturdy and capable, ambitious and a little sneaky, hard-working and thoughtful."

My eyes widened at his list. "How do you know this? Have you even had a full conversation with the man?"

"First, you should know, I know all." He stretched his weathered hands wide in a silly, mystical gesture. I chuckled as he continued. "Second, he's come to see me. He came the first time he visited last November, and I met his partner, Ms. Ritter. He has come back every few months to stop in and say hello, catch me up on things."

The energy building in my chest with each word he

spoke shot down into my legs, and I jumped up. "What? Wait... *What?*"

He gave me that obnoxious, charming grin again and folded his hands together, apparently relishing my dismay.

As I paced the small living room space of his room, I babbled. "Why did he visit you? What has he said? What have *you* said? Why haven't you mentioned this before?"

He pinned me with his Morrison blues. "*Aflutter.*"

I huffed, but stopped and waited, arms crossed.

"I'm not going to recount our conversations as they were just that—*our* conversations. I can only tell you that I respect the man, I think he's good for us, and I think he could be very good for you."

I made a strangled, choking sound as I swallowed down my disbelief.

"I never mentioned it because you've shown nothing but total disdain for the man. It didn't seem relevant until just now."

CHAPTER THIRTY-THREE

Jonas

Her walk gave her away.

Leonie always walked with purpose, energy, intent. But if one applied a verb to her approach down the sidewalk, even with her grandfather at her side, it could be said she *stormed* down the way.

A small part of me wanted to slip into a shop and disappear out the back. While at times her rage called to me in a primal, fiery way that made me desperate to quell it with tenderness and physical placation, today I had little left in my tank. I'd spent the morning turning myself inside out getting the surveyor to clear his schedule, and I could admit it hadn't been the most upstanding thing I'd ever done. But he'd be here tomorrow, and I'd get what I needed to push things forward.

I also hadn't slept much because of that, and the decision I'd made late Monday when Leonie had come to my office. I'd decided I wouldn't tell her about the details of the hotel project again. It only caused tension between us as she clearly wanted the project delayed and I felt keenly it should be completed as soon as possible to increase the visibility and capability of the resort.

I was right. She had her reasons, whatever they were, but I knew the business, the industry, and I knew this place needed a hotel. I was right, and I'd have my way, and everyone, including Leonie, would be better for it. That thought might make me sound like a condescending jerk, and maybe I was, but the board had approved the move for a reason.

Facing her wrath for now seemed a monumental task I wasn't quite up to. Selfishly, I wanted the Leonie who'd come to dinner this past weekend. I wanted her quiet voice and her gentleness, just for a minute.

"Hello." I greeted her as she came to a halt in front of me, then turned to the older man at her side. "Mr. Morrison, good to see you."

"And you, Jonas."

"Why didn't you tell me you've been seeing Grandpa Will?"

Her voice held a frantic note. What had seemed like rage on approach now showed itself to be... fear. *Strange.*

"I didn't know I needed to report on all of my interactions with your family." My own tone bared an edge.

She breathed in a halting, odd breath. "You don't."

I looked to her grandfather, then back at her, attempting and failing to decipher what an appropriate next response might be.

"We're just off to lunch. Can you join us, Jonas?" Mr. Morrison smiled and set a hand on Leonie's wrist. She blinked at him, then back at me.

"Unfortunately, no. I have a conference call in a few

minutes. I've just grabbed some takeout." I held up the bag of food.

"Ah, then we won't keep you. But I hope you'll plan to join us at the Morrison home for Thanksgiving in a few weeks. My son and daughter-in-law will be back, and I know they'd love to have you, too."

Leonie's tight smile and raised brows told me she hadn't expected this invitation. I hadn't considered my plan for the holiday, though it was still three weeks away, and I didn't normally make a big deal out of it. If Leonie didn't want me there, nothing would convince me to go, not even the excellent gentleman extending the welcome.

"Thank you. I'm not sure what I have planned, but..."

"Just let Leo know, but we'll plan on you." He waved a hand and they started walking.

"I'll see you..." I said, trailing off because obviously I'd see her. We worked in the same building, though it was large and we could avoid each other if we wanted, as she'd proven effectively over the last year. Now that she'd stopped avoiding me, we actually saw each other a few times a day, at least at a glance.

She nodded, no words for me, and let her grandfather usher her away. I watched them go, tension and irritation tightening my chest, then turned and stalked back to the lodge to get back to work.

I did not, in fact, see Leonie again until Friday afternoon. I'd decided not to seek her out since the interaction on the street two days ago had been so fraught and uncomfortable. Maybe I'd missed the subtext. Maybe I'd done something horribly wrong. But if I had, I didn't know what it was, and I'd decided to give her space.

Honestly, I'd given myself some space too. I didn't want to feel angry or frustrated or annoyed at her. I didn't want to constantly be under suspicion anytime she learned something new about me. I thought we'd gotten past that way of interacting, and yet the scene on Main Street with her grandfather had been steeped in the old approach.

If I functioned as I typically did, this would be it for me —I'd sign off and wash my hands of all of this—of Leonie, of Silver Ridge, of Silverton as a whole. But because I'd evidently become incapable of reason and because this woman had my guts in a vise, I couldn't just walk away.

I could give her space, and I'd decided to give it to her until she came to me because, well, wasn't it her turn? I'd done the pursuing thus far, and if she was interested then she needed to show me.

Except.

There had been that look in her eye, and it'd been new. If I didn't know her better, I would've thought—I *had* thought—it was fear. But that didn't make sense. And why on Earth would me visiting her grandfather cause that reaction in her?

I didn't know, and I'd grown tired of not knowing. Rather than continue to leave her alone as I'd planned, I pressed in by visiting her hall in the lodge and knocking on her door at three on Friday afternoon. Frankly, my feet took me there without my permission.

"Mind if I interrupt?"

She startled at the sound of my voice and scooted back from her desk, then nodded. "Of course."

"Thanks."

She sat once I took the chair across from her desk, the

scene from Monday reversing, except this visit hadn't started with a kiss. Discomfort hovered around us this time, no easy smiles or sweet blushes rising to her cheeks. Her eyes were cagey, but she didn't seem angry, or upset. She seemed... well, damn if she didn't seem unsure.

"Can I ask—well, uh, how are you?" *Great delivery.*

She straightened in her seat, scooted the chair closer to the desk. "I'm fine."

"Are you?"

Her eyes skated side to side, then, "Yes."

"The exchange on Wednesday was..."

"Odd. I know."

I wouldn't have said odd, exactly. But yes, odd too. "Has something changed?"

"How so?"

"Has something changed between us? Now that you know I've visited with your grandfather, does this change things between us?"

Her lashes fluttered and her throat worked as she swallowed. "Um, no. Not for me."

Relief flooded from my head down to my ankles in a warm wave, and a small smile escaped. "Good."

She nodded, biting her lip with a smile.

"So... are you still available tomorrow?"

"Of course."

She said it like it was so obvious—like I should know that of course we would still spend the day together. I wished it had been obvious to me—I might've slept better, might not have spent the day yesterday pacing the hallway toward her side of the building debating whether I should ask her that very question or not. Might not have been tempted to book a flight out of here and never look back purely to remind myself I was still in control of myself.

No matter. Not if nothing had changed for her.

"You'll give me the whole day?"

"I will."

"The whole night?"

Her cheeks reddened and her blue eyes practically glowed. "The whole night?"

Then, I heard it. I registered what she thought I meant. I cleared my throat. "I mean, for dinner. And... dessert. And... just..."

I inwardly groaned at my awkwardness, frustration warring with pleasure at seeing her face as she watched me and the smile that grew as I fumbled.

She chuckled. "I get it, Jonas. I'm yours—all day... and night."

CHAPTER THIRTY-FOUR

Leo

I woke frustratingly early the next morning, more than ready to spend a day with Jonas.

It'd been a weird week. I'd felt restless, upset... unhinged.

The knowledge that Jonas had been visiting Grandpa Will had thrown me for a loop I couldn't have anticipated. The primary emotion wasn't even confusion or surprise—those came first, but they didn't hang around.

No. The first and overriding emotion I felt was, by far, fear. Because if he really was that determined to go out of his way to be nice to an old man, to honor my family's legacy, then he wasn't the bad guy I'd thought he was all along. Most of my experiences with him thus far were proving that anyway, and this addition only intensified the reality that he was *nothing* like I'd assumed.

And more than that, more than him not being a *bad* guy

was the news that, even beyond what I'd already discovered, he was a very, *very* good guy.

He visited my grandfather. Not just once. Not just to meet the man who established the lodge and brought skiing to this little town on the heels of his experience in World War II. He visited multiple times, and it sounded like fairly consistently. He and Grandpa had a good rapport, they... they were friends.

Seeing him on the sidewalk had drilled it home for me. I was in grave danger of falling for Jonas Bauer, and that was very, *very* bad and also extremely amazing, thrilling, and terrifying news.

I'd always wanted to fall in love. I wanted the full story, just like I'd seen my siblings and friends experience. So much of the wistfulness and angst I'd felt these last few months as I saw each of them finding their own love story was the longing I had for my own.

In the last few weeks as Jonas became not just a curious possibility but a genuine prospect, I'd embraced this fact: I didn't begrudge my dear friends and siblings that they'd found their partners and were moving on to a new phase. If at some point I'd felt resentment or self-pity, I could safely say those feelings had dissolved, and left in their place was the knowledge that I wanted my own story, my own partner, my own love.

And somehow, Jonas' visits with Grandpa Will cut to the quick—I might just get that story after all. And yet how could I even begin to consider such a thing when I knew... *I knew* being with him would compromise my plans. The vision I'd had for my life would take a flying leap if I ended up with Jonas, and that was on top of the fact that though he continued to prove himself a good guy, my gut wasn't usually wrong. My reaction to him last year couldn't have been *that* off.

Could it?

I shoved away those thoughts, determined to be happy and up for whatever he had in store today rather than bogged down by the sudden and ferocious fear of falling for a man I didn't actually fully know, had suspected of being the villain in my story, and who *ohLordhelpme* might just be the hero.

He knocked on my door at exactly eight, just like he'd said he would, just like I knew he would. I grabbed my jacket, hat, gloves, and small hiking pack.

"Where are you taking me?" I asked as I stepped out the door to find him in hiking boots, pants, a black jacket unzipped a few inches at the top, and sunglasses. Inevitably perfectly stylish and expertly dressed, even for an early morning late-season hike.

"I thought we'd take the low path around and into the canyon—see how far we can get. Then come back along Meier's Pass and end at my house for lunch. I went over that way recently and it was in good shape."

This time of year, hiking could be iffy. The ground had frozen and wasn't likely to thaw until spring, but occasionally some parts of trails could wash out with autumn rain and mud, or if they were particularly wet with the freeze, you'd end up on an ice path which kind of ruined everything. Sure, you could use your spikes and get serious—of course people hiked in winter, but it was early for that, especially since the first real snow wouldn't arrive for another few days.

"Sounds great."

I waited for him to turn and head down the stairs, but

he just stood there, and since he wore sunglasses, I couldn't see his eyes.

"Jonas?"

He stepped into me then, crowding me and seeming taller than ever even though we both wore hiking boots. Two cool fingers touched under my chin and urged me to look up just as he leaned down and placed a quick, searing kiss onto my lips. He broke away and pulled me into a hug just as fleeting, and then stepped back.

"Okay. We can go now."

Warmth glowed from my chest out to my fingertips as I followed him down the stairs.

We spent about an hour and a half hiking as the sun continued to rise and finally crested over the mountains as we sat for a coffee and pastry break, watching the beams of light shoot through the gray-blue of the fall morning.

"This is great. I never hike this late in the season."

"No?" he asked, sitting on a fallen log next to me.

"I don't like going alone this time of year, and in the past everyone I would have gone with was busy. Danny and I used to but we haven't the last few years for some reason."

He held up the thermos he'd brought coffee in and I nodded, so he refilled the small mug I cupped in my hands. I could feel his eyes on me as I took a sip and stared out at the sky.

"Thank you for coming with me." His voice came low and quiet, like he wanted to tell me, but didn't want to disturb the moment.

I glanced at him, then stalled as I caught his gaze. "Thank you for bringing me with you."

We'd ensnared each other, both of us caught up in the weight of the moment which seemed like far more than just a shared mug of coffee on a short hike in the early

November morning. But I couldn't be sure what it meant, so I blinked away and stood.

"Probably time to keep going, right?"

From there, we continued up, adjusting course when we hit a rough section that wasn't worth traversing, and ending on a path that I knew for certain did not put us back at the lodge. The trail leveled out into the valley that made up the north side of Silverton's unincorporated area, the fields at the foot of Silver Ridge Peak and its sisters seeming like bowing supplicants to the mountains above them. Just a few miles to the south and we'd be standing at the base of Silver Ridge Resort.

He'd mentioned stopping for lunch in just a few minutes, but we weren't near his home, not by a few miles.

"Uh, Jonas?"

He led the way, clomping down the trail a few feet in front of me since it'd narrowed enough that we couldn't wander side by side.

"Yes?"

"You know we're nowhere near the lodge, right? I mean, we're not, like, too far off, but we won't be there in the next few minutes..."

"Yes, I know."

Oh. But... did he? He didn't strike me as the kind of man who couldn't admit being mistaken, but maybe I'd read him all wrong.

"Then, um... were we just going to picnic lunch it? Did you bring stuff with you?" I hated to sound whiney, but clouds had descended on us, and though no rain or snow were in sight, my skin had soaked in the cold and I was ready to thaw out inside. Preferably somewhere heated.

"We're almost there."

But... where? We weren't near anywhere I knew, and I didn't...

"Just through here," he said, holding open a well-made wooden door in the middle of what looked like a fairly elaborate stone wall.

"Uh..." I said dumbly, then saw the funny look on his face and decided not to continue questioning him. I wanted to ask if he knew where he was and if we were allowed to enter this gate onto what had to be private property, but that was all fairly redundant given that he knew about the gate in the first place and had opened it.

I wandered through, taking in a large house not far down a gravel path. Mature trees dotted the land to the left, like they'd been there for years, though this house had to be new considering I had never seen it before.

Then I realized, as we rounded the corner to the front and I saw the cobblestone driveway—this was a house in Jamie's neighborhood. This was smaller than Jamie's by a fair amount, but it was still towering and every detail I noticed spoke to the quality. Whoever owned this home had to be wealthy—just the land, not to mention the building requirements Jamie and Julian had placed on the neighborhood to create the draw for wealthy owners, were nothing if not extravagant.

"Whose house is this?"

I followed him around the yard and onto a small path that led to the front door. He raised a brow as he pulled out a key, opened the door, and said, "Whose do you think?"

CHAPTER THIRTY-FIVE

Jonas

Leonie's eyes widened as she blinked repeatedly. "Are you saying this is *your* house?"

"Yes."

"This is your house."

"Yes."

She turned, looking up at the entryway ceiling, a two-story entrance a bit much for my taste, but I liked the large windows that meant the upstairs and entry level benefitted from natural light.

"But—"

I watched as her thoughts stopped and started a dozen times. This was the second time in a week I'd broken her brain, and I had no idea why either time.

"Have I never mentioned my house?"

It seemed highly unlikely, but perhaps not. Evidently not. It wasn't yet inhabitable and I wasn't in a rush to move out of the mountain manager's cabin as it was so conveniently located. Though this place would be all of a ten-minute drive to the lodge, so still not a real commute compared to living in the city or even in other ski towns where I'd spent seasons.

"Uh, yes. You mentioned that you'd bought a house in the neighborhood to get to Julian Grenier about the land." She wrapped her arms around herself as she continued to slowly circle and take in what she could see from where we stood.

"Will you come in? The fireplace and chimney are completed—the builder said it's safe to light a fire. I thought we'd have lunch here."

My hand on her back, I guided her through the house to the living room, currently a wide-open space that connected with the kitchen and centered on a massive stone fireplace.

"This is going to be incredible. It already is." Her blue eyes tracked around the room, taking in the floor, the huge windows, the copper hood and pressed ceiling of the kitchen, the unfinished cabinetry and missing countertops.

"Still a ways to go, as you can see."

"Are they going to finish before the season? It looks so close."

She followed me into the living room where I unpacked a blanket and laid it out in front of the fireplace. Then I set to work on building a fire with the materials I'd placed last night.

"No. They had a delay with more than one thing—in fact, my contractor has been fired due to negligence. It should have been done a month ago, even with some of the issues, but he was dragging his heels. Grenier actually identified the issue and told me so I could handle it. Fortunately, I have a place to live and wasn't in a rush, so I am able to wait for the new contractor's schedule to clear. It should be ready in the new year."

The fire sparked to life and the logs slowly caught and burned. It'd be a few minutes before any heat came from the flames and I realized with a cruel rush of reality that this idea was far less romantic and far more uncomfortable than I'd planned.

"If you're freezing, we can go. I didn't anticipate the day being quite this cold, and it'll take a while for it to warm up—"

"I'm not in a rush."

Her blue eyes sparkled with a small smile, and the familiar pang of affection hit me in the ribs.

"Good."

Feeling unaccountably shy—not a sensation I was accustomed to—I retrieved the cooler I'd dropped off earlier and unpacked the lunch I'd made that morning. I poured her more piping hot coffee from a new thermos, then poured us bowls of warm soup from another and split a sandwich between us.

"Nothing fancy."

"It's perfect."

We ate in silence, the crackle and pop of the fire the only soundtrack. She finished her soup, then leaned back on her hands and pinned me with her stare. I quirked a brow at her, waiting for whatever lay behind those lips.

"So you're like... super wealthy."

I chuckled low. "I have enough."

A sputtering sound burst from her. "Don't be dainty about it, Bauer."

"Oh, I see. You're a snob."

Her mouth dropped open. "Me?"

"Yes."

"How am *I* the snob here?"

Her eyes glowed with the reflection of the flames in the fireplace. Though the room was large, the relative darkness outside made the space press in around us and feel more intimate. The trace of a smile at the corners of her lips told me she was enjoying this just as much as I was despite the topic of conversation.

"You're clearly going to like me less if I tell you that I am absurdly wealthy."

She tucked her lips between her teeth before arching a brow at me. "*Absurdly?*"

I nodded, the corners of my mouth pulling down. I wasn't ashamed of my wealth. I'd worked hard for what I had, and that would benefit her eventually. In many ways, it already had. The resort hadn't been sold off for parts like it might've been if the *unnamed investor* hadn't stepped in.

"So you buying the land for the hotel wasn't, like, your life's savings?"

"No."

"And this house isn't a... gift from someone?" Her voice had shrunk, and the laughing glint in her eye retreated further with each question.

"No."

Her face sobered completely and she muttered something under her breath as she sat up, legs crossed and her plate with a few remaining bites of sandwich in her lap.

"What was that?"

She shook her head slowly, then looked at me with brows dipped low in a troubled wrinkle.

"I said it's like my own personal billionaire romance." Then her grin burst wide and she laughed. "This is ridiculous."

"I wouldn't say *billionaire*. Just multi-millionaire."

Her jaw dropped and she laughed again, more loosely this time. "This is insane."

I inched closer to her, let my hand slide over the slope of her shoulder and down her arm. "What's this about a billionaire romance? Should I be concerned? Are you only after me for my money?"

The delight on her face flashed before she tucked it away in favor of a stern frown and squinting eyes, assessing me. "Maybe."

"Harsh." But I couldn't hide my own smile at the exchange, a delightfully playful version of some of our more antagonistic encounters over the previous months.

She brought a finger to her chin, tapping it as though thinking hard. "Well, your money, and your body."

She meant it as a joke, but desire flooded my chest down into my gut. I could accept that, if that was all she wanted. I would take whatever she'd give me, which should have concerned me on a very real level. It didn't. Especially not when she looked at me like that, all heat and wanting.

Liebe Guete, this woman was radiantly beautiful. Even sitting on the floor in a dimly lit room after hours of hiking and a light rain, she just.... My stomach knotted with how insanely lovely she was, how much I wanted her.

Her hands rose to either side of my face and her blue gaze poured into me. "I'm just joking, you know."

I stared back offering only the tilt of my chin, unwilling to do anything to break her attention, the closeness, the little smirk playing at her lips.

"I also like your accent." She kissed one cheek.

"I don't have an accent."

"Sure." She kissed the other cheek, then slowly, my forehead, my left temple, the corner of my mouth. "I like how you clench your jaw when you're frustrated and trying not to say anything."

She said this in a low almost-whisper at my ear, then placed small kisses on my jaw, then around my ear.

"I'm never frustrated."

She chuckled against my neck, and my eyes shut at the feeling, the lines of sensation sizzling out from where her lips brushed my skin.

"I like how delusional you are," she said at the base of my neck now, a smile in her voice.

I shook my head at this and reached for her, pulled her face to mine. "Sounds like you're fairly fond of me."

She shrugged one shoulder. "A little."

We were inches apart, and finally, *finally,* she brought her kiss to my lips. I held her by the back of her head, wishing for a couch or a bed—anything softer than the stone floor seeping cold into our bodies beneath the blanket.

As it turned out, this was not my best plan. We should've gone to the manager's cabin. Or her apartment. Anywhere, really, other than this wretched half-finished house.

I'd wanted to show it to her—get the conversation out of the way. It being early November, I'd assumed the fire would do enough to warm us. How wrong I'd been, especially if her shivering and the slight bluish tint around her lovely lips were any kind of clue.

I brushed a hand over her head, smoothing little flyaway hairs down as I went. "I wish the fire had done more for us, but I can tell you're freezing, and I am too."

"Let me warm you up then, Jonas."

Oh, but I would. Just not here, and not now, as terrible planning would have it. Even her suggestion, which should have lit me on fire, only served to reinforce the decision to go—her voice had shuddered with a shiver as she'd spoken. *Time to go.*

I coaxed her into leaving with little more than a promise of resuming our close contact later. "After dinner, we'll cuddle up, and you can keep me warm in a room that is climate-controlled."

CHAPTER THIRTY-SIX

Leo

Jonas left me at my place and took his car home—turned out it was only about a twenty-minute hike from his house to mine. Well, his new, not yet finished house.

His mansion, if we're being honest.

It wasn't as huge as Jamie's or Julian's for sure, but it was still massive, especially considering he was a single man, no family, no pets. What did he need all that space for?

I'd already suspected he was wealthy since he'd bought the land, but we hadn't discussed it. He'd forced the issue by showing me the house, and part of me was glad.

The other part of me felt annoyingly intimidated and young. I was several years younger than him at least—I'd turn twenty-five, this year on Thanksgiving, and he was at least thirty... but he could be a few years older than that. Not a huge gap, but just, the whole thing—his worldliness, his wealth, his general distractingly severe good looks and a demeanor that said *You'll never know if I hate you or want to make out with you...* challenging.

What I couldn't escape was how much I did like him. I liked everything about him. I liked how he didn't shy away from admitting he had money. He'd demurred a bit but not in a way that made it seem like he didn't get that it was a big deal or that he was ashamed of it. He owned it, but not in a flashy manner. And thinking of his wardrobe, car, the things in his home... they were all top quality, but none of them flashy. The fanciest thing he had was his car, and even that was an Audi Sedan in black that was always, somehow, meticulously clean, and this only stuck out because not that many people in Silverton owned luxury cars.

As I combed through my freshly showered hair and debated if I wanted to wear makeup or not, I pondered these things. The whole day had left me feeling like fog had rolled in and softened the edges of the scenes we'd wandered through. The hike was gorgeous—a little adventure, a lot of natural beauty, excellent coffee and pastries. Score one for Jonas.

He'd handled the change in hiking trail well. Another point to him. He'd let me in on something personal—his fancy pants house. Again, points to Jonas. And then the whole kissing, wanting to keep me warm situation... *all* the points to Jonas.

I liked that he'd insisted on taking care of me, but had done it in a way that included me. He wasn't a toss-me-over-the-shoulder kind of guy. No, he relied on logic and expected me to as well. While I didn't love the idea of abandoning the opportunity to be close with him, he was right. I'd been shaking for a while, and the fire, soup, and coffee had done nothing to help the cold. In fact, it wasn't until a full five minutes of steaming hot water in the shower that I'd finally felt my skin warm and my core temperature rise enough to relax the hunched tightness at my shoulders caused by shivering.

He'd promised I could keep him warm tonight, though. I planned to do just that. After my shower, I rested in bed and tried to nap for a while since I hadn't slept well the night before and had woken early. The hike had worn me out, and I didn't want to be sleepy and out of it tonight. But my mind was too busy reviewing the day, even though I wanted to enjoy every minute of our time together without being tired and having to call it an early night.

That was one weird thing I'd noticed. I felt a ticking clock in the back of my mind with him. The more I knew of him, the more I liked him, and yet I felt an urgency to be with him, learn more about him, kiss him... and it didn't seem like the urgency of new love or some such nonsense.

It felt like somewhere inside me, I sensed we didn't have time together.

Seeing his house today should have calmed some of that in me—clearly, he planned to stick around. And knowing he visited Grandpa Will should, in theory, reassure me he wasn't burning bridges while planning to ride out of town with the deed to Silver Ridge Lodge in his hands.

But I knew myself. As much as I liked Jonas, I'd *always* dreamed of the family business being mine. No matter how good he was at the job. No matter how much I liked him or his kisses or his attention or his silly German curses. Eventually, I'd be taking the job—his job—when all the pieces came together, and then what?

The ticking clock was not a real surprise.

This was all the more reason to enjoy him now. Enjoy these last few weeks before things became truly insane and I spent hours and hours on the mountain teaching and skiing and soaking up the best thing on Earth, and then we'd see. Maybe we'd be close enough by then he'd see it my way, and I wouldn't have to take it from him.

Maybe.

∼

"That was amazing, Jonas. Thank you." I set my napkin on the empty plate in front of me and leaned away from the table. Of course he could cook, because I definitely needed one more thing to like about him.

"You're welcome. Thank you for coming to me."

"Of course." Like I wouldn't drive the five minutes to his house, but instead demand he pick me up? Crazy. Plus while I'd slowly showered and pondered our relationship and every interaction we'd ever had over the course of the afternoon, he'd been cooking a four-course meal for us.

No, really.

Salad. Then homemade roasted carrot soup which I wouldn't have thought much of but it. Was. Mind-blowing. Then a main course of schnitzel and potatoes and red cabbage. I didn't know the plan for dessert but I had no doubt it'd be amazing.

He'd joked he wanted me to have a taste of his German side. I told him I'd gladly taste his German side any time, and then blushed furiously until we both burst out laughing at the double entendre.

"Do you want dessert now?" he asked as I rinsed dishes and he continued clearing the table. I'd made him promise I could help clean up since he'd refused me that participation last time.

"I'd take a little, if you want some too."

I loved dessert and didn't want to pretend otherwise.

What good would that do? I was sincerely eager to find out what he'd bought or made for dessert; on my visit to Germany years ago, I'd eaten dessert not once but *twice* a day thanks to their afternoon cake-eating tradition known as *Kaffe und Kuchen*—basically a totally genius plan to have coffee and cake and chat during the mid-afternoon hours when everyone is depressed and losing focus anyway.

Maybe we could institute that around Silverton. I'd have to bring it up at the next town council meeting.

Anyway... the other reason I wanted dessert now, despite my mostly stuffed belly thanks to eating every single bite of food he'd served me thus far, was that I wanted what came after dessert. I wanted him close and I didn't want excuses or interruptions.

I finished rinsing dishes and placing them in the dishwasher, wondering if his version of fastidious extended to things like how a dishwasher was loaded. Would he change the way I'd put in the dishes later? Probably not, as he was also someone who valued his time and wasn't likely to redo something that worked well enough.

"Ready?" he asked, two bowls in his hands.

I gasped at the sight of pale white and brilliant red in the bowl. "Is that what I think it is?"

He chuckled and walked to the table, me trailing behind. "Depends on what you think it is."

"Is it *Heiße Liebe*?"

He placed a bowl in front of me, and I beamed at him, physically biting my tongue to keep from professing my love for him. It'd be a joke, a kind of fun exclamation, but the more time I spent with him, the less funny it'd be. The more confusing it could be. So, no declarations tonight, but true, deep, abounding appreciation for what he'd just put in front of me.

One side of his mouth kicked up as he watched me raise my spoon and hesitate over the small bowl full of vanilla ice cream and hot raspberries with raspberry sauce. Simple enough, but it satisfied on a soul-deep level, I would swear it.

I'd ordered it every time I saw it on a menu when I traveled in Germany or Austria.

"You sound almost... reverent. Should I be concerned?"

I took a bite and closed my eyes as the cold, smooth ice cream slid over my tongue followed by the tart tangy warmth of the raspberries. "No. I just *love* this. It's my favorite."

"I know."

"What? How?"

He took a bite, swallowed, then set his spoon down in his bowl. "I heard you tell Bel one time at *Rise and Shine*. I don't remember the context, but I remember hearing *Heiße Liebe* come out of your mouth and being struck dumb for a good five minutes."

I raised my eyebrows since my mouth was full of another bite of the delectable dessert.

"It's true. I don't get to hear German very often, and then you come along, looking like you do, shunning me entirely, and then speaking my language? I had no chance." He fiddled with the spoon, then lifted his gray eyes to meet mine.

I abandoned the dessert, rising from my seat and coming to stand in front of him. He scooted back, watchful. Placing my hands on his shoulders, I stepped between his legs, my heart racing. "You had no chance at what?"

"Resisting you."

I bent to take his mouth, claim him, confirm his resistance was indeed futile. As was mine. I'd been drawn to him the moment we met and though I'd tried to keep my distance and build a wall between us, our togetherness had become inevitable.

He tasted like dessert. *Heiße Liebe—hot love—*aptly named. Our kiss was sweet and decadent and caused my belly to twist with heat. We kissed for long enough that when we came up for air, my ice cream had melted into a swirl of red and white goo.

"I think it's clearly time you stop worrying about resisting me."

CHAPTER THIRTY-SEVEN

Jonas

We sat curled into each other on the couch, fingers lacing together and separating in a mesmerizing, dizzying dance. The fire flickered in front of us, the flames a perfect mimic of what my chest, my mind, my whole body felt.

After dinner, and kissing, and abandoning dessert, we'd moved to the couch, though the brief breath to rinse bowls and load the dishwasher had broken the spell. In other circumstances, it might not have—as adults who were clearly attracted to each other, there was no reason to insist on moving slow.

But after Leonie's admission that she'd been discarded by men who found her to be too much—a pretty face but not enough to keep them around once they got to know her, I wanted to make sure we did plenty of getting to know each other before things progressed too far physically.

She'd snuggled down into my side, head on my shoulder, and we stared out at the little flakes beginning to fall outside.

"I love the first snow."

Mein Gott, having her close, that voice speaking to me gently in the quiet of the night, it made my heart race and jump.

"It's late for the first snow, no?"

"A bit, I guess. It already snowed up top on the peaks of course, but down here it can come as early as beginning of October. Usually before November, so you're right, it's a little late. But I'm glad I get to see it with you."

I ducked to kiss her forehead, the sweetness, though she refused to accept that she possessed any, forcing me to connect with her in some physical way.

"Me too."

After another minute, she sat up and my heart lurched at the thought of her leaving. I didn't want the night to end. I wasn't sure when we'd be together like this again. We were both busy, I had people coming to visit, her family would be arriving in town in another week or so for the holiday... I didn't want her to go yet.

I didn't want her to go at all.

So rather than let her possibly assume I wanted her to go, I said, "Tell me why you and Liam are always at odds."

She gave me a look conveying how out of nowhere my question was, but I simply waited, hoping she'd give a little. Thus far, I'd done most of the confessing—about my family, my money. Time for her to take a turn.

"People like to say it's because we're too alike."

I shifted on the couch, resting an arm behind her where she'd relaxed against the cushion and taking her long honey braid in hand. I'd never see her hair down completely—

there was always some of it pulled back or knotted or braided or weaved in an intricate pattern to keep it off her face and out of her way.

I distinctly wanted it in my way. I wanted it surrounding us. Yes, *us*. I wanted it wild and clutched in my hands. I wanted it loose and free. Yes, I'd allowed her hair to become a symbol for *her*—a signal to the sign, perhaps, but it didn't change the fact that as I felt the smooth, tight rope of her hair, I wanted to pull it.

"And what do you say?"

"I say... I've always loved him and envied him."

"Envied him?"

She nodded, swallowed. "I'm the youngest, and I always wanted to be older. I wanted to be running around with the *big boys* as my parents referred to them. Even though Danny's only a year and a half older, he got to go with them most of the time when I had to stay home, stay behind, have a nap, whatever."

"Poor child."

She narrowed her eyes in a futile threat. "Liam was always sweet—really they all were, except when they weren't and acted like big doofus brothers, terrorizing my Barbies or hiding plastic bugs in my bed, but once he hit his teens, something changed."

She took a big breath and let it out on a long sigh. "In retrospect, I see that it was all normal. But he got busy—sports, friends, girls, jobs, and then he was off to college, and then he was gone to the Army. All the while, I just wanted part of him for myself—I wanted my biggest brother to be there, to check in. And he did, but it always felt like I came last, just like I always had—the youngest, the girl, all that. So I spent a few teen years hating him, then feeling guilty for hating him, especially while he was deployed and was an actual hero."

She rolled her eyes dramatically and we chuckled.

"I'm sorry to say, I like your brother quite a bit." I tugged at her braid just slightly, then released.

"Don't apologize. He is the best. It's true. He has the reputation of being generally loved and helpful and charming and wonderful because honestly? He is. He has a hero complex, and Danny and Jamie have always given him crap for that, but it's something I love about him. But the last few years especially, he lost some of himself, and he could never see that what he wanted so desperately to get rid of was exactly what I—"

She stopped dramatically, her eyes flaring wide, then shuttering for a moment before a pasted-on smile covered her lips.

"Was exactly what you..."

A shake of the head, slight frown. "It was what our parents had wanted for him, and he didn't want it. That was okay, but he made it out to be this huge burden."

She folded her hands together and shoved them between her knees like she was tucking herself away.

"That would be difficult to watch."

"It was. Really frustrating. Especially because my parents and Grandpa Will never made him feel bad for wanting to do something else. Our dad isn't like that. He'd never guilt Liam. But Liam couldn't ever see past his sense of duty, and then his need to be the savior of the family business once it became clear it couldn't survive if we didn't change things."

I let that last thought hang in the air, hoping she could hear herself. That she believed it. Because if I was anything for Leonie and the Morrisons, I was both symbol and deliverer of change.

"So... good thing you came along when you did." Her tight chuckle had me inspecting her.

"I'm honored to be a part of the business."

A fleeting close-lipped smile, if it could even be called that, and then she was looking down, inspecting her hands. "Couldn't have done it without you."

I waited for her to look at me, to lighten the mood, *something*, but she was lost in her thoughts, and I couldn't keep my laughter in. I let it ring out in the room, hoping she'd see the humor in the situation.

"What are you laughing about?"

"That last statement sounded like someone talking at gunpoint. I'm amazed you got it out without crossing your fingers."

Her eyes flashed, and she seemed to realize I was poking at her, drawing her out of wherever she'd gone that had caused the somber mood. Whatever she was keeping close wasn't something I could pry out of her just yet, and so it was time to move away from all that seriousness and into something else that might make her stay a little longer.

"I won't deny that complimenting your involvement would have been darn near impossible for mc months ago."

"And now?"

"Now I can admit you did something no one else could have—you took us out of our tunnel vision and you've given us hope."

Her earnest eyes glittered up at me, and my heart must've grown arms and rattled the cage of my ribs at the sight. Having been on the receiving end of those eyes casting me death glares and frustration and disappointment, having her look at me with this calm, hopeful gaze shook me.

"Leonie, I—"

Her hands rose to hold me on either side of my head like she'd done earlier, but she brushed her soft, pink lips over mine to quiet me, and the effect was nothing short of mind-numbing.

I chased her as she pulled away, pressing against her mouth and nipping at her lower lip.

"I should go," she whispered, breaking the spell, though her voice wrapped around us in the quiet room and her fingers knitted together behind my head.

"You should not."

"I should. It's cold enough, the roads will ice."

"Then you should definitely *not* go." I wrapped my arms around her waist, my hands resting against her back. "Too dangerous."

Her body shook. "You sound pretty desperate."

"Maybe I am."

She took a big breath. "This is kind of like that Christmas song 'Baby it's Cold Outside.'"

I jerked back and we turned toward each other. "It is not. I'm not coercing you. You are free to go at any time, Leonie."

My voice came out a bit harsh, but that song was nonsense.

"I'm joking, Jonas." A half-smile pulled at her gorgeous, full lips.

"I'm not. Go if you want, please. I don't want you here against your will. But if you want to stay, let me be clear. I want you here as long as you'll stay. I want you to cuddle up here on the couch with me and watch a movie, and then I want you to fall asleep next to me, and wake up next to me."

My eyes searched hers as I watched warmth rise to her cheeks and her chest rise and fall. She swallowed, then bit her lip as she studied me right back.

"Which movie?"

"Your choice."

"What do you like?"

"You."

She chuckled and shook her head. "Not a real answer."

"How about, I want you to stay as long as possible, so I want you to choose a movie that will make you want to stay."

Her open-mouth stare made me want to laugh and kiss her and throw her over my shoulder on the way to the bedroom.

I didn't do any of those things, but rather waited for her expression to lose its surprise and warm up. Once it didn't, I spoke.

"When will you realize how much I want you?"

CHAPTER THIRTY-EIGHT

Leo

We watched *Pride and Prejudice*, the 2005 version.
Foolishly, I thought it'd work to quell the rioting desire pummeling my brain into stunned verbal failure, but no. Of course it wouldn't. It was subtle and funny and lovely and oh so romantic. It was my favorite movie.

It was also a kind of test. Would Jonas be the kind of man to roll his eyes or complain about a period drama?

No. Of course he wouldn't. He simply said, "Oh good, I haven't seen this," and pulled me close so his arm draped behind my shoulders and my body rested against his.

If that wasn't a kind of emotional catnip on its own, he then laughed and seemed to delight in the movie, commenting on how he didn't expect it to be so funny. This, naturally, forced me to give a small lecture on Jane Austen's brilliance and discuss why her books had lasted with such staying power, which he listened to as though my words mattered to him.

That was another thing. He *listened.* He listened so carefully and thoughtfully and *fully* it made me second guess my words. I liked to talk, so I could be caught babbling on and he'd sit there, rapt attention on me.

It was thrilling and terrifying and so unfamiliar. I'd never had a man give me his undivided focus unless he was related to me or trying to kiss me. And though I knew with full confidence Jonas wanted to kiss me, he showed me moment by moment that he also wanted to hear me, be near me, be close to me, *know me.*

The whole night was a heart-exploding dream. By the end when Lizzie and Darcy are *incandescently happy,* my little heart had trotted down a path full of hikes through green fields and snowy peaks and evenings spent just like this with *this* man.

When the movie ended, he took my hand and led me to his room, where I'd been before but this felt very different. It *was* different.

He stopped next to the bed and turned me to him, his gray eyes searching mine. The darker shade of his brows gave his gaze a fathomless look to them—cliché or no, his were eyes I could get lost in.

His hand cupped my jaw, the other fiddling lightly with my braid at my back. His touch, his focus on me, the overwhelming reality that my feelings for him had ballooned out of control in just a few short weeks, made my pulse pound and my breath come up short.

His lips fell to mine like an inevitability. A fleeting thought made me wonder how I'd ever not kissed him—how had I thought I hated him? How had I seen him as an enemy when he now embodied so much loveliness and joy and irresistible pleasure?

As he pulled me to him, his lips skimmed across my jaw and down my neck, each soft, warm kiss causing blood to thrum in my veins. My hand threaded into his hair, searched over his arms and back, alternately clutched at his shirt and urged him closer.

Our kiss ignited between us, and the idea of leaving and venturing out into the now-driving snow was nothing short of ludicrous. Staying was its own kind of madness, but I couldn't think of any other insanity I'd welcome more.

"Stay tonight. No pressure. Just... sleep next to me, and wake next to me."

"Are you going to tell us what's going on with you and Jonas?" Wells wiggled her eyebrows and eyed me.

Mia chuckled next to her. "You guys seemed pretty cozy when I saw you at the grocery last weekend."

It'd been two weeks since I'd spent the night at Jonas' house. I'd spent the night but not *spent the night.* As much as it seemed like that would have been the next step, he'd kept us from going that far, and part of me was glad. It was wise to go slowly, especially for someone like me who'd never been involved with someone like him—who'd never felt anything like what I'd been feeling. The time together had been perfect, and a definite step forward into truly exciting and unknown territory for me.

Waking up next to him had been a foreign experience. I'd awoken before him and wondered if I should sneak out to avoid any awkwardness, despite not actually feeling uncomfortable. Just full of anticipation and joy.

Once he opened his eyes and hit me with that gray gaze, I decided it, second only to the mountains just outside the window, was my favorite view.

I should have recognized that thought for the harbinger of doom it was, but of course I'd ignored it, because he was staring at me like I was *his* favorite view right back.

We'd grabbed a quiet lunch midweek, snuck in dinner four times, and each of us popped into the other's office as often as we could. Maddeningly, we both had a lot of extra-work activities going on—meetings, interviews, pre-planned events we couldn't just beg off nor could we share with the other person. In some ways, that was probably good—if I'd had my way and spent every waking moment with him, he'd likely be sick of me already, and then where would I be?

Lovesick and desperate, not unlike you are anyway.

We hadn't meant to be secretive about our relationship, and strangely enough as I sat at the table at *Basta* with my sister-in-law and my two friends who would become the same eventually, I realized we hadn't defined our relationship. But we hadn't been public—not at work, though we weren't exactly sneaking around, and not in town, primarily because we didn't spend much time in town. We were at his house, or work, because they were close by and convenient.

I didn't need to worry. Jonas wasn't the kind of man to date multiple women, nor would it be possible in a small town like this. It would be good to name what we were doing—*dating*, in a relationship, committed to each other.

That thought made my chest flutter. We were committed to each other, weren't we? I didn't know exactly what that meant, but that was precisely why we should talk about it. What did he want, in the end?

I knew what I wanted, and I could see it unrolling with Jonas, even though I wasn't sure how we'd reconcile what I wanted out of life, and what he seemed to. But again, we could figure that out.

"We are dating. I mean, we haven't defined the terms or anything, but yeah… we're seeing each other." The smile on my face felt ridiculously large, and based on their answering ones, it was.

"This is awesome. I love this." Wells clapped her hands.

Bel eyed me, a thoughtful, though happy, look on her face, while Mia held her wine glass up.

"To Leonas, may you be infinitely happy."

I burst out laughing. "*Leonas?*"

Her dark eyes sparkled back at me. "Have you not heard that? Danny suggested that be your power couple name."

"When did he say that?"

When had my brother noticed me and Jonas?

Mia's Cheshire cat grin filled her entire face. "I think it was after he saw Jonas kissing you against your office door last week?"

My jaw dropped and my cheeks burned. Wells applauded more insistently and Bel cast me a delighted albeit shocked look, then dramatically shook me by the shoulders.

"How did you not tell me you were with him? You're making out at work and I didn't know?"

Her words were rushed and celebratory, but I thought I detected a bit of hurt around the eyes where she wasn't smiling.

"I know. It's been kind of… overwhelming. I'm not great a talking about this kind of thing, and—"

Bel held up a hand. "I don't see how you get a pass on this."

"A pass?"

"Yeah. You wheedled your way into each of our relationships, meddled around, and in some cases even caused trouble," Bel continued.

Her sharp look was unnecessary since I still felt bad for how I'd interfered with Wells and Liam, and for that matter, to some degree, even Mia and Danny when I'd doubted Danny's ability to commit.

"And now, here you are, hoarding your thoughts and feelings like a stingy dragon and we're left in the dark."

A giggle escaped before I could address anything she said. "A stingy dragon?"

We all laughed, then Mia held her glass up again, and we all joined her with hands raised to the center of the table.

"To Leonas."

After a few more jokes and receiving our food, we settled into an easy rhythm of chatting and catching up. I'd been let off the hook when Wells asked Bel how she was doing in LA and how she was liking taking on more clients. Then conversation shifted to Mia and Danny's wedding and reviewing the things we each needed to do to help prepare.

When Wells updated us on the hotel plans and Liam's brewery, I couldn't help the twinge of unease that slipped in. Each of them had jobs that complemented or at least cooperated with their partner's. How could Jonas and I work if I wanted to take his job?

And how could I look at myself in the mirror if I just gave up on that dream, and let him have what I'd always wanted, simply because I loved him?

As though she read my mind, Bel's voice cut through my thoughts. "So Leo, really. How is it going with Jonas?"

I pushed the last few tubes of penne around on my plate before surrendering my fork. "It's really good."

They all beamed back at me.

"I just..."

They sobered, all in unison. It would have been completely hilarious if they didn't seem like they'd been waiting for my doubts.

"I'm just not sure where it can go. I know he likes me. I definitely... like him. I just don't know how well we fit together long-term."

Bel narrowed her eyes at me and pressed her lips together. I couldn't decipher the look but she spared me much detective work when she shook her head and started speaking.

"You don't know how you fit together long-term?"

"Why is that funny?"

"Leo, you're talking about a man who takes no crap—none of *your* crap. He's not intimidated by you. I don't know the ins and outs of what your time alone together is like, but I'm guessing, based on how happy you seem, that it's pretty great."

I attempted a bored look, but my mouth formed a grin of its own accord. Apparently, I couldn't even think about being with Jonas without smiling like a dolt.

"Your point?"

"My point is, I think you know where you want it to go."

Mia and Wells watched the two of us, silent. I wished one of them would interrupt, or change the subject. I could finally understand why they'd resisted my meddling in the past.

I heaved a sigh, reluctant to say what I wanted aloud. Somehow, I knew if I admitted to them what I wanted, soon after I'd have to tell Jonas. And that meant dealing with a mini Pandora's box of problems I didn't want to have to deal with while everything was so fun and happy.

"I do know. I do." I frowned again.

"What is it?" Wells asked, all kindness in her voice.

I didn't want to admit this, but these women loved me, and I needed help. This nagging notion in me wouldn't just disappear.

"He thinks I'm sweet. I mean, he knows I'm not, but I know he thinks it anyway. Like, he called me sweetie in German."

Bel made a sound of mild disgust and rolled her eyes. "Woman! How many times do I have to tell you being *sweet* is not a problem?"

Mia and Wells looked on, but I couldn't let them misunderstand.

"It's not that I think it's a bad thing. *You* are sweet, Bel, and you, Mia, are the sweetest, and Wells, you're like... *so sweet*. But me? I swear I'm not trying to sound like an idiot, I just... I don't want him to be disappointed." I didn't need one more thing that could come between us before we ever begin.

Bel grabbed my hands and her green eyes bored into mine. "I'm going to say something, and I need you to really hear me right now. Can you do that?"

"Yes."

She shook her head. "No, *really*."

I huffed a little, a smile pulling at one corner of my mouth at her bossiness and the little burst of love I felt in my heart.

"You *are* sweet—no!"

I pressed my lips together, biting back my interruption at her refusal to hear it.

She glanced at Mia and Wells as though to loop them into the conversation, and they both nodded as she continued. "You are, my friend. You care for your people so well.

No, not always, of course. And dang, girl, you can get salty in a heartbeat. But as your life-long friend and devoted fan, I have to tell you, you do have sweetness in you. It's not a bad thing. Being strong *and* sweet is what I love about you, and I want you to embrace it."

Wells smacked the table. "Completely agree."

Mia raised her glass. "To strength and sweetness, a beautiful combo."

Bel gave me a soft smile. "Jonas *sees* you, Leo. The rage, the salt, the sweet too. That's worth remembering."

CHAPTER THIRTY-NINE

Jonas

Leonie Morrison would be the death of me.

I'd lost all focus. I could hardly stand to work in my office knowing she was down the hall working in hers, or out on the mountain checking out where we'd made snow, or talking with Danny or any number of her instructors or teachers....

I had been so distracted yesterday by thinking about Leonie, who I'd just seen laughing with Jane, her lead child-care worker, that Karla had hung up on me. It had taken me several minutes to realize she'd done so. When I called back, she had been unamused, but not as angry as she justifiably should have been. Karla was an extremely busy woman and didn't have time to coax me into consciousness.

She'd confirmed she'd be here for two days next week, just in time for Thanksgiving. She wasn't one to celebrate holidays, and had forgotten completely, particularly after having been in Europe for the last month or so. Now I had the awkward task of deciding whether to bow out of the Morrison family Thanksgiving meal, which I was fairly sure I was still invited to since Leonie and I were dating, or finding a way to invite a guest to a dinner at which I myself was a guest.

I wanted to go to that dinner. I wanted Leonie to see me with her family—the people she loved most—and see I could fit with them. I fit with her, and I'd fit with them. After that, she'd be ready to really be with me, and we'd move ahead. She'd embrace the changes with the hotel, and we'd work together to make this place great.

It was all going according to plan, but I didn't want to miss the dinner. And I didn't want to invite a guest of my own. But Leonie would likely do that for me, once I told her when Karla would be here.

It was six days to Thanksgiving, and I'd be busy all weekend. Julian Grenier was here yet again, and though I wasn't certain why since he seemed to be the most in-demand person I'd ever met and yet had come to Silverton no less than three times in the last three months, I couldn't pass up an opportunity to meet with him. More than that, Leonie would be with Bel Paxton and Wells Bryant-Morrison for a surprise bachelorette party for Mia Parker, and apparently, it was a weekend-long event.

I did my best not to let Leonie see how undesirable spending an entire weekend away from her sounded. I didn't mind her knowing I was completely gone for her, and she seemed, if not equally interested, then close. I wanted the next week to solidify things between us. Perhaps if she had time with her friends, she'd be able to come to the conclusion that she felt as strongly for me. Then she'd be ready for what I had for her.

I'd planned out my weekend so it was filled with work, meetings, physical training, and more work. I'd meet Grenier for lunch on Saturday, and my evenings would be spent working ahead on all of my non-Silver Ridge Resort obligations so that I could take a few days, and Thanksgiving itself, off before the season began a week from today and life became fuller and more demanding for the next few months.

I couldn't wait.

I had everything I never knew I wanted. Of course, I'd wanted Silver Ridge, but I hadn't known how. I'd had no idea I'd want it this way, in a hands-on, day-to-day way that demanded time and energy, not just money. This revelation paired perfectly with the reality that I'd succumbed almost entirely to my desire to be with a woman I shouldn't ever have started dating, and yet now that I had, I couldn't fathom an alternate course.

Fortunately, I'd see Leonie for a few minutes tonight before she left for the surprise party for Mia. I'd soak in every second with her and hope it'd fuel me for the weekend so I wouldn't be pining for her like the sap I never realized I was until she came along.

Her knock came at six, just as I pulled on a pair of soft denim pants and dried my hair after a shower. I'd run on the treadmill, a terrible way to run but the only option this time of year when sidewalks iced over and the air became truly impossible to breathe as the sun went down, and had managed to get showered and changed just in time for her.

The door opened and she launched, arms wrapped around me and body pressed to mine like that was where it belonged.

This is *where it belongs.*

"I've missed you," she said, breathless and smiling between kisses.

"And I you."

My hands slid down to rest at the curve of her lower back just under the end of her fitted puff coat and savored her lips on mine, wishing we had more time.

"Are you sure you have to go to this thing?" I mumbled.

She pulled back and narrowed her eyes. "Are you trying to get me to ditch my friends?"

"Never. I know they are important to you. But I won't pretend I'm not jealous for you."

Her bright blue eyes slayed me, heating and widening as they searched my face and landed on my lips, then flicked up to meet my own eyes. "Jealous? Of my friends?"

"I'm jealous of anyone who gets time with you when I don't."

She frowned, but didn't speak.

"I don't mean I begrudge you the time with friends, or family, or whoever it is you're spending time with. I only mean I would be perfectly happy to be around you all day, and all night."

Her lips parted again, then pulled into a broad smile. "You are sneaky."

"What?"

"You've got stealthy words and they're sneaky. I think you know it, too."

I responded with a somber face, unwilling to give her anything. I hoped my words affected her even a fraction of the amount she affected me merely by existing.

A sound strummed from her phone, and her face dropped. "I have to go or I'll be late. That won't work for a surprise party."

Her genuine reluctance buoyed me, just a bit. I didn't

want her to wish she wasn't going, but seeing her wishing we could have just a few more minutes helped me feel less like I was too far gone. Maybe I wasn't the only one dreading the weekend apart, even though I enjoyed my work and the things on my list. I'd much rather be doing all of them with her.

"Should I be concerned about this party?"

Her smile returned. "Concerned how?"

I straightened, pressing her to me but ignoring the sizzle in my blood at her nearness. There was no time to enjoy that properly. "Will there be strippers? Anatomically shaped pasta? What are you in for?"

"Do you think that's something Mia would enjoy?"

"I wouldn't pretend to know what women enjoy for such events."

Her eyes flared wide. "Do you think *I* would enjoy that?"

"Would you?" Something about the intensity in her eyes made my stomach drop.

"No. I'm not interested in random strippers, and I prefer penne pasta."

"Are you interested in *specific* strippers?"

She threw her head back and cackled—no other word for it. Then hit me with a look with so much... *Heiliger Strohsack*, it looked like love. Not just tenderness or affection, but love.

Couldn't be. I didn't anticipate love between us for another few months, once we'd worked through some of the issues, once she knew everything. I might have been heading in that direction, but she certainly couldn't be, not with her as resistant as she'd been to me and everything between us.

Leonie wouldn't be one to love easily, but I suspected,

based on the way she behaved with family and close friends, once she did give her love, it would never be lost.

I cleared my throat against the crush of longing for her, for that love between us, and watched as she calmed from her laughter and shook her head with delight in her eyes.

"If you're offering, I suppose I'd consider it."

With no time to properly address that comment, I stole a kiss, then very reluctantly released her. "I'll see you... Monday?"

Yes. Monday. Approximately sixty hours, not that I'd thought about it too carefully and not that I'd be counting down the minutes until I saw her again.

CHAPTER FORTY

Leo

Mia was totally surprised, and the weekend turned out perfectly.

We spent it at a little bed and breakfast and spa tucked way out east of Silverton. The place was ridiculously idyllic and apparently a getaway for extremely wealthy people. Jamie had told Bel about it, and once she'd mentioned it, we knew we had to go.

I couldn't believe I'd never heard of it, but once Bel filled us in on the details, it made sense. It had originally been set up as a luxury rehab location for wealthy patrons struggling with various addictions. Because of the location, though, and the challenging winters this high in the mountains, it'd shut down a few years back. Then, once Jamie and Julian Grenier had begun surveying and building out their neighborhood, someone had purchased the facility and revamped it into a destination spa.

It. Was. Gorgeous. Set out in a meadow with fields— most of which Wyatt Saint owned, we learned after arriving —and looking up at the far side of the Silver Ridge range and the east face of Silver Ridge Peak in the distance. I'd never seen it from this side other than in the car on the way to Wyoming, but it was just as marvelous, if a bit mysterious, from this angle.

And it was exactly what we all needed less than a week before the mountain opened for the season. It was bold to take the time away, but everything was ready, and though the week leading up to Thanksgiving and then opening day would be insane, it was worth it to have this little getaway.

Kai was staying with Danny, Bel had arrived last week and was spending the time with me anyway, and Wells had hired a manager for the inn since they had so much business and she couldn't do everything herself, so her manager was covering her this weekend.

"Are we sure we have to go back to real life tomorrow?" Wells sighed where she sat in a cushioned chaise longue, snuggled under fluffy down blankets, hair swirled in a towel on top of her head and eyes covered in slices of cucumbers.

"I wouldn't mind another few days here, though I think my body is confused." Mia spoke from a similar state, then sipped cucumber mint water from a glass straw.

Nothing cheap here. Nothing plastic. Everything was supremely and fastidiously comfortable, beautiful, and relaxing. It was almost overwhelming how forcefully the place took rest and relaxation.

Upon arrival, our car had been parked for us. The small bags we'd packed had been snatched by the bellhop even before we'd entered the building. Though there were other patrons in the place, we never *ever* saw them. We were in our own little party, a perfectly appointed room with a gorgeous, huge bathroom. Spa treatments in the mornings, and time to explore the other amenities including Turkish baths, pools, steam rooms, saunas, yoga classes, a glorious library filled with cozy couches and chairs and books floor to ceiling. The place was amazing.

We applauded Jamie more than once over the course of the weekend—he'd funded the getaway since none of us could have, even split four ways. That was why he'd mentioned it to Bel, in the end, and I would have to tell him how much we had all enjoyed it. I was sure Bel would too.

"What do you mean?" Bel's sleepy voice brought me back to the moment.

"I mean it's confused why I'm treating it so well," Mia answered. "Massages, pedicures, facials, manicures, relaxing in ergonomically designed lounges and chairs... it knows November is not a time for peace, and yet here I am."

They all laughed, and I with them. The weekend had been a blissful retreat, and I'd been more relaxed and in the moment than I had in... maybe ever. I didn't remember the last time I'd felt this happy—just simply happy.

Some of that had to do with Jonas. His send off—searing kisses and a confession that he'd miss me in a way that only Jonas could say—had left me aching to be with him, and yet all fluttery at the thought of reuniting, even if it would be at work on Monday. I'd blocked out those confusing feelings about moving forward with him. Somehow, up here in this fancy little world with my best friends, I was able to function as though it'd all work out.

Wishful thinking, perhaps. But I clung to it and embraced the calm which had become more and more rare as I'd fallen farther and farther for Jonas.

As for the weekend, we'd spend much of the time simply relaxing, talking about trivial things, updating each other on life even more than we already had at dinner days before. We only had a few hours left before we'd make the drive back to Silverton, though fortunately, we had the whole day to enjoy the place and we'd unanimously agreed we wanted to just lay around as much as we could.

"I think I've finally gotten over the feeling that Kai is about to bound in here and dive on top of me and ask for lunch."

At the sound of her voice—smiling and kind of wistful—I pulled off my cucumbers to see her face. A small frown curved her mouth, and she stared at the gigantic fireplace roaring in the corner—there was one in just about every relaxation room in the building.

"You miss him?" I asked, snuggling down into the blanket and taking a drink.

"I do. This is actually the first time I've ever been away from him."

"Wow, that hadn't even occurred to me, but I don't know why—I'm sorry. Are you doing okay?" Wells' concern shone through her voice.

"I am. I've been ready for something like this for years, frankly, but I've never had someone I trusted to watch Kai while I was away. Obviously, I trust Danny, so this is great. But I do miss him. It's an odd tension."

"I'm so glad you came, Mia."

We had taken her to dinner on Friday at a place up the canyon, and then had given her the choice. Danny had packed a bag for her and kept Kai with him, but we didn't want her to feel trapped or like she couldn't say no. Fortunately, she said yes, and it'd been one of the best weekends of my life thus far.

We hadn't talked much about me. That was fine. I wasn't sure I had anything more to report after our dinner last week, and I hadn't talked with Jonas about what we were doing. But in four days, he'd be at my house for Thanksgiving as my date. Either before or after that event, I wanted to nail things down. As much as it sounded like a nice idea to not worry about labels, I wanted a label. I wanted to call him my boyfriend, even though calling Jonas Bauer *boy*-anything seemed ridiculous.

But after a weekend of pampering and relaxing and eating healthy, gourmet food, I wanted to return to work. If there'd been a true love in my life to now, it was Silver Ridge. My love was in bloom November to April, and there was nothing like the first crush of it when the season opened.

"What are you doing for your birthday, Leo?" Bel asked later that day as we all slowly packed our things.

It was time to go, and we knew it, but leaving this place wasn't easy. I patted a perfect synthetic down pillow with pristine cover that lay next to my small suitcase on the bed before answering.

"Just family dinner. I'm guessing Ma will have a cake, but you know it's going to be crazy. And you'll all be there with me. But I kind of considered this weekend my celebration too. And you all insisted on toasting me several times last night." They'd surprised me with a little cake as well. It was a perfect celebration.

"But what are you and Jonas doing?" Wells asked.

"Oh, I don't think he knows it's my birthday."

Wells stared at me, horrified, and even Mia and Bel looked surprised.

"What?"

"I'm big on birthdays. I always assume everyone else is too." Wells shrugged, fiddled with the zipper.

"I like my birthday, but I mostly like the beginning of

the season. Plus this year it falls exactly on Thanksgiving, so it's not easy to make it a whole separate thing. I'll be happy to have everyone together, and Jonas is coming to dinner, so it'll be great."

Bel and Mia exchanged a look, then Bel said, "You're right. That'll be nice."

Later that night, I messaged Jonas to tell him I'd arrived home safely. The reception hadn't been great out there, but I'd sent him a few messages, not wanting to seem needy or overly attached with my phone.

I fell asleep waiting for his responding text, too tired after the weekend away to stay awake despite the whole trip being focused on relaxation. I dreamed of mountains and snow and soft pillows and gray eyes.

CHAPTER FORTY-ONE

Jonas

L eonie shook Karla's hand, giving her a broad smile. "It's great to see you again."

"Likewise." Karla returned Leonie's handshake with equal fervor, then cut me a look that said she approved.

Leonie looked exceptionally beautiful today, and just seeing her sent my pulse racing. Pathetically, I felt a drop of disappointment at having to share her with her family, and my friend.

"We should probably get going. The sooner we get there, the sooner the appetizers will start and then maybe we'll get out of there before midnight." Leonie gestured to invite us out of my house, so Karla and I followed.

Karla had met me at my house, then Leonie had joined us, and I'd drive us all to the Morrisons' home. If Leonie was concerned about Karla being at my house, she hid it well. She needn't have had any concern at all, which I'd told her in no uncertain terms two days earlier when we'd spoken about Karla's visit and I'd broached the subject of Karla joining us for dinner with her family.

She hadn't seemed worried at all. More curious. In fact, she'd said, "My parents love having a big group for holidays, and I look forward to getting to know this person who has known you for so long."

Kind of... cryptic? Not quite that, but something. It'd left me feeling restless, like she wanted to dig around and figure me out, but I'd already been showing her who I was.

"So was Jonas always so..." Leonie trailed off as I started the car.

"Serious?" Karla offered from the front seat next to me.

Leonie had insisted she sit up front.

"Yes. That's it, in one sense."

"Then yes. He has been. He's always been driven, and it's part of why I was happy to take a chance on partnering with someone so young."

Leonie caught my eye in the rearview mirror as I shifted into drive. "Was he very young when you started Bauer Group?"

"Indeed he was. Twenty-two. We're just eighteen months out from our ten-year anniversary. It'll be perfect to celebrate with the resort hotel here building out, and a few other projects we have going on elsewhere, before we mark ten."

I heard the sharp intake of breath, but couldn't chance a look back as the roads were snow-packed thanks to the snow that had dumped for the last forty-eight hours. My stomach plummeted and dread pinched at my jaw and temple.

"The hotel?"

"Yes. Silver Ridge's hotel? On Jonas' new land? I'm thrilled we can list that under our consultations results."

Karla smiled over at me, but the moment she saw my face, she sobered. "O-of course, it's certainly—"

"The hotel won't be completed by this coming summer." Leonie's words emerged certain and challenging.

"Ah, well, I—" Karla struggled to find words, and I clutched the steering wheel to keep from covering her mouth with my hand.

"We'll discuss it after dinner, yes?" I made it sound like a question, because I couldn't very well refuse to speak to her, but this was not the time. Why did Karla have to bring up this *one* thing that caused problems between Leonie and me?

I eyed Leonie in the back seat, her face the picture of betrayal and frustration, then she nodded.

"So, er, what is your mother doing for the holiday, Jonas?" Karla's change of subject, however obviously awkward, was much appreciated.

We chatted, our amiability forced at this point since we could both feel the black hole of energy coming from the back seat. I didn't want to face this conversation before we walked into her family's holiday meal. I didn't want anything between us, but I doubted she'd let it rest until we found a moment alone.

I parked and saw Liam and Wells walking up the porch steps to the inviting home complete with a wreath on the door and a wooden *welcome* sign propped on the porch.

At the same moment, Karla said, "I see Wells and Liam. I'll just—"

She exited the car before anyone could object.

I unbuckled my seatbelt and twisted around to face Leonie, who sat with a dull affect on her face that sent my heart galloping with alarm.

"Why is Karla talking about the hotel like it's a done deal?"

"Because Karla has been informed about the project in detail. She had an interest in the development of the—"

"Which means it is moving forward this summer? You're going to take that risk before we've even had a more successful season?"

"It's a calculated risk, and one I whole-heartedly believe in. If you would consider my perspective, I believe you'll see—"

"I don't need to see your perspective, Jonas. What I see is you doing what you've always done—barrel ahead with a plan despite my opinion. I realize I'm just the *daughter*, just the youngest, just a *woman* with a feeble mind for business, but I have reasons for resisting this timeline and you know it. If you can't respect my opinion about something like this, if you just plow ahead while letting me think you're doing what we agreed upon, how can I ever trust you with *anything*?"

Hurt shone in her eyes, and it threatened to gut me. I hated that I'd put that there, even while I fully believed in the project.

"You know I don't see you as feeble or *just* a woman, or any of that other nonsense. I respect you, but on this we disagree, and the board voted this summer to move ahead. I'm not going to apologize for pursuing this project or finding a way to make it work on the timeline I'd originally set out, which was not easy, for the record. I regret that you see this as a negative development, but I can assure you it's a good thing for the resort, for your family, and potentially for you."

Her brow furrowed and she sat forward, a mixture of

emotions warring on her face. "How could it be good for me?"

Just then, Kai knocked on Leonie's window, and after a double take, she beamed a smile at him and opened the door. "Well hello there, my favorite almost-nephew!"

She shut the door behind her and I slowly inhaled, calming my breathing and grabbing the bottle of wine I'd brought to give the Morrisons.

"Jonas, Karla, have you known each other long?" Alice Morrison, the matriarch of the Morrison family, asked with a warm smile.

She'd been very welcoming, saying how pleased she was that Karla and I could come. The problem rested in the fact that Leonie hadn't let me get near her or touch her since we'd entered the home. I was being punished, and though I couldn't blame her for feeling frustrated, or even a bit betrayed if I took her perspective, I couldn't understand her not standing by me.

I'd walked in and introduced Karla, since she was technically my guest, and Leonie had lagged behind, uncomfortable as that was. I'd hoped she'd grab my hand, claim me as hers, but she hadn't. Did the Morrisons believe Karla and I were together, there at their dinner table as mutual friends of Leonie?

Meine Guete, I hoped not. I'd have to make it clear.

"We're distant cousins. We've been close friends most of my life and have been partners in business for just shy of a decade." *There.* Should be clear enough now.

"Oh! Forgive me, I thought perhaps you were romantically linked." Alice Morrison flushed and shared a regretful smile, but Karla and I both waved it away.

"Happens all the time," Karla explained.

"No, not at all," I said uselessly, wishing Leonie, who sat across from me, might interject.

"Leo, come on," Liam said, from down the table.

She shot him a glare. A truly brutal look that would wither a lesser man. My stomach clenched, familiar with the occasional animosity with which these two treated each other. They'd been better the last few months, but it didn't surprise me to find they butted heads at the family table as well.

"What? Don't give me that look. You're being obnoxiously silent." Liam's voice came out critical and sharp.

My hackles rose just as Leonie spoke. "Stay out of this, Liam."

"You're being rude."

I couldn't stay silent any longer, my blood racing through my veins in protest at his censure of her. "Please. It's nothing."

Liam eyed me, evidently trying to puzzle out what I meant.

"Truly, don't concern yourself. It is not for you to tell her how to treat me."

Dead silence filled the table. No—not just the table. The entire room.

If I were a different man, I might have shrunk in my seat, or slithered off to the bathroom to alleviate the pressure in the space. I was a guest, and I'd just essentially reprimanded the oldest son of the host family, a man who had at one point been my employer and was now in charge of the board that determined my ability to perform *anything* in my job.

Brilliant.

Leonie cleared her throat and gave me what I would heretofore refer to as *the death glare.*

"Jonas, may I speak to you privately?"

My gaze swooped around the table with a tight attempt at a smile, then stood. "Of course."

I followed her through the kitchen, around the corner, up the stairs, and into a small room with posters of Picabo Street and the US Women's Ski team plastered on the walls. Despite the circumstances, I smiled inwardly at the peek inside Leonie's childhood bedroom.

"*What* are you *doing?*"

Her voice cut through any thought I might have had about kissing her, asking who her favorite skier was, what she was like a child.

"Your brother is too harsh with you."

Her chest rose dramatically like she sucked in a large breath, then deflated. "Sometimes, yes. But he was right. I was being rude."

She studied her shoes—an enticing pair of heels that paired with the deep blue cocktail dress she wore like a weapon. At least, it served as a weapon for me—a knife to the jugular just looking at her. If I breathed too deeply, her beauty, loveliness, extreme allure, would slice me.

I stepped toward her, reaching for her hand, then dropping mine when I remembered the argument about the hotel. "I'm sorry for not telling you."

She shook her head once. "I don't want to talk about that now. I just want to... I needed a minute. So... minute complete. Let's go back, and I won't pretend I hate you, and you don't have to worry about me disavowing any knowledge of you. Deal?"

Amused at her use of *disavow* and yet tremulous at the

thought of her considering the notion, I nodded. I scrambled for some way to reconnect, not wanting to return to the table without some sign she'd do more than ignore me. "Could I... could I hug you? Kiss you?"

Her crystalline eyes nearly glowed with unspoken words as her lips pressed into a line. "You can hug me."

I scooped her up immediately, wrapping my arms around her back and holding her there for a moment, two, breathing in her fresh, warm scent before I released her.

She stepped back and opened the door. "We'll talk more after."

With another nod, I followed her back to that table. We found the family and their guests chatting amiably, Jamie and Danny ribbing their father about something I'd missed.

I ignored the pang of missing my own father, a familiar feeling this time of year. He'd always loved Thanksgiving. Sometimes, I thought my mother and I should have made a better effort to get together and celebrate the holiday in his honor, but she made excuses or claimed to have other plans anytime I mentioned doing such a thing.

No one drew attention to me or Leonie the rest of the meal, for which I was grateful. They'd all felt the tension between us, and I'd stepped in with Liam, so I couldn't blame them for wanting to avoid any further drama.

But by the end, Wells had coaxed me into speaking a few times, and Karla had answered a few questions and conversed with ease. Leonie stayed quiet, which seemed odd considering how vocal she was at work or any other time I saw her, and yet she wasn't subdued. She appeared thoughtful.

I knew at least some of what she pondered, and had to work fairly hard to keep my knee from bouncing as I thought about the conversation we'd have after dinner.

"Ready everyone?" Alice Morrison asked as she walked in, a towering cake covered in glowing candles.

Will Morrison started singing, and everyone else followed. *"Happy birrrthday dear Leo, Happy birthday to you!"*

Applause filled the room as Alice set the cake in front of Leonie. I caught her eye, my face a white sheet of mortification and frankly, a bit of horror. I had no idea it was her birthday. I'd planned nothing.

I had nothing for her.

I had no way to make her feel special.

She held my gaze, then shut her eyes and blew out the candles.

Everyone offered her congratulations on another year, and she seemed to glow from the attention—questions about her goals for the next year and her favorite moments from the last. I'd have to make it up to her, and I prayed she'd let me.

Though she'd been joking about the night ending at midnight, we stumbled out into a bitterly cold night at half past eight and a small part of me wanted to cry. It made no sense that the family who operated a ski resort known for opening the day after Thanksgiving did *anything* late on this Thursday. And no, eight wasn't all that late, but it was when you considered that I intended to get up around five to make sure absolutely everything was under control. And more than that, that I needed to clear the air with Leonie before the day ended and the madness began tomorrow.

Karla and I talked quietly on the ride back to the inn where I'd leave her for the night. She'd ski opening morning and return to the valley and the airport later in the day. Fortunately, we'd completed all our business earlier so she didn't have plans to extend her trip.

Not that I didn't want to see my friend and catch up, but ultimately, we communicated every few days via e-mail about Bauer Group matters, and I wasn't entirely sure I wanted her opinion on Leonie. In truth, the evening had been a strange one in terms of our dynamic, and until we talked through the hotel business, and likely a few other things, they wouldn't return to normal. I didn't need Karla here in the midst of getting beyond that. Plus the birthday failure, which I hated to add to the pile.

I parked in front of Leonie's house and walked her to the door. We didn't speak. My nerves had fired up with a mixture of need to clear the air and need to touch her after being deprived of contact for what felt like months. Of course it hadn't been that long, but there would be no contact until we worked through this. I only hoped we'd get through it tonight.

The door swung open and she held out a hand, that same gesture she'd used earlier. "Will you come in to talk?"

CHAPTER FORTY-TWO

Leo

If he'd stop looking at me like that, it'd make it a whole lot easier to maintain my list of reasons the hotel was a bad idea. I'd be able to keep my anger at him and not just start begging him to define our relationship.

I didn't want to be in that position—the weak one, waiting for him to give me what I needed like I was begging. He didn't need to know he had that much power over me. In fact, he *couldn't* know that—I couldn't let him.

"Do you want something to drink?"

I unraveled my scarf and pulled off my jacket, hung them both on a peg inside the door, then held out a hand for his. He quickly shrugged out of his coat and handed it to me, our fingers brushing and sending a thrill through me. Just that little contact, and my heart tripped.

"No, thank you. I would like to talk about the hotel, if you're ready."

I slipped out of my high heels and sat on the couch, then patted the spot next to me. Surprise flickered across his face, and my weak little insides found that completely adorable. How could he feel so unsure?

Well, to be fair, I'd been a total jerk at my parents' house, and I wished we could have hashed this out before dinner. But I wished even more that he would have told me what was going on instead of... whatever it was he'd actually done.

He sat, a cushion of space between us, and I launched.

"Why didn't you tell me it was still happening?"

"To be fair, we've made an effort to table work discussion in our private time together."

Private time together made my chest flutter, which I promptly told it *not* to do. We had business to discuss before we got to enjoy any of said private time.

"Okay. I can see that. But last I heard, the surveyors couldn't come before the winter, which would have delayed it. I thought that was a done deal, and I suppose sort of foolishly assumed there was nothing else to talk about."

He clenched his jaw, then eyed me, those steel-gray eyes plucking at my heartbeat. "I purposefully omitted telling you when I was able to reschedule. The following week, we didn't see each other much, and since then, we haven't been focusing on the things that cause conflict but rather—" his gaze dipped to my lips, "—the things that we can agree upon."

I swallowed. "Right."

We sat locked in a fraught staring contest. Well, fraught for me since my emotions were pinging all over the place. I wanted to forget about the hotel and just kiss him. But I also kind of wanted to shake him and yell at him and tell him he couldn't build that hotel because if he did, what would *I* do?

How could I take over as mountain manager if there was this huge element I couldn't manage?

But I couldn't say any of that, because I couldn't exactly admit that I wanted his job. That was the one thing I wasn't being fully honest with him about, and I hated it, but I just couldn't... not yet.

"I'm sorry you are upset by the schedule. Could you explain, again, what your objection to the hotel is? I want to understand, and I want you to understand why I see it as an essential step for the success of the resort."

I shifted on the couch, tucking my legs under me and leaning my elbow on the back of the couch to face him. "I'm concerned it's too much too soon. I worry we'll overextend and build this massive, expensive hotel, and then not have people to fill it with. Then we're bleeding money from something we didn't need to begin with."

"But we do need it, Leonie. We do. We cannot expect people to drive as far as they have to and spend a few hours skiing. Some will, but to get the tourism dollars we need, we've got to give people a place to stay."

I nodded, irritation pinching at my shoulders. "Wells is building on the same timetable, but she's been planning it for almost a year—seriously for at least six months now."

"Yes. I'm very happy for Wells, and I think an expansion of Silverton Inn will be excellent for her business and the town. But another twenty rooms, or however many she'll add, will not even put a dent in what we're hoping to build. If we're serious about growing this place to be a world-class international destination resort, we'll need dozens of hotels. It's going to change things here."

His words weren't said in harsh tones, but they struck me like a blow. Everything would change, and yet his talk of building the resort so it drew the attention I'd always believed it deserved... my heart clenched and I wished I could have both—the draw for the resort and mountain that I loved and wanted people to discover, and yet not the change.

This had become my reality lately—wanting two opposite, incompatible things. Change, growth, and yet no change. Jonas, a relationship with him, and yet the job as mountain manager just like I always had.

"I know things will change. They already have." If my voice sounded a bit wobbly, I didn't let it stop me. I didn't try to hide *that*, at least. "I just... I'm concerned about how the staff, and... everyone will handle all the change."

"It was always a stipulation of the original investor's— the lack of available land wasn't a deterrent, but it was a matter of time."

My mouth slackened, surprised by this. I hadn't realized it'd been a part of the original deal. The first investor who'd expressed interest had stipulated land be available for a hotel before they ever agreed to invest, and that's when everything had fallen apart with Liam and Wells... *what a mess.* In the end, Liam went back to Jonas and said we didn't have land, nor could we get it, and Jonas had pulled this other investor out of his magician's hat—one who didn't require land for a hotel expansion. But apparently, that hadn't been indefinite.

"I didn't realize."

He nodded, a small frown on his face. "I'm sorry it came as a surprise. I understand a small resistance to change, though I'll admit I'm confused by your desire for the business to grow and stay the same at the same time."

I huffed, frustration welling up, which I swallowed back down. "I don't either. I know it doesn't make sense."

He held out his hand, and I immediately took it. He tugged just once, and I slid over, bringing us close.

"It feels like the more these things change, the less ownership my family has. And I get the investors are helping provide the means to make these changes and expand things, but I dread a scenario when we, the Morrisons, don't ultimately control things. You're in charge, but you're still beholden to the board. And forgive me, but after sixty years of owning and managing it, I don't want that lost. I want it in my family for my children and their children."

His eyes softened. "What would your family do without you?"

Those kind eyes, the generous words, they cut through my frustration and sent the last embers of my frustration fizzling into dust just as the thought of nearness to him with no argument between us lit a new flame.

My body swayed closer without thought, then I pressed up to take his mouth with mine. I needed the connection, and as jumbled as I felt, I didn't doubt my feelings for him. That, maybe more than anything else, was most confusing and yet reassuring.

As soon as our lips met, he pulled me near and wrapped both arms around me, one hand at my back and one sliding into the hair at the nape of my neck. He tilted my head and deepened the kiss, controlling the sensation with dizzying slides of lips and tongue. After a moment—or maybe minutes, because he'd obliterated my sense of time passing —he pulled away.

"I'm sorry I didn't know it was your birthday. I had no idea, and I can't help feeling I should've."

"How would you know? I never told you." I pressed a hand against his hard chest, and a little sigh escaped.

"I should've noticed it in your file. I knew your address, but not your birthday... stupid."

I shook my head. "It's not like you were combing it for personal data on me. I didn't expect you to know *or* do anything."

"Still. I want you to feel celebrated. You deserve all the good wishes and celebration."

"That's sweet, thank you. You can buy me lunch at work this week if we can find a moment, okay?"

He nodded. Then, "I should go."

I squeezed him closer into a full embrace, resting my head on his shoulder. "You should stay."

His chest dropped as though he'd sighed, though I didn't hear it. "I shouldn't. It's late."

I hugged him tighter. "It's my birthday. You should stay."

He clutched me close, both of us holding on for dear life for some reason, and then I felt him drop his cheek to rest on mine. He nuzzled my ear gently, effectively releasing a little flock of butterflies in my stomach. He nipped at my earlobe, then pulled back and set me away so he could see my face.

The look I found there devastated me. So serious and sincere and almost anguished—why? I raised a hand to touch his cheek and smooth it over the curve of his jaw. My strange thoughts voiced themselves without permission. "I've started to dislike fighting with you, and I hate that we won't have time together."

"Is it so wrong, to dislike fighting?"

"No. I shouldn't be fighting with my boyfriend."

His brow arched. "Who's this? Boyfriend?"

Nerves shot through my belly and my hand dropped from his face. Was I completely off base?

"Uh, well, I guess, to be fair, we haven't really addressed that, but it seemed like—"

His low chuckle would've made my toes curl if I hadn't still been shaky with uncertainty of my statement. "You can call me boyfriend."

"And what will you call me?"

"Any number of things, but I suppose girlfriend is a good enough label for now."

"Good enough? That doesn't sound very enthusiastic."

He touched his forehead to mine. "It's not nearly permanent enough. It's not binding. But I suppose for now, it'll do."

I'd have to unpack that, what it implied and what it actually meant, on my own. I couldn't do it now while he looked so intense and beautiful and was so close.

"I don't look forward to time apart, but we'll see each other every day." He took my hand in his, held it to his face again, then turned his head to press a kiss into my palm.

"Not like this. Not alone."

"We'll make time. Are you working weekends after this week?"

Basically everyone on staff would be around this weekend to make sure things got off smoothly, especially since it was always a huge weekend for us, so I was looking at seven straight long days of work.

"No. I'll take next weekend off because *kinderski* starts the following weekend. Then I'll switch to Mondays off and usually work in a half day one other day, depending."

His disapproval came through clearly as he shook his head then grasped at my shoulders. "That's too much. You need two full days off."

I chuckled. "Not realistic."

"But you do. You can take the time."

"I try, but I'm usually filling in for someone—a kinderski teacher, or an instructor. Plus then I have a few clients who come and request me, and I always take them if I can because they're all great tippers and I enjoy those lessons. I love a good day off but most of my private lessons are really fun guys who are intermediate-advanced so I can ski the whole mountain."

His gaze darkened then and he pursed his lips. "So we'll spend next Saturday together."

"Fine."

He frowned at my clipped response until I started laughing. "I mean it. It really is fine. I think I'm just... spent. I need sleep before we get going in the morning—you're right. So.. get out of my house already." I grabbed his lapels and pulled him in for a rough, quick kiss.

A brilliant smile flashed his perfect teeth at me, and my heart thudded in my chest.

I liked him so much.

At that moment, I knew I *loved* him, in fact. And I wanted us to stay together, and be together, and have all the... togetherness.

"Fine. Since you asked so nicely, I'll go."

CHAPTER FORTY-THREE

Jonas

Five days after opening day, things were looking good. Late November was never the busiest time for a ski resort because students were still in school and families weren't yet beginning holiday travel, and often the snow wasn't significant enough to open the whole mountain.

This year, the snow gods had been generous and we had a solid base at the bottom of the mountain. Snow-making machines ran overnight to shore up the base, and the weather had remained chilly enough to continue that work so that by the time Christmas and the New Year arrived, we'd be fully operational, whether there was a white Christmas or not.

But like all mountain lovers, I hoped for a white Christmas.

I'd wondered, in my daydreaming moments, if I'd spend Christmas with Leonie. I hadn't spoken to my mother yet, but I didn't usually go home, and it was unlikely I would this year. Working in the ski industry made Christmas vacationing all but an impossibility.

But the daydreams had become vivid, and on that note, quite uncharacteristic for me. I could imagine waking up next to Leonie and sliding the present I'd already purchased over to her. Maybe I'd just leave it on the bedside table.

In either case, my foolish heart assumed I'd be waking up next to her. And I wanted that desperately. Saying no to her last week had been torture, except I'd known what awaited us in the ensuing days. But soon, we'd spend the day together, and I'd decided it was time for an advancement between us on more than the physical level.

Where we'd landed with the hotel was unclear. She understood my perspective, I believed, and yet I knew she didn't want it. I knew, too, that whatever had her so resistant to the timing must be more than simply fearing change. Leonie may not have liked change, but she wasn't fearful. I wanted to get to the heart of whatever that issue was, but I also knew that I wouldn't be able to give on the matter. Whatever her fear was, she'd have to adjust.

And, part of me reasoned, I was still keeping something fairly large from her. I should just tell her—just admit I now owned essentially sixty percent of her family's business thanks to the forty percent I'd bought into as their first investor, and now as the new owner of dear Jim and Carlos' company which owned what amounted to another twenty.

My original plans to take the resort in hand, build it up, and sell it at a massive profit to some tool from the Colorado resorts or another conglomerate was less appealing by the day, and Leonie's fears about losing the business her family had built...

It shouldn't affect me, but it did. *She* did. In a way no

woman ever had. And I couldn't pretend she didn't matter, or that I didn't want to factor her in.

Karla's call earlier this week hadn't done anything to assuage my guilt or my mixed-up feelings. Staring out at the falling snow in the plaza where the last few skiers were tromping along with skis and poles in tow, exhausted and happy after a full day of early season skiing, I recalled her words.

"I can't believe you."

I didn't respond because she would tell me what she meant eventually, and sometimes, with Karla, silence proved to be the best strategy.

"You're going to destroy that girl when you sell the place."

"It won't destroy her. She's strong."

She scoffed. "Perhaps, but she'll never forgive you. She could barely handle the discussion of a hotel that will improve the entire city, let alone the resort itself. She will *never* forgive you."

My swallow felt more like a dramatic gulp as I let that thought settle heavy in my gut. "I'm not certain."

"I am. She's not the kind of woman to let this go. I don't know why you bothered to take up with her in the first place."

"I don't mean that. I have no doubt, especially now, that she would eviscerate my memory and any affection she may have for me if I sold the place."

A pause, then, "*If?*"

"As I said, I'm no longer certain."

Silence filled the line while she presumably waited. But I had only just begun to think the thought, so finding words to explain wouldn't come naturally.

"I don't understand, Jonas. This has been your plan

since the beginning—since you bought in and kept it all cloak and dagger knowing they wouldn't accept an aggressive investor even in their dire state."

"I know. Being here has..." How to explain? "Changed me. I'm beginning to think about different things."

She sighed long and loud into the phone, and I could picture her scrubbing her hand across her brow, a gesture she only made when she was working to understand something but mostly wanted to yell at someone. Perhaps I knew the look well because it wasn't the first time I'd elicited it.

"I'm behind you, whatever you decide. Bauer Group will benefit, whatever you do. But Jonas, you need to decide now. Before your change of plans becomes more conspicuous."

That ominous comment had me pacing around my small office. "Why would a change of plans be conspicuous? If I decide not to make a move and sell, who's to know?"

Another sigh. "You know how word of mouth works, no? You are aware you have a stellar reputation in all things? Bauer Group has the reputation of rehabilitating through consultation, finding investors and enabling businesses like Silver Ridge to experience a resurgence and even a revival. But your investment group also has a reputation for selling the next big thing. I haven't said anything—"

"Not even a hint?""

"Not even a hint. But you can't be so naïve as to think Silver Ridge hasn't popped up on various radars. The choice to maintain the investment past the usual year or eighteen months won't go unnoticed."

"I will handle it."

We'd parted with amicable farewells, even though she clearly disagreed with my waffling. Recollecting the conversation didn't help the pit in my stomach. If I didn't sell, I'd be stuck. I'd be compromising all the rules I'd set for myself years ago. It'd be a kind of surrender that gave me heartburn and had me clenching my teeth, which I could not be doing because that often led to migraines if I didn't catch myself and take evasive measures.

I rubbed my temples as I stared out, unseeing, at the plaza, now emptied of everyone but Jiff and his handful of people working the gondola, and a few patrollers coming off their final sweep down the mountain.

A hand slid from my shoulder down my back, and I startled.

Leonie's laughing face greeted me as I turned. "Did I scare you?"

"I was chasing windmills, I guess."

"Any particular windmill giants you're slaying?"

A half-smile pulled at one corner of my mouth. "Only work."

"Ah. I can't say I'm surprised."

She glanced at the doorway to my office, then leaned up with chin raised to give me a soft, sweet kiss. A band of tension eased in my mind and chest with just that simple action.

"Would you be interested in a sleep-over on Friday? I know we'll both be exhausted, but I want to see you and—"

"Yes. Absolutely."

Her answering smile blazed with satisfaction. "Great."

"Your place? Mine?"

"Either way. I'll plan to run home and shower because I'm skiing all day Friday with lessons, so you can come to me or I can just meet you back here."

My phone buzzed loudly on the desk and I grabbed it, then cleared the call. "Sorry, Grenier's pestering me."

"Anything important?"

I shook my head, then gave in to the need to pull the ends of her long braids. She wore two braids whenever she skied. They drove me insane. All of her braids did, but seeing her like this in ski pants and boots, a tight sweater shaping to every curve, and the braids... *Meine Guete*, they did me in.

"You like the braids?"

She looked quizzically at me, and then I knew. She didn't realize what torture I found these braids to be. "I love them."

Her brows raised in surprise. "*Love* them, huh?"

"Yes."

"You like the braids best?"

"Yes." But then, I'd not seen her hair down completely, so, "Maybe."

"Well, out with it. Tell me where this is going."

"I love the braids. But I haven't seen you without any braids in your hair, so I may like no braids better. Best. Hard to say."

"I had no idea you were so concerned with my hair," she said, biting her lip to hide the smile lurking.

I dipped my head to close the space between us. "I'm concerned with everything about you."

CHAPTER FORTY-FOUR

Leo

The last few students from my afternoon group lesson zig-zagged down the face of Spring Run-off, one of the ski runs that fed directly to the gondola and plaza in front of the lodge.

Their group had done well, but after working seven days straight, I was more than ready to get home, cleaned up, and back to Jonas.

"Great job guys. You should be all set for a fantastic day tomorrow." I slapped high-fives with several of the men, all about my age from the looks of them.

"Any chance we can get another lesson tomorrow?" the one with sparkly movie star eyes and too-perfect skin asked.

I'd not managed to remember his name because he had a twin brother in the group who was literally indistinguishable from him. He was "one of the twins" and that was as good as I could get.

"Sorry. No can do, gentlemen. I've got plans." Plans to *not* work and spend the day laying around with my boyfriend-slash-manfriend for whom I'd become desperate.

Truly, I'd never felt this kind of *need* to just be with a person. I loved my family, loved my friends, but I never missed them like I did Jonas. It never felt like my ribs might cave in if I didn't see them like it did with him.

And I knew that was ridiculous since I worked several hundred feet from him when I was in the lodge and I knew where he lived and I could track him down when I needed to, but I also couldn't just stop life and go stare at him. We'd both been insanely busy, and I could also admit that I'd been attempting to resist the pull toward total ridiculous codependency with him.

I didn't want to let on just how much I cared for him—loved him. Not yet. Especially when we'd made no commit-ments. I knew he found me attractive, and he'd said he liked me, but so often I'd been the one to like another person more than they liked me—they never liked me enough to deal with me, to really know me.

I'd gone farther with Jonas in that regard than I had with anyone else by a long shot—I'd admitted just that. I'd told him how I'd been rejected for not fitting in a tidy, sweet little box, and he'd been unfazed.

But at Thanksgiving, I'd been a jerk. I'd let a legitimate frustration and disappointment get the better of me, and I'd hurt him. He hadn't demanded apologies, and we'd left that night on good terms, but I wanted time together. Uninter-rupted, uncomplicated *time.*

We were about to get exactly that, if I could get the boy band version of a group lesson over here to say goodbye.

"Are you sure? We can't tempt you with amazing tips and even better company?" One of the other men loosed a shiny white smile that was truly startling in its beauty. The name was... Bri? Something... I honestly couldn't retain it because I had one man on my mind.

"Seriously, we'd love to have you again," said Sam, the one I'd come to think of as the leader and one of the nicest, most charming men I'd had the pleasure of interacting with in recent memory.

But no. I didn't go for gorgeous boy band groups with sparkly smiles and charm for days. I put in for grumpy half-German workaholics.

"Sorry guys. I truly hope you enjoy your stay in Silverton and have a great weekend skiing. Look me up if you visit Silver Ridge again, and don't forget to tell all your friends to come ski with us."

With a wave of the hand holding my poles, I lifted my skis with the other and began the walk to the employee locker room. The heel-toe action of my ski boots propelled me forward and their impact on the cobblestones of the plaza had me eager to feel the warmth of my slippers. We had little heaters that fed into our boots in the lockers, but I always hooked them into my slippers so when I finished skiing I could slip into warm, lined shoes. It was one of a hundred small things I loved about skiing, and as I reached for the locker room door, I savored the fact that this was my life.

Somewhere mid-shower, I'd grown nervous.

Not a little nervous. Mild hyperventilation, shaky hands and knees, can't totally remember what I'm supposed to be doing kind of nervous.

Not. Ideal.

But rather than let that keep me from going to Jonas' house, I pressed on, intent on *not* spending this night with my face in a pint of Ben and Jerry's and another viewing of *The Proposal* on my TV.

I wanted this time with him. I wanted this step with him. And yet, my stomach felt like it might crawl out of my body. There was little in it, nothing to empty out, thankfully, or I might've been in deep trouble.

Jonas opened the door looking delectably fresh and tousled, like he'd run a towel through his hair just before answering. He wore well-worn jeans, a T-shirt that did marvelous things for his chest and arms, and that messy hair that made my stomach clench in a more than pleasant way.

"Come in. It's freezing out there."

He hustled me over the threshold and shut the door behind us, then quickly unwrapped me by pulling my hat and scarf from my head and hanging them, then unzipping my jacket and tugging it from my arms. Once he'd hung the jacket, he pulled me into a hug, then stood to his full height so my feet dangled just off the ground.

I pressed my chilled nose into his warm neck and he shuddered.

"Ah, *Liebling*, that's a mean trick."

I spoke into his neck. "*Liebling*?"

He pulled back and smiled down at me, his eyes tired but pleased. "It's a term of endearment."

"What does it mean?"

"Does it matter? It means I care for you, *Liebling*, and I want my language to reflect it."

I shook my head. "Sometimes you're so American and other times you're so... *not*."

"Because I use German words on occasion?" He pulled

me to follow him, all the way through the house to the couch in front of a hearty fire.

"No. Of course that's part of it, but it's more your cadence, the words, and then even the ideas you have. I don't know. I'm not explaining it right."

He sat, then pulled me to sit on his legs, perpendicular to him. "Well I'm American, but I've got influences that aren't, so I suppose this is not a surprise. And language matters. The words we use matter, the names we call each other matter, and sometimes German words are simply better than English words."

"That I believe. I've found *Donnerwetter* to be an incredibly satisfying first German experience."

A small flame lit in his eyes, and he leaned in to run the bridge of his nose along the curve of my jaw, then back behind my ear. "How would you like to have an incredibly satisfying *second* German experience?"

A delighted giggle burst out of me, shocked and pleased at his wordplay. His laugh rumbled in his chest, but he didn't stop the assault of kisses on my neck, and the levity fizzled into nothing as heat and anticipation crackled between us.

I tilted my head to grant him more access which he greedily took, his attention lingering behind my ear, then at my pulse, then at the dip of my throat.

"Jonas." My breathy voice would've made me roll my eyes if it had been someone else. How could kisses on one's neck change the sound and quality of one's voice?

Well, this was how. Each press of lips to skin sent my blood racing, my heart pumping faster, the breath in my lungs somehow too much and not enough.

"Yes, Leonie?"

He mumbled these words into my shoulder, where he now focused his attention.

The sound of my name on his lips, those same lips searing a trail of wanting into my body, made me laugh in a desperate attempt to gain composure.

"Dinner?"

He raised his head to study me, gray eyes inspecting each part of my face—eyes, nose, lips, chin. "Are you hungry?"

This was my chance. A moment to take control, slow the progress or stop it altogether, breathe and not feel rushed or nervous. But did I want that? I'd been waiting for this moment, for uninterrupted time with him, and I wanted him body, mind, heart, soul. I could end this now and follow the nerves, the doubt, the insecurity, or I could be brave and claim him.

"No, actually, I'm not."

CHAPTER FORTY-FIVE

Jonas

Hours after she'd arrived, Leonie and I lay side by side on a blanket in front of the fire, a picnic of cold pizza and room temperature Silver Ridge Brewing beer our feast.

I'd never been happier to eat cold pizza.

"Do you have any special traditions this time of year?" One hand propped her head up while the other traced the veins in my wrist.

"My American friends never seem to celebrate Saint Nicholas day. You set shoes or boots out on the porch the night before, and then in the morning, they are filled with small gifts from Saint Nicholas."

Her lazy smile looked pleased. She raised my wrist and kissed the inside, my heart glowing with the action.

"That sounds nice. I bet kids love that."

"They do. I always did."

"Anything else?"

"We open gifts Christmas Eve. I'm not sure that's uniquely German, but it was my mother's tradition more than my father's. The *Christkind* brings the presents that night so we open them then."

"We always did Christmas Day."

We watched the fire crackle and pop, each quietly sipping our drinks or nibbling at the pizza. I rested my head on a pillow and watched the light flicker over her face.

"You are so beautiful."

Her eyes cut to me and simmered with blue heat. She leaned over and rested a hand by my head, her chest melding against mine. She dropped her face close and planted a lingering, sensual kiss on my mouth that launched a thousand little ships of desire for her for the hundredth time this night.

"You're beautiful too."

She beamed at the face I made, which was admittedly at once pleased and perplexed by the compliment.

"You don't believe me?"

I chuckled. "I believe you think that, and I'm glad for that."

"But you don't think you are?"

I brushed a hand back over her head to tame the wild, loose strands, loving the sweep of each lock against my hand —perhaps even better than a braid. No, certainly better, knowing so few saw it this way, and no one but me could run fingers through it. I traced her eyebrows with the pad of one finger, still delaying my response, which caused her brow to furrow. I smoothed down the wrinkles with my thumb.

"You do know you're, like, painfully attractive, right?" Her voice held a note of genuine concern.

I stretched my neck up to steal a kiss. "I am delighted if you think so. I feel very much the same about you."

She shook her head, then set about showing me just how attractive she found me. When we came up for air, the night had closed in and we were both clearly exhausted. I stood and pulled her up, then wrapped an arm around her and took her to bed.

I woke to darkness, the early winter day cold outside the window. Leonie lay curled on her side toward me, her hands tucked under her head, her knees nearly to her chest. My hand itched to roam over her, to map the curve of her hip and the smooth slope of her back, but I wouldn't.

No, I would breathe in this moment. I would relish her warmth next to me, the sweetness of the last twelve hours, and the low, inexorable pulse in my chest that told me I loved this woman. Completely. Irrevocably.

Sooner than expected, but I had no doubt. She'd folded me, end over end, and if she ever flattened me out, I would show indelible creases from her influence. A terrifying thought, if one considered she may not feel the same. An exhilarating, life-altering reality, if she did.

She woke with a start, then focused on me and smiled. "Are you staring at me while I sleep?"

"Unabashedly."

Her smile grew. "Should I be concerned?"

I pulled her to me, crushing her against my chest as my unruly heart nearly burst.

"I love you, Leonie," I said against her hair.

When she leaned away, her eyes were wide and soft. "I love you, Jonas."

~

At breakfast, we talked of our families. At lunch, we spoke of food, our favorite adventures in travel, and a hundred other small things, and by late afternoon, I felt she knew me in a way no one ever had. She knew nearly everything about me. And I felt as though I knew her.

"Did you always want to work in ski education?" I asked, surprised to realize I never had before.

She sipped a cappuccino from a bright blue bowl masquerading as a mug. We sat at *Rise and Shine* near the window, the table I usually took and where I had so often sat waiting to get a glimpse of her before I began the day in earnest.

"No, not at all."

"Really? You're the best instructor I've ever seen."

"When have you seen me instruct? Did you watch the group lesson with the boy band on Friday?" She shook her head at the memory and sipped her drink.

"Boy band? Uh, no. I watched you instruct the *kinderski* sessions last year."

She straightened. "Last year?"

"Yes. I came to town at Christmas, if you recall, and made sure to observe every aspect of the business. One of those things was you. You were so good with the children, and later I watched you with an adult lesson and the same was true. I've yet to see you do anything but excel at whatever you try."

"I never saw you." She frowned into her coffee.

"I made sure of it."

Her face broadcasted disappointment, and it caused a familiar ache. The desire to right wrongs for her, to change anything that made her unhappy, laced through me.

"Why, do you think?" Her question emerged quietly, with something like pain in her voice.

"Why did I not announce to you I was observing you? To that point, your reception of me had been less than agreeable, and I didn't want you to feel I was observing with judgement."

"No, I mean why do you think we started the way we did? From where we sit now, it feels like we lost so much time." She spoke to her hands cupping the drink, not sharing her face with me.

"I suppose because I was, from the outset, representative of everything you didn't want." I reached for her hand and linked our pinkies.

She sighed and her shoulders slumped a bit. "True. And then, you became the representative of everything I did, and therefore took what I wanted, leaving me with nothing."

My stomach dropped at this, though I couldn't be sure what she implied. "Tell me what you mean, please."

She retracted her hand and sat taller in her chair, then pinned me with her glorious blue eyes, full of sadness now. "I haven't always wanted to be head of ski education. I grew up wanting my dad's job, and then Liam's job. I've always, *always* wanted to be mountain manager. My degree is tailored to it, with a minor in early childhood education because I knew we needed to expand our childcare options. But I didn't get that degree to be the woman in charge of childcare and education forever. I got it to help the lodge."

About eleven things happened at once, not the least of which was me realizing that all along, she'd been lying to me. Not in a malicious way, but in a profound one, to be sure. She'd avoided this subject more than once. She'd purposefully kept this dream of hers out of our conversations, and now I knew exactly what it was that kept her just a little aloof from me. I'd felt it more than once over the last day but had chosen to ignore it, certain that those moments when she'd start to speak, then stop herself, *censor* herself, had more to do with strong feelings or a self-consciousness in a relationship than it did with something like this.

Would this be what came between us?

"Can you say something?" Her voice pleaded, and yet frustration twined through.

"What can I say? How can I solve this problem when I apparently have what you want and have always wanted? I don't know what you expect me to say."

And then, Julian Grenier sauntered in with the ring of the bell and came directly to me.

"Bauer."

I cleared my throat, wanting to delay what I could see barreling toward us. "Leonie, you remember Julian Grenier, your brother's colleague..."

She smiled, and nodded. "Of course. Nice to see you."

Grenier's eyes shifted to me with no real acknowledgement of Leonie. "I'm done playing coy. I want your shares in the resort. I know you hold a majority and I intend to buy you out. We needn't conduct the business in person, but I can't continue this e-mail, phone tag nonsense. Let's wrap it up before year's end."

He turned to Leonie, whose face had drained of all color, and nodded. "Ms. Morrison."

And just like that, he exited, the cheery jingle and shudder of the door's closing at odds with the chaos raging in my mind, all through my body.

Leonie's eyes fluttered as she stared after Grenier, then swooped to me. "What does he mean?"

I swallowed, internally scrambling for a way to explain this that didn't seem like total and utter deceit to her.

Her chest rose—she must have been taking a huge breath. "Just tell me. How could you own any amount of the resort?"

"I've invested in the resort."

"*How?*"

"I'm the investor Bauer Group recruited earlier this year."

A choking sound came from her throat, and her hand balled into a fist as she crossed her arms over her chest. Before she could ask anything else—before it looked like I was trying to keep anything else from her, I spoke again.

"I also recently acquired a small investment firm, Piqued Peak."

Her inhale was audible. Not a gasp—just a disbelieving pull, like she'd been holding her breath.

"I have no plans—"

"That's enough."

She shot to her feet, grabbed her jacket and scarf, and was out the door before I could stop her. I fumbled around, gathering my jacket, the sack with a fresh loaf of bread we'd planned to have with dinner later, and the hat she'd dropped on her way out, and hustled down the street.

I caught up to her, though not easily, since she was nearly jogging back up toward the lodge despite the wintry air. I grabbed her arm to get her attention. "Leonie, you have to listen to me."

She whipped around.

"I do *not.*" She huffed out a breath, the air emerging from her an opaque cloud. "Fine. Tell me. Leave nothing out."

Surprised she didn't storm away again, but relieved, I started talking. She began walking again, so I followed after her.

"I did plan to acquire a majority share and sell the lodge. But I've started to doubt that plan. I've felt differently here than I have anywhere else, more like I'm at home, at peace, and that's valuable. I was just telling Karla I don't know if I'll sell. Then the last week or so has clarified it for me, and if it hadn't, then the last day certainly has. I won't sell. I know what this place means to you, and I don't want... I wouldn't take it away from you."

We'd slowed to a stop just outside the Silverton Inn. I reached out to her, intent on taking her hand in mine and reassuring her, but she pulled back, disgust and wariness coloring the move.

"You know how much it means to me..." she said, her voice watery and pained.

"I do."

"And you wouldn't take it away from me."

"No. Never."

She tilted her head, her eyes piercing against the afternoon sky. "But you would have. You've been planning to. Even after we started dating, you've chosen to make this happen. How can I possibly believe anything you say?"

"I haven't lied to you."

"You have. Repeatedly. It's called lying by omission and you've done it masterfully—to me, to my family, to this town. I don't think I have anything else to say to you."

She turned, burst through the gate to the inn, and shuffled up the stairs and through the door.

I stood looking after her, my chest caving in, my mind a flat line, wondering how the hell I could recover from this.

CHAPTER FORTY-SIX

Leo

He didn't follow me, but he took a while to leave. Maybe five minutes, like he was thinking about following me inside.

Tala at the reception desk never looked up from her book, but just said, "They're not here," and went back to reading. She must have assumed I was there to see Liam and Wells, and how she knew I was here for them without looking up or asking, I'd never know, but the woman had the knack.

I wandered around the small library area with a roaring fire and cozy furniture, wishing I could sit down and enjoy the room and forget what I'd just learned.

I didn't feel a thing. I knew the feelings would come, but just this minute, I didn't feel a damned thing, and I wanted to hang on to that as long as I could.

I read the spines of the books Wells, and probably

before her Tilda Saint, had stocked in the built-in shelves. I admired the brocade on the sofa, the leather of a set of chairs, the weave of the rug. A couple wandered by, ski pants swishing and boots clomping down the hall, which shook me out of my mindless study of the room.

As I turned to go, a familiar voice met me.

"Leo? What are you—what's wrong?"

Wells grabbed me by the shoulders as my mind skipped like a broken record.

"What happened?"

I swallowed, then again. "Jonas essentially owns Silver Ridge. He just admitted it."

"*What!?*"

"I know. And I'm... I don't know. I can't think. It's like my brain flat-lined. I don't..." I trailed off as I looked into her kind, bright eyes. My throat thickened and I cleared it, both wishing for and not wanting tears. "I don't know what to do."

She pulled me to her and held me. Tight. When I would have pulled back, she consoled me with a pet to my head. "It's okay. We'll figure this out."

I nodded, words failing me, and clung to her, my chest and stomach tensing, but still finding no real outlet.

I inhaled deeply, then pulled back. "I should go. I feel like I need to sit with this a bit."

"Okay. But we're here. You know Mia and Danny are too. I guess... should I tell Liam?"

"I guess so. We've all been lied to long enough."

Reluctantly, I wound my scarf around my neck—I'd never put it on after leaving *Rise and Shine*—and after one more quick hug, shouldered out the door.

I trudged up the hill toward the lodge, toward Jonas', still unable to nail down a thought. It felt like someone had scattered words and thoughts all around me, but I couldn't reach any of them to pick up and inspect or use.

So I kept walking, my chest tightening as I worked my way up the hill, past the packed-full parking lot for the resort, then into the small parking area reserved for the manager's cabin. No sign of Jonas, so I slipped into my car, glad to avoid him and anyone else.

I drove home, where I undressed and showered and cleaned my kitchen sink. By eight that night, I'd effectively wasted the afternoon and avoided all coherent thought. Troublingly, I *couldn't* summon thoughts. It felt like I hardly remembered Jonas' words, but I'd never forget them —how could I, when they were what I'd always expected and dreaded to hear from him?

When I checked my phone at half past eight, the edges of my state of mind began to fray when I saw a series of messages from him. The first was a voicemail from about an hour after we'd parted requesting I call him.

And then the texts.

Please call me.

I see your car is gone. Please let me know you made it home okay.

We need to talk. Please respond when you're ready.

It was that one that made me stop. When *would* I be ready? When would I even be ready to feel what I knew would be a crushing amount of hurt, and beyond that, when would I be able to process this?

A fleeting thought to call Bel, or even Liam, slipped through my mind, but it slithered right out again. Wells would tell Liam, and she'd probably tell Mia and Danny too. Liam would call Jamie... So I sat on my couch and tried to read, thought about starting a movie, but in the end went to bed by nine.

The next morning, waking to a sunny sky, realizing I'd slept in far later than I ever usually did and that I'd woken alone in my bed, without Jonas, with a new understanding of him... that's when it hit.

Everything I'd suspected about him had been true. He *had* been out for himself. He'd worked his way into our business, into our lives, and all the while he'd been buying up the pieces of our family legacy with the plan to sell it. To sell it not just for his own profit, but right out from underneath us.

And he wouldn't have had a majority share if he hadn't pushed for a second investor. He wouldn't have been able to do it without considerable planning and plotting. This was no accidental occurrence but a premeditated maneuver to benefit him and ruin the Morrison family legacy.

I should have felt fury. Rage. Hate. All the things I'd felt for him before I really knew him. But I couldn't conjure those feelings. They wouldn't come. The only thing I could feel was the collapsing of my heart in on itself, like the chambers were folding up, quitting, and the whole room, the whole house, the whole world was moving in slow motion because of it.

Instead, I felt hurt. I felt so sad, I could hardly take a full breath before it broke open into a sob. I pressed my face to my pillow to stifle the sound, but eventually just let myself lay there and cry.

I cried because I did love him, and he'd said he loved me, but he'd lied for so long, how could I believe him? How could he say he loved me but still keep this huge truth from me?

It seemed like he'd told me everything, but that had only happened because he'd been forced. If Julian Grenier hadn't walked in and declared he wanted to buy Jonas' shares, I never would have known Jonas had *any* stake in the business beyond being an employee and wanting the best for it.

Yes, he'd bought the land for the hotel *from* Grenier, which was confusing considering now Grenier wanted to buy the lodge. What? I couldn't pretend to understand that odd man, but that wasn't the point.

Jonas had planned to take everything from us, just like I'd feared. He now held the job I wanted, and from what it sounded like, he controlled more than half of the company. He claimed he wouldn't sell it, and how had he put it? He'd never take it away from me.

How could I trust that? How could I possibly believe anything he said when he'd kept this huge secret?

I slumped to the side on the bed, wondering how long I could stay just like that. I didn't want the headache that threatened as I cried some more, feeling the painful mix of betrayal and doubt and hope warring in me.

He'd done a number on me, hadn't he? He'd gotten me wrapped around his capable fingers and then he'd told me what I'd wanted to hear—that he loved me. Why would he say such a thing if all the while, he planned to take away the thing I loved most?

I closed my eyes against the tears, the crush of emotion pressing in on my chest. I didn't have to decide anything or do anything now. I didn't have to sort out how I felt or would act, I didn't have to know what I wanted. I could wait for all of that, because soon enough, it'd be unavoidable. Maybe at some point in the next eighteen hours before I had to show up at the lodge for work, I'd magically figure out a way to feel and think about all of this that didn't hurt quite so much.

Until then, I'd let myself wallow and hide. I didn't want

to be brave or brash. I didn't want to see Jonas and whip him with words—I didn't have any of that in me. And I couldn't listen to any more of his words which were likely all lies. I'd failed miserably at sussing out what was true and what was fabricated between us, and until I could figure that out, I couldn't face him.

CHAPTER FORTY-SEVEN

Jonas

I knocked on Leonie's office door at eight forty Monday morning.

I'd given her the weekend without showing up at her apartment, but I couldn't wait any longer. I understood needing space, but I'd convinced myself, right or wrong, that if she'd hear me out and let me explain, or more fully convince her that I really wasn't going to sell the place, all would be well.

I knew she kicked off any lessons at eight thirty and usually made it back to her office, assuming she wasn't filling in for an instructor, ten minutes later. I didn't want to risk the day slipping by, the week swallowing us whole. The more time that passed, the more distance between us.

As things stood, there was a gulf I'd have to bridge and I hadn't figured out how except to plead my case and assure her I meant what I said.

The fact that Karla had warned me about this and I hadn't dealt with the problem ahead of time, whatever that might've looked like, had nagged at me all weekend.

She didn't answer, so I knocked again, even though I could see perfectly well the light wasn't on behind the door. I checked my phone for the umpteenth time since we'd parted ways Saturday afternoon, then turned to head to my office.

She rounded the corner and saw me just as I saw her. My heart thudded in my chest like it usually did when I caught sight of her, but this time there was a desperate plea attached to the sound. *Please listen to me. Please believe me. Please forgive me.*

"Oh."

Not an ideal greeting, but at least she didn't ignore me and turn the other way. I wouldn't have been shocked by that reaction, especially since I'd grown accustomed to her ignoring me the first six months of our acquaintance.

"Please let me speak with you."

She shuffled her feet, then looked at me with a face full of regret. "I'm not sure what good that would do."

I stepped closer, wanting to touch her, but stopped short when she stiffened at my approach. "I understand why you'd say that, but I need to talk with you."

She swallowed, glanced back down the hall, then sighed. "Fine. Let's talk later. I don't want this to bleed into work."

I nodded as she passed me, then disappeared behind her door. I flipped open my phone to answer the call buzzing in.

"Yes?"

"I told you, I want the place. Name your price."

Grenier. Excellent timing, as always.

"Sorry. It's not for sale. I'm keeping it."

"Why?"

"Why do you want it? You just sold me the adjacent land."

"Never mind. Best of luck."

The line went dead, and that was all. People accused me of being short and to the point, but Grenier had me beat by a mile. I wasn't surprised he wouldn't explain his motivations to me, but I'd never seen a man shift from making a multi-million-dollar investment to simply cutting the call.

Okay then.

I plodded back to my office and slumped into the chair behind my desk. It wasn't quite nine a.m. and yet I was exhausted. I hadn't slept all weekend thanks to my mind running laps around what I'd say when I got Leonie on the phone, how I'd explain myself, how I'd reassure her that I wouldn't sell the company.

I'd attempted to get Grenier on the line to clarify that with him, but he'd been uncharacteristically unreachable, so at least I could check that off my list thanks to his call this morning. I still needed to connect with Karla, who'd no doubt give me a well-deserved *I told you so*, but in the end I could take it. Might as well get it over with now so I could take the next few hours to mentally prepare to talk with Leonie and grovel as much as I needed for her to take me back.

"Jonas. I wasn't expecting your call. I'm just heading to an early lunch."

I could hear city sounds in the background, and the relief I'd often felt in the last few months returned. I didn't miss it.

"You were right."

She was silent for a beat, maybe muting the phone, then

her voice came through clearly. "I'm sorry. I don't celebrate this victory."

"I'm not selling. I'm keeping it. I'm staying, and I'm keeping it."

"If you're sure."

"I am."

"Fine. We'll discuss details another time."

"Good."

Just like that, I'd wrapped up that end. I knew I could count on Karla to accept the change. She had to have known I didn't plan to leave Silverton, not after so long being in the job, and especially not after being with Leonie. I didn't know what my work for Bauer Group would look like, but I knew she'd support me.

My head dropped down on my desk and I let out a sigh. Dramatic, but necessary. My guts were in knots. All I wanted was for this to be over.

It wasn't as simple as her believing me, though. I'd come to that conclusion after a long first night without sleep. I'd realized that what she'd said before Grenier approached and dumped a heaping pile of mess on our table also presented an issue, as had my poor response to it.

She wanted my job. Or, perhaps a better way to say it was, she'd *always* wanted my job. How her own brothers didn't seem to know this was a mystery—how could she have kept that to herself for so long? If it'd truly been her desire to take over as mountain manager, if that'd been her plan for so long, how did no one involved in the management of the mountain know that?

It didn't make a bit of sense. Leonie's character had proven, over and over, to be direct, clear, and without preamble. I couldn't imagine her not marching into Liam's office at some point in the last few years and staking a claim on the job.

But she hadn't. No one had mentioned such a thing to me, and even she had kept it close and not hinted at it in conversations we'd had the last few months. I couldn't say why for sure, but I would bet her reluctance to accept the hotel timeline had something to do with that goal as well.

We'd have to talk about it. I didn't know what the solution might be there, but we'd figure something out. She was young and had plenty of time to pursue whatever she wanted.

I held my head in my hands and exhaled slowly.

We'd talk about it. We'd listen to each other. We'd work it out.

We had to.

At exactly five, Leonie knocked on the frame of my door.

I bolted up from my seat. "Come in. Please."

She sat in the chair across from my desk like so many times before, but her energy, or lack thereof, felt off. Not the go-getter, not the ball-buster, not even the shut-down, angry version showed on her face. This Leonie was subdued in a way that hit me like a punch to the gut.

The quiet between us crawled up my neck and threatened to drive me mad. Even when all we did was fight, we'd never had trouble finding words for each other.

But then, inevitably, we spoke simultaneously.

"How was your day?"

"Let's just get on with it, if that's okay."

I swallowed down the disappointment. "Of course."

She waited.

"I want to make clear that I will not be selling my parts of the company. I had already decided I wouldn't, even before Grenier showed up, but I let him know it's not an option."

Her only response came in the form of lips pressed together and a slight nod.

"I know you must be thinking I've lied to you this whole time. I haven't thought of it that way. I viewed being an unnamed investor as essential because of the animosity you personally showed at the outset of our consulting, and because I didn't want to be seen as..."

She arched one brow.

"I didn't want to seem aggressive. Like I had plans for the place beyond revitalization."

A slow blink told me the irony wasn't lost on her.

"I know. I *was* aggressive. I'd planned to be aggressive, so shielding my investment was sketchy and wrong." I cleared my throat. "I mean, ultimately all the things I wanted to do for Silver Ridge are the same. I wouldn't change anything I've done now that I'm keeping it—I hope you know that, at least."

She nodded, but still nothing.

"By the time the Piqued Peak guys came, you and I were still at odds. We were forced to work together for that event and that's what pushed us to get past all the barriers we had."

"Ironic that those barriers came about from me mistrusting your motives."

My jaw clenched hard in frustration, but I couldn't say anything. What response could I give?

"I am sorry. I recognize that I should have been honest with you about my stake in the company. I also realize you have every right to be angry with me. But I will also admit that I expect the reality of my confession, contrition, and resulting plan to maintain the business will have some influence on our ability to proceed."

She crossed her arms, cradling herself close and creating a visual barrier between us, as though I couldn't tell how little my speech thus far had done to warm her to me.

"I'm not sure what you expect, Jonas. I asked you weeks ago not to lie to me—I told you I hate it. So on one hand, I have that shoved in my face—this man I trusted and shared parts of myself with lied to me. But the reality is, we both lied. We've *been* lying, consistently and over time, and we only confessed to those lies when backed into a corner. Even if I take you at your word and believe that you won't sell, I'll still always be wondering what else you're lying about. Will you, in fact, not sell? Do you even care for me at all?"

"Of course I do. You know I do."

"And beyond that, there's my issue. You have what I want—exactly what I want."

Her voice wavered and her eyes shone with tears. My throat closed, instinctively knowing whatever came next would be terrible.

"I may love you, Jonas, but I love Silver Ridge more—I've loved it all my life. It's in my blood... in my soul. I haven't been able to figure out how to make *us* work and not give up the dream I've had since I can remember. I can't make those things work, and that tells me one of them has to go. All of this—the lies, the drama... that clarifies things for me."

"That's not... it's not either or. It doesn't have to be."

She stood, tension in her body, but surety in her face. "See you around, Jonas."

CHAPTER FORTY-EIGHT

Leo

Thankfully, most of the staff had left by the time I shut Jonas' office door and dragged myself to my car.

I kept it together until I got home, but by the time I unlocked my door, my face was wet with tears and my heart felt like someone had taken a hammer to it.

I didn't like what I'd told him, but it was true. After all the hurt, disappointment, and sense of betrayal, what was left? There was no way for us to be together anyway. Even if he didn't plan to sell the company, which I wanted to believe and thought I might actually believe, we still had the problem of him having my dream job. It was a small company—there weren't that many other options. And if he was willing to leave his position, which felt like an oddly anticlimactic and disappointing way to get the job I'd always wanted, why wouldn't he just say so?

I filled Bel, Wells, and Mia in via text, kept it short and

sweet, welcoming their efforts to console me, but knowing it'd take time. I insisted I was fine, though I knew it was a matter of hours before one or all of them hunted me down.

As life would have it, Grandpa Will was the first person I actually had a conversation with after the breakup. I arrived at Silverton Springs on Thursday night with a bag of *Guac* takeout. We'd planned a little dinner date weeks ago. Jonas was going to come too, but I'd confirmed he would not be there when I'd spoken to Grandpa earlier.

"You look terrible, darling granddaughter."

"Why thank you. You look annoyingly chipper."

My bad mood had hung around me like a weight, and there was nothing I could do to shake it. I felt justified in my bad moodiness, and frankly didn't feel like shaking it. It was my form of mourning, and if it meant I was unpleasant to be around, well... some people thought I was unpleasant all the time, so what difference did it make?

"I gather all is not well in the land of love."

I huffed. "Is it ever, really? I mean it. In real life, is *all* ever well with love?"

His bright eyes studied me with a gleam while he unwrapped his food. "You know, you can talk to me."

"I know."

He opened the plastic container and see-sawed a fork through his chimichanga. The low hum of his fridge and the distant sounds of people talking in the hall accompanied our food preparation soundtrack.

"Jonas came by yesterday."

"What? Why?"

"He came by. He told me about the mess he made."

I forced an awkward laugh-slash-snort and frowned at my plate, then scooped a pile of guacamole onto a chip and chomped it in one bite. Maybe a healthy serving of guac could patch up the leaky atriums of my heart.

"And you think I should take him back? Believe he isn't going to act on his sneaky, money-making take-over and forgive the fact that for the majority of the time he's been here, he's essentially been plotting to screw our family and ruin the Morrison legacy—a legacy *you* started, by the way?"

My cheeks flamed with shame and frustration as I inhaled and prayed I could calm down. I didn't want to sit here and yell at my beloved grandfather over lunch, especially when he'd done nothing wrong.

"It's up to you if you'll forgive him, young one. My admonition is not so much to do with him."

"What do you mean?" I picked up my fork, though my appetite had fled.

"He also told me you shared something with him he thought I should know. He wouldn't say what. I wonder if you know what he was talking about?" His soft words were filled with kindness.

My heart skipped a beat, and my stomach turned to cement. I didn't want to talk about this. I didn't want to talk about any of this.

"Leo? I want to know what's going on." He patted my hand with his weathered, dry one.

Inexplicably, my words stuck in my throat and tears jumped to my eyes. "I—I'm sorry."

"Why are you sorry?"

"I haven't been honest. With you. Or with anyone, really."

"Tell me, please."

I inhaled slowly, then let the air billow out, feeling an odd mixture of defeat and relief. "I want the mountain manager position. I always have. I've never said anything, and I should have."

He studied me, his blue eyes smiling though his face stayed neutral. "You're worried this is news to me, darling?"

"Isn't it?"

"Oh, dear. No. I've seen it in your eye since you were single digits, child."

The tension in my chest burst out of me in an odd choking giggle. "What?"

"I assume we all did. Plus you weren't very subtle when you'd tell your Da things like, 'when I run the lodge, we'll have donuts at the cafeteria every day.'" He beamed at the memory.

I laughed in earnest now. "Why did I feel like it was such a secret?"

"I don't know."

I scooted a chunk of chicken around on my plate. "No one ever talked to me about it like they did Liam. It was never 'when Leo takes over' like it was for Liam."

Grandpa tsk-ed. "He's eight years older. I think your father assumed you'd come into it when you were ready, just like I did. Things haven't gone the way any of us predicted this last year, but that doesn't mean you can't still step into that role eventually."

My face darkened at the mention of the events of this year, even as my chest cinched tight over my lungs, making normal breaths hard to come by. "I might never have a chance if Jonas sells."

"He assures me he won't."

"He said the same to me. But can we believe it? He's been planning to for so long, and we're supposed to accept that something has changed so significantly for him that his whole business plan has altered?" I dropped my fork and slumped back in the chair.

"He convinced me, but it sounds like he has some land to cross before he can convince you. I'm not as concerned about that, because I believe him to be an honest man, at his heart. Just like I believe you to be an honest woman, even if you've not been upfront with your family about your dreams."

I ducked my head. "I wish I had been. Maybe if I'd said it aloud as an adult, I wouldn't be in this position."

We each poked at our food, him eating happily and me wondering how I'd lost my appetite when that had, to this point in my life, never been a thing.

"What position is that?"

His words were infinitely gentle, yet a balloon of frustration burst in me. "I'm in love with the guy who has my job. A man who, until a few weeks ago, was going to sell my family's business out from underneath me. Even if I believe he's changed his mind about that, what kind of future do we have?"

Grandpa's sympathetic frown made me squint, trying to stay the tears threatening to spill over and probably roll out uncontrollably. I didn't want to start *again* because I didn't think I'd stop. Not now that I'd finally admitted what I really wanted and felt fairly stupid for it, considering apparently everyone knew all along and yet never told me they did.

"Can I give you a word of advice?" He squeezed my hand, then released it.

"Of course."

"Don't sit down in the impossibilities. If you love him, and you believe him, you can find a way forward. Don't fool yourself into believing that the circumstances mean you can't be together. That's your fear of taking the risk talking, and it's not the Leonie Morrison I know."

I swallowed hard, my head dropping forward before I let him see the tears that had in fact sprung loose. I wiped them, suddenly furious with myself for being a coward for so long, and still feeling so tied to the hesitation and fear I'd felt.

Who was I if I wasn't determined and focused and unwavering in the pursuit of my goal? I'd lived so long waiting for my turn, and then everything with Jonas had happened. He'd thrown me into a tailspin of fear and worry as he'd come in to change things, then to take Liam's job, and then as I faced the truth about my feelings for him.

Would I let that stop me—either from loving him or from figuring out a way to run my family's company?

No.

The truth resounded in me, clear as a blue-bird day on the mountain. There was no way I was laying down and letting him or my dream go. I had no idea how I'd make it work, but I would. And I'd pray with everything I had Jonas would still be here once I did.

Hopefully, I could believe him. Because if I could, that meant he really did love me, and we might just have a chance of being together.

CHAPTER FORTY-NINE

Jonas

The week after my conversation with Leonie was a cruel thing. I wanted to see her, be near her, convince her we could get through this, and I could do some of those things if I just walked around the building and looked closely enough. It was just that last part that seemed impossible.

Each day that passed—four interminable ones, for the record—placed me more and more at the mercy of my emotions. This was not a place a man who prided himself on his logical and professional prowess liked to live. And yet, I couldn't escape the swirling pool of anxiety, frustration, desperation, and sadness.

But I didn't suffer the idea of supposed impossibilities without a little pushback. After she'd left my office with a fond but brutal farewell, essentially saying she probably could forgive me with time and effort, but that she didn't believe there was hope for us anyway, the wheels had been spinning.

And spinning. And spinning. Until I wanted to punch something. But I'd avoided any more migraines, and I'd managed not to succumb to the temptation of begging her to give me another chance.

I'd never felt the drive to sink to my knees in front of someone like I had that afternoon. I'd *never* begged. Frankly, I'd never had something worth begging for.

Not until her.

Listening to her decide that not only did she likely not believe me but *if* she did, it didn't matter anyway? I'd wanted to beg. I'd wanted to grovel at her feet, arms wrapped around her waist, and convince her that if we worked together, we could figure this out.

We could. I knew it, without a doubt. I just had to convince her, and the fact that she hadn't said she hated me as Karla predicted she would... well, I counted myself lucky indeed. Now the job was to work out a way to show her we could be a team, and we could stay together.

I was not a man who loved easily. In fact, I'd never loved anyone but my parents, and perhaps Karla in a familial way. Romantic love had not been a factor in my life until Leonie shook my hand last November, and after that, I was done for.

I won't claim it was love at first sight. For her, it might have been hate at first sight. For me, I just knew she mattered. That whatever happened between us, it would be important. It was why I was constantly seeking her out in a room, on the street, at the coffee shop. I'd had to limit myself from doing so to avoid becoming a creep.

There was an inexorable draw between us. We'd both resisted it initially, but once we gave in, it was... I sighed, massaging my temples, and shifted in my ski boots at the memories flickering through my mind. *It was everything.*

The plan I had in mind had the potential to blow up in my face in a spectacular way. But it might also result in exactly what I wanted, which was Leonie with me for good.

The gondola rumbled over the line and into the station at the top of the mountain. The doors swung open and I waited for the couple across from me to exit, then did the same and grabbed my skis and poles from the outer compartment. I hadn't been up the mountain in a few days and felt the need to be on it. Nothing provided perspective like being at these heights, and though I could see the mountains perfectly from my office window, I too easily lost track of the view amidst paperwork and e-mails.

The crowds were thinning as it was Friday afternoon by the time I made it to the top and clipped my boots into my bindings. Up here, I had anonymity. I didn't worry about calls or texts, didn't have to deal with e-mail, didn't have to face the disappointment in myself for how badly I'd messed everything up.

The crisp cut of skis into perfect snow accompanied my descent, the shifting rhythm of hips and knees staying loose, weight forward, poles planting like walking sticks a satisfying flow down the mountain. I stopped at the ridge just before the continuation of the slope that led to the final section of the ski run and pulled in a slow, frigid breath as I took in the astounding view in front of me.

This was home now. This glorious vista had burrowed into me without my knowing, and it wouldn't leave. I didn't want it to. I'd seen countless mountain ranges and ski resorts, and something about this place had stuck. There was no avoiding it, and I didn't have to. I wouldn't.

With new determination, I pushed off, savoring the

scrape and crunch of my skis on the snow. Just when I was about to make a turn, a small streak of a person shot past me, clearly wild and out of control. The child's weight was behind him, but the skis ran away in front, over a small dip in the hill, and then left the body a crumpled into a heap just past it.

I cut to a stop just above the child, hoping to keep any other skiers from running over him since he was just past a sloping jump. I searched the mountain, but didn't see any skiers who looked like they were rushing to the child's side, so I lifted my goggles and bent to help.

"Are you okay?" A stupid question after seeing the fall, but what else would I say without knowing the little ski torpedo?

"I think so," came the tearful reply as the child—a girl, I could see now, based on the long brown hair snaking out of her helmet. "That's gonna leave a mark."

I chuckled under my breath and stopped one of her skis from slipping away down the hill. "You fall often?"

"No." The sharp retort told me this skier was not happy to have fallen—not that anyone ever was.

"Of course not. Are you hurt? Can I help you?"

She pushed up to sitting, then pulled off her goggles. "Thanks for saving my ski."

"Of course. Can I call someone, or—"

"Sara, are you okay?"

Leonie stopped without skidding, coming to a perfect halt next to the girl, below me.

My stomach dropped, then tightened at the sight of her, the sound of her voice, even the finesse with which she came to a stop on her skis. *Meine Guete*, she was glorious, made only more so by being in her element.

"Jonas? What are you doing?"

"I—I stopped to help."

"He saved my ski," the girl said.

"That was nice."

Our eyes caught, and I didn't dare look away, unsure of when I'd get to look at her so freely again. She nodded and mumbled something again.

"What?"

"Nothing."

"Can you help me get my ski back on, Miss Leo?"

She shook herself, as if coming out of a daze. "Of course, Sara."

"I'll be off. Glad you're okay, Sara. See you soon, Leonie."

I glanced at her once more before skating back to the main thoroughfare more determined than ever to make my plan succeed.

CHAPTER FIFTY

Leo

Seeing Jonas help Sara had confirmed it. I loved him. I wanted it to work.

He stood there, eleven feet tall and more handsome than any man on the mountain, even with his black ski helmet making everything but his sharp jaw and perfect mouth unseeable.

I still had it bad for Jonas Bauer. It was miraculous I hadn't made a fool out of myself. I'd had the insane vision of pulling off a glove and running my warm fingers over his cool lips, then guiding his chin down to my face. It had flashed across my mind just as he turned to go, thank goodness, or I might've satisfied that fantasy, which then would have been very awkward considering I'd broken up with him earlier this week.

Also logistically, kissing in ski helmets wasn't ideal.

The larger point was, I didn't want that. I didn't want to

stay in this horrid place of separate but not separated—we still saw each other, had to function together, or would very soon, and I still loved him.

That was what it came down to, and what kept me up nights running through scenarios where we could be together and not require me to give up my life-long goals or him just give up a job he seemed really good at and suited for. I hadn't figured it out yet, but seeing him, feeling the heart-melt as I realized it was him helping Sara after her fall... I had to.

It struck me as he skied away—who did I think I was, after all this time? Why was I moping around, wallowing in the thought that I couldn't find a way to make things work with Jonas?

I was Leo Morrison! I didn't take no for an answer. I fought for what I believed in, despite the odds.

I'd spent too much time keeping my dreams and goals to myself. I'd hidden my thoughts and feelings away and determined to make everything happen on my own. But that wasn't real life, was it?

We need other people—we're made to live in community and to learn from others, to ask for help and let others ask the same of us. I loved nothing more than butting into my friends' business and helping them with their problems, whether they asked for it or not. Why would I think I didn't need the same from them?

In this case, the person I needed help from was Jonas. I needed to know how he felt, and then I needed his help to figure this out. I'd made little headway on solving our problem because I didn't know what *he* wanted. I didn't know his perspective, and isolating myself from him just didn't make sense.

No more waiting around expecting life to hand me

what I wanted without ever saying the words. It was time to stop acting like a fool and be a woman.

I worked Saturday and Sunday, had some great lessons and could feel the season ramping up already in a way it didn't always by this early in the month. People were showing up and doing it in groups. They were staying all day, eating lunch at the cafeteria and at the top of the mountain... things were looking good. It was far too early to tell if this would be the season we needed to keep momentum going, but now that I knew it was Jonas who'd invested in us so heavily, some of the pressure to impress the investor was off. He knew the ins and outs well enough to know it was too early. He wouldn't be expecting a drive-by summary of the first two and a half weeks of the season and scoff at the numbers.

Although, it was also possible that if the season didn't get off to the start we all hoped it would, he'd jump ship.

No. He said he wouldn't.

My mind contradicted me even as the pit in my stomach opened wide. Not that I knew why... not exactly anymore. I wanted to believe Jonas, and something about seeing him with Sara, seeing him out on the mountain instead of his office, watching his beautiful form slide down the slope... it'd given me hope. After my revelation that I'd take what I wanted, I'd gone to find him, but he hadn't been in his office. And I'd lost a little of my gusto. So I'd decided to give it the weekend and hunt him down Monday.

By the time my day off rolled around, I wasn't sure what to do with myself. It felt too early in the season to take the day, but in truth, it'd be harder to come by days off as the holidays closed in, so I needed the rest. I slept in, made a large breakfast and feasted on it while reading a new book I'd been saving—I may or may not have been procrastinating finding Jonas.

I decided to go visit Wells since she often took Monday mornings off. I could talk things through with her and calm my nerves a bit before I went to find Jonas—maybe I could catch him on his lunch break.

I gathered my jacket and a few layers of warmth, stuffed my feet into my boots, opened my door.... And nearly tripped over a small basket sitting on my welcome mat.

A small basket with tissue paper covering the contents. *Hmm.*

I picked it up and was about to drop it inside the door and continue on my way when I saw a small note.

Happy Saint Nicholas Day. Love, Jonas

My heart, the one that had been walking along its normal path through the morning, took off like a mustang over the salt flats at a leave-nothing-behind bolt. I shut the door shakily and hurried to my couch, tearing the bow and tissue paper away to reveal... a leather portfolio.

Okay. Admittedly not what I was expecting, though I couldn't tell you what I expected in the first place. Just... probably not a folder full of... yep, paper.

I fanned the document... it must've been forty pages, maybe more. They weren't numbered. What was this that Jonas was giving me? Some kind of good news report on resort numbers thus far?

I flipped through, my heart pounding in my ears now, wondering what he meant, hoping his *Love, Jonas* was as significant as I wanted it to be.

And then, I saw it. A little plastic yellow flag with *sign here* on it. I flipped to the document.

I hereby accept the terms of the asset transfer in the amount of the entire existing ownership of shares in Silver Ridge Lodge and Resort from Jonas M. Bauer.

Asset transfer?

I scrambled, searching through the documents again.

It couldn't be.

It. Couldn't. Be.

Tears of disbelief, amazement, and overwhelm tracked down my face as I fumbled for my phone and dialed Jonas. It rang, and rang, and rang, then cut to voicemail.

"You've reached Jonas Bauer."

I chuckled through my tears because of course that's all his message said—spare, essential information only. Nothing in excess. How completely opposite to the man himself.

Not his outer appearance or the way he presented himself professionally, but his insides. He was so kind and lovely and generous and—

"Jonas. You're a crazy person. You're just an absolutely insane man and I don't—" I broke off and sob-laughed. "You need to call me back, okay? I'm coming to the lodge, and we're going to talk and... you're just... I'll see you soon."

I hung up and raced around the room, grabbing my things, and rushed out the door. The five-minute drive to the lodge felt insanely slow, but I made it. I outright ran from employee parking into the building, down the long hallway that led to Jonas' office. I knocked.

No answer.

I knocked again and waited, wondering if somehow he hadn't gotten in yet. He always started early, but maybe delivering my little basket had thrown off his schedule. Or maybe he'd gone to get a snack. Or a coffee in town. Or had a meeting.

My phone rang and I answered it immediately. "Hey!"

"Uh, hey. What is going on with Jonas resigning?"

Liam's voice shocked me into stillness. "What?"

"I just sat down at my desk and I have an e-mail in my inbox with Jonas' letter of resignation. He sent it to the whole board."

"I haven't heard anything about this. I haven't really talked to him since last week."

Which was entirely my fault. He would have talked to me, but he was probably giving me space. I knew he had more to say, more he wanted to work out. Why didn't I let him?

My feet came unglued, and I nodded and smiled as I passed the people milling around the lobby of the lodge, doing my best not to let my impatience at their clueless, directly-in-my-path meandering show on my face.

I burst out the door and jogged across the plaza and around the corner to the manager's cabin—to Jonas' house, all the while listening to Liam.

"This is bad news, Leo. I don't know what's going on between you two but him up and leaving tells me something very bad has happened, and I don't like it. We need him here."

I reached the door and knocked. Knocked again.

"All I can tell you is yes, we broke up. But it wasn't... horrible or anything. And I... I was going to talk to him today. But he's not at the office, and I'm here at the cabin and he's not answering."

"He's gone. At least that's what his e-mail says."

"How is he gone? Why would he go? *Where* did he go?" Panic filled me. Had he really just signed over everything to me, left his job, and then left *me*?

I knocked on the cabin door again, knowing the futility

of the action and yet unable to walk away. I tromped through snow and around the corner to peer into a window on the far side of the building, and my stomach sank through the icy ground.

Empty. The house was empty. The blinds had been left open and through them, nothing but bare hardwood and stone, and beyond, the kitchen. No furniture, no rugs, nothing.

"Give him a call and let's figure this out. We don't want to lose him."

I don't know if I said something or not, but Liam hung up and I stood staring into the empty cabin for a while longer before I reanimated and trudged back to my car.

Once inside, I took out my phone with still-shaking hands and pressed the call button. This time, it went immediately to voicemail.

I pulled in a shuddering breath, closed my eyes, and let it out.

He'd left. He'd cleared out without a word, dumping everything he thought I wanted in my lap. The only problem with that was he'd taken the thing I'd finally realized I wanted the most, and without a backward glance.

He'd taken himself, bridges an inferno behind him as he went.

CHAPTER FIFTY-ONE

Leo

The next few days plodded by with a pace so mind-numbingly slow, I could hardly breathe through the more mundane moments.

My hope held out the rest of the day Monday. I'd assumed Jonas would call me. *At least*, he would call.

He didn't call.

Then I started worrying. What if something had happened to him? What if he was sick? Or in a car accident. Or he'd been kidnapped by international financial terrorists and *made* to sign over all of his possessions, leave his job, and never speak to me again?

Okay, so maybe the romantic suspense novel I'd been reading had spilled over into my imagination when it came to Jonas, but still. Why wouldn't he just answer the phone?

Wednesday evening, I got a text.

I'm sorry I haven't called back. I'm swamped here, but I'll be in touch soon.

Where was here? When was soon? I wanted to call him and yell at him and *make* him talk to me. But I didn't since clearly, he wouldn't answer.

I'd decided to be patient, which was not really a thing for me. I'd also decided that if I was going to convince him to come back and take me back and settle for a life in Silverton, I couldn't very well unleash the simmering rage that threatened to boil over every time I thought of him leaving without a word.

By Friday of that week, a boulder-sized hunk of fear and sadness had taken up residence in my belly. I couldn't stop wondering what Jonas would say when he did get in touch. I'd let my mind extrapolate all kinds of scenarios. Everything from him helicoptering in and proposing to me over megaphone to sending another text that said *You're just a little bit much.*

It was that last one that had my chest aching. What if, after all of this, he'd decided that I was the problem, and the fastest way to divest himself of me and my *little bit much* was to give away his investment and disappear across the country or world?

I'd talked to Bel, who'd assured me that wouldn't be it. She'd reminded me of the things I'd told her about how Jonas had said he accepted me for me. But then I countered with how he seemed to always find a reason to call me a nickname which probably meant something about me being sweet, and that he had to have finally realized I'm just not and that wasn't what he wanted.

At which point, Bel had told me to slap myself across the face and get a grip, and we'd both laughed. I could laugh because in my heart of hearts, I didn't really believe that. I hadn't given up hope that when we did talk, we could find a way forward.

By Friday evening a little past eight, I was plunking dishes into the dishwasher when my doorbell rang.

My pulse picked up as I scampered across the apartment to answer. The door swung open and...

There he stood. Tall, serious, gorgeous, with snow gathering in his hair and at his shoulders.

"Come in," I said and held the door wide for him to enter.

He stepped through, but stayed right by the door as I shut it behind him.

He smelled *cold*, and like himself, that minty, citrus scent I'd forever associate with him. His eyes found mine as he ruffled his hand through his wet hair and my heart thumped in response. *Oh, hi, you're home*, it said, all breathy and stupid. Fortunately, I didn't say anything aloud.

The room was silent, though I wondered if he could hear my pulse as it pounded away in my neck.

"So how are you—"

"I'm sorry it took me—"

We both broke off and chuckled at our talking at the same time.

"Please," I said, gesturing to the couch.

We both sat, and I stuffed my hands in my lap to keep an eye on them. I could see them going rogue any minute and reaching out to grab him.

"I'm sorry it has taken me so long to get here."

"I—it's okay."

His gaze searched my face and he swallowed, which was when I registered he seemed nervous. Why would *he* be nervous?

"Did you get the paperwork?"

"The paperwork that seems like it says you're giving me your multi-million-dollar stake in my family's business?"

He nodded.

A laugh burst out of my chest. "Yes, Jonas, I did get those."

"Good."

I waited, sure he'd explain everything now, but he just sat there looking unsure, snow melting into his black jacket.

I reached for his hand where it rested on his thigh, unable to stand the separation and the awkwardness that packed into the corners of the apartment. "Please explain this to me. I don't understand what's going on."

He laced his fingers with mine, which alternately set me at ease and made my breath feel short.

"I have made a mess of things between us. I wasn't sure you believed that I didn't have plans to sell, so I figured if I gave it to you, you'd believe me."

I laughed at this, because it was completely ludicrous. "You decided you'd give it to me."

"Yes." His brow furrowed like he had no idea why I'd need to repeat that.

"Jonas, you can't just give someone something like that. It's too much."

"Yes I can. I already did. Did you sign?"

"No."

His look was thunderous. "You must."

"I'll decide what I must do."

We stared at each other until just the corner of his mouth twitched. "Fine."

I huffed out a breath, but didn't speak, afraid my smile would take over my face. "Please continue."

He squeezed my hand, then did as I asked. "As you

must know, I also resigned from my position as mountain manager."

"That part I don't understand at all."

"Don't you?" His gray eyes pinned me with a meaningful look, and I wanted to cry.

"You left it for me? I mean, I know you did, but why?"

"Leonie, I love you. You told me being mountain manager was your dream, and then later clarified that you saw no way for us to be together even if I didn't intend to sell my part of the business. You made it clear there was no way forward for us if I kept the job."

All color drained from my face. "It wasn't as an ultimatum—I never meant it that way. In fact, I've spent the last two weeks trying to figure out some way around this. Some way to fix it."

He brushed a hand along my cheek. "That's what I did. I solved it. Done."

"Just like that?"

"Yes."

"And now what do you do? Where did you go? Why did you move out without talking to me? Why didn't you stay to talk about this?"

"I wanted no room for doubt. I don't want you to have *any* doubt about me. Over the last year, I've discovered that my investment here goes far beyond financial. Even if I hadn't fallen for you, I would've felt tethered to this place. But now...."

His gray gaze searched my face, so loving and gentle, I couldn't help but lean close and capture his lips with mine. Relief coursed through me at the contact. We both sighed into the kiss, but I pulled back, intent on understanding everything now.

"So if I sign, I own your part of the business?"

"Yes."

"You realize you can't actually be done as mountain manager? We have to transition. If I was ready today to take over, we'd still have to find my replacement. There's too much to do for you to just abandon us."

"I would never abandon you. But I wanted it clear—the job is far less important to me than you are."

Tingling warmth spread through me. "You must really like me."

"I really like you, and I really love you."

This time, our kiss blazed wild before it calmed, his hand running over my head and pulling me close.

"I missed you."

"Where did you go?" I sat up so I could see him, though I kept hold of him.

"I went to New York. I put my apartment up for rent, moved out what I didn't want to leave, and met with Karla to formulate my coming back to a more active role in Bauer Group."

My chin dropped. "How did you do that so quickly?"

"Honestly, I'd been planning to deal with the apartment and had been dragging my feet with getting it done. My house will be ready in the new year, and until then, I can find somewhere to stay. Plus, I needed to talk with Karla now that I'm not working here." He dipped his head and kissed my jaw, then spoke into the skin of my neck. "I had to find something to occupy my days until you get home from managing this place."

"Well, on that note, what about the hotel?" I asked, savoring his attention.

"I won't change my mind on that. I urge you to let the plan move forward. You'd have to get the board's approval to delay it as it is, but—"

"Please stop talking to me like you aren't in this job. You can't just be done. I want the job, and I'm not going to demur and not take it, but at whatever point it makes sense for me to take over, I'll need your help to transition and learn the ropes."

"I can do that, of course. I should've allowed for that, but I got tunnel vision on the dramatic gesture." He gave me a sheepish little grin.

"Adorable. But not actually as helpful as you sticking around and giving proper notice, in reality."

"No, I suppose it's not."

I hugged him tight, then released him. "You should know that part of the reason I didn't want the hotel was because I know I'm not equipped to manage one. I really don't have experience there, and I was concerned I'd be less attractive to the board when I tried to oust you."

His eyebrows jumped and a sly half-smile graced his lips. "Now we come to it. I knew you were plotting against me all along."

"I can't say I wasn't."

He shook his head, but the look on his face was nothing short of cherishing.

"But seriously, I don't know how to manage that. But you do, don't you? Couldn't you stay on to manage the hotel portion? Or something? I don't want you to just throw it all away for me and resent me. It's romantic as all get out, but I'm afraid of what'll happen when the dust settles, never mind how angry the board will be."

"I enjoyed the job, but it wasn't my dream, Leonie. My dream has always been to find a home, and I believe for me, that is here in Silverton. *That's* my dream. And you are. But beyond that, I can continue doing what I've always loved doing through Bauer Group and my other investments, and that can be done from anywhere. Frankly, in many ways it'll be easier from here where I'm closer to many of the prospective clients."

"That makes sense, I guess."

He cupped my cheeks. "It does. And if you and the board decide you want me involved for the hotel or anything else, then it's done, *Liebling*."

With my hands behind his neck, I pulled his face to look at mine. "You're insane, Jonas Bauer. But I love you, and I'm glad you're mine."

"I'm yours, huh?"

"Yes. Completely. Don't you think?"

"Certainly."

CHAPTER FIFTY-TWO

Jonas

Danny and Mia Morrison were married two days before Christmas. Leonie, Wells Bryant-Morrison, and Bel Paxton were bridesmaids, and Danny's brothers and father were his groomsmen while Grandpa Will presided over the ceremony with his flair and charm on full display. Kai Parker, soon to be Morrison when the formal adoption process was completed, escorted Mia down the aisle, and it choked even me up when he jumped into Danny's arms to hug him and then took his place next to William Morrison.

All in all, it left me feeling... eager.

I wanted the same for myself, but to see Leonie walking toward me, her father on her arm. I wanted to celebrate a union of our lives with my mother and Leonie's family and everyone we knew in town in attendance.

My mother, as it happened, had eagerly accepted our

invitation to spend Christmas with us, even knowing Leonie and I would both be working long days for the holiday itself. I'd moved back into the manager's cottage so she took the guest room.

The smile on my mother's face after Leonie had embraced her tightly for what seemed like a surprisingly long hug upon her arrival had spoken volumes. Leonie had been warm and lovely and *sweet* and tough on me as usual, and my mother's eyes had shone with veritable glee as she watched us interact.

All that, and then her repeated declarations that she loved Leonie and had always wanted a daughter spelled out her feelings well enough. I'd known they'd get along, but their fast friendship folded me over again, creasing me indelibly, marking me for Leonie in yet another way.

If I had my way, it'd be a matter of time before we had our turn at this, and not a lot of time at that.

"Are you next?" Grandpa Will asked, a sly twinkle in his eye.

The man had a mischievous look at almost all times. It was that forever smiling mouth and the wrinkles around his face like he'd spent years laughing.

"If she'll have me." The truth, and nothing but. If Leonie would have me, I'd marry her today.

"She will, I'd guess." He clapped me on the shoulder.

He wandered off, chatting with every person he encountered along the way. I couldn't help my smile as I watched him go, but then Liam Morrison wandered up and I sobered.

"You're going to marry my sister?"

His face was stern. Not typical of the oldest Morrison sibling, but I couldn't pretend to be shocked that all of the drama had reached him, and that he held no fond feelings for me.

"Is that right?" Jamie Morris said as he sauntered up and hung an arm around his brother.

"Oh yeah. They've been hot and heavy for months now," Danny said as he joined the conversation with a wide grin. "We call them *Leonas*."

I coughed at that. "Uh, well, I haven't asked her yet, or anything, but... I'd like to."

They looked at me, three pairs of bright blue eyes, so like their sister's, bearing down on me.

Then Danny cracked a signature beam. "Good. Do it soon."

"Yeah, Bauer, get on it." Jamie nodded sternly, then winked as he turned to find Bel waiting for him.

Liam lingered, his face still serious. "You shouldn't have hidden the fact that you were the investor."

Shame colored my cheeks as I faced the man I'd deceived. I wouldn't ever live that down. "I understand if you're angry."

"I'm not angry, Bauer. Not anymore. You gave it all up for Leo, and any man who actually sees her, knows her, and loves her? That's a man I can get behind. So, like Dan and Jamie said—get on it."

He reached out, and I clumsily offered my hand a moment late. We shook, then he turned to find Wells.

"What was all that?"

Leonie's warm hand took mine and she leaned up to kiss my cheek. Her long, golden hair flowed down her back in waves, and the silver dress made her look astoundingly beautiful and angelic, even. Of course, I'd learned over the last few months that almost everything made her look so to my eyes. Ski clothes. Sweatpants. Nothing.

Especially that.

"They were asking when I'm going to ask you to marry me."

She choked on the sip of champagne she'd just taken. "I don't think you're supposed to tell me that."

"Why not? It can't be a surprise I want to marry you."

Her eyes softened and she bit her lip, then she swayed toward me to place a lingering kiss on my lips. "I don't suppose it is."

We smiled at each other, happy to be together on this night celebrating love and family and the future, which looked incredibly bold and bright.

"So when should I expect the proposal?" she asked, an arch to her brow that told me she thought she was funny—that she thought it was still a ways out.

I leaned close, glanced at her lips, and said, "Could be any time now, Leonie. Better be ready."

EPILOGUE

Leo

Bel looked the kind of pretty only she could look—delicate and polished and astoundingly lovely in her simple silk sheath wedding dress, and yet kind of flower-child, carefree too. She wore a flower crown the owner of *Bloom* had woven out of early spring daisies and stephanotis over the waves of her caramel hair. Bel had refused to use fancy flowers despite the fact that she was marrying a millionaire who would've imported tropical flowers from the farthest reaches of the globe at her word.

Jamie wore a black tux with a white shirt and thin tie, though this surprised no one since he wore the same thing to any formal event. Only the little flower pinned above his breast signaled this was a different affair, and his hair was a little less disheveled in the knot at the back of his head. Well that, and his demeanor, which had shifted from generally broody and mildly mysterious to the outsider to an overall aura of joy. He positively exuded it.

The best thing each of them wore? Smiles stretching the outer limits of their faces, making their cheeks wrinkle and their eyes shine and everyone in attendance laugh from the pure elation rattling around the room as the minister announced them married and presented *Mr. and Mrs. Jamie Morris* to the world.

That was an interesting thing—the *Morris*. I wasn't surprised Bel had changed her name—she'd mentioned feeling absolutely no conflict about ditching the name of her childhood. Her relationship with her parents had everything to do with that, but it was her choice. I was a little surprised she wouldn't be Bel Morrison, but of course Jamie was Rockstar Jamie Morris now for anonymity's sake, and so of course she would be too. I just hadn't thought about it until right that moment.

I hoped Jonas didn't expect me to become a Bauer. I had no plans to be anything but a Morrison.

My stomach clenched at the thought of him, followed by a familiar refrain in my mind. *If he ever asks...*

After Mia and Danny's wedding, I'd sort of expected a proposal to follow fairly soon. The way he'd talked about it made me suspect he might have a ring in his pocket at that very moment.

But that would have been crazy. I mean, not *totally* crazy because I would have said yes then, but still a little quick if you considered we only really started spending time together purposefully in October. Two months? *Fast.* And yet it'd been a year since we met, and in many ways our relationship had felt like it'd been on fast forward, despite the madness of the ski season.

I did see the wisdom in waiting, though I hated the

process. Leave it to Jonas Bauer to be perfectly content to plod his way toward the altar and leave me tapping my toe at the front of the church.

That was also an unfair depiction. Jonas' methodical approach to things was part of what I found so attractive about him, and in the same breath, he could be alarmingly hasty once he'd made a decision. See his choice to sign over his shares in the company, quit, move, and leave the state in a matter of days once he decided that was how he'd win me back...

My point? I wanted to marry the guy, and I wanted him to ask me. Soon. I didn't care about being traditional regarding a lot of things, but on this one, I did. I wanted him to ask me so I could say yes.

The couple and the wedding party had processed out into a heated tent and now mingled in an area set up with bistro tables and bars at odd corners. Only I had a date who wasn't in the wedding since Wells and Mia were married to the groomsmen.

"A lovely ceremony." Jonas' smooth voice came from just behind me.

My heart leapt at the sound as I turned to find him smiling down at me, gray eyes glittering behind those clear glasses, his tailored dark gray suit, white shirt, and a tie that matched my dress completing the picture.

Basically devastating.

"Yes," I said, folding my hands together behind my back, hoping he liked the bright blue dress Bel had chosen for me. She'd selected different shades of blue and different cuts for each of her bridesmaids. I wore robin's egg blue with spaghetti straps and a flared skirt with a fitted bodice. It was happy and ridiculously feminine, and I loved it.

Wells wore a shade lighter than ocean blue in an A-line

style, and Mia wore a baby blue sheath that was gorgeous on her. Everyone looked fantastic, honestly.

"Would you like a drink?" Jonas asked, handing me a flute of champagne.

I accepted it immediately. "Of course."

His arm curved around my back and his free hand rested at the base of my spine. The simple, familiar touch sent my pulse skittering. I hadn't seen him much lately as the season came to an end—what would seem like a slow time turned out to be very busy for him as manager. *Yes*, he was still mountain manager, but we were working on the transition and had our first round of interviews for replacements for my position in a few weeks.

And the last few days had been all wedding madness. I'd missed him.

"Will you come with me a moment?" He dipped his head and spoke close to my ear. The general hubbub in the room made the words feel intimate, shared only between us.

I nodded, then followed his urging as we stepped outside the massive event tent that had been erected in Jamie's beautiful backyard at his house in Silverton. Jonas reached for my hand and I walked after him, attempting to hold my champagne steady so it wouldn't slosh over the side, particularly since his pace had nearly doubled once we'd exited the tent.

"Is something wrong?" I asked, scurrying on tiptoes after him—no point in bothering setting down my horrid heels as they were an inch taller than I liked and were generally terrible. I'd have to remember I didn't want pretty shoes for my own wedding unless they were comfortable too.

He glanced over his shoulder at me, his face serious and a small frown pulling at his mouth. "Yes."

A flag of alarm waved in my mind. What could be wrong? What could be so wrong he'd be nearly jogging down this path to where Jamie's decks overlooked a low valley and held the best view of Silver Ridge Peak on his property, but that also had him wanting us to both be juggling champagne flutes on the way?

He offered his arm to me as we reached the stairs, and though I knew he could see the questions in my eyes, he didn't speak as he escorted me down, down, down the stairs and different levels of the deck until we reached the one farthest from the house and tent and hoopla.

His shoulders rose and fell in a great sigh as he looked out at the mountains for a moment, then turned to me.

"Leonie."

My breath caught. The way he said my name, as always, made my chest flutter, and yet, something about the look on his face... I knew. I couldn't explain it, but whatever it was, I knew *this* would change me.

The night seemed to shift then, the light fading another touch so the mountain became more shadowy and indistinct, and only small fairy lights weaved on the branches above us lit the space. The late spring air was cool, but I only felt my heart racing.

"Jonas," I said, though my voice emerged weak and wispy, my body shaky and unsure in the context of his intensity.

"Something is wrong."

Okay.... How did he expect me to respond? I stared back, showing him I was ready, he could tell me, we could fix it.

His gaze settled on me, heavy and full. "Everything is wrong when I spend the night without you. Everything is wrong when I wake and you aren't in my bed. Everything is wrong when I have to tell you goodnight and watch you leave. Everything is wrong when we eat breakfast separately or make lunches in different kitchens or fold laundry on different couches."

My heart thud-thud-thudded in my chest and my breath came too shallow. My mind filled with his words as I watched his stern, lovely face confess.

He set his glass on the railing of the porch and took mine from my hands to join his. Then, he took my hands and kneeled, never breaking eye contact.

"Leonie Morrison, everything is wrong when you're not mine and I'm not yours. I didn't plan to do this here—I had something else in mind, but I don't want to continue pretending I'm satisfied with anything less than being with you and calling you mine. If you feel the same way, please make me the happiest fool on the planet and marry me."

A laugh-sob burst out of me, a flood of emotion so strong and uncontrolled, I could hardly stand. I dropped to my knees in front of him. "I do feel the same way, Jonas, but you didn't ask me a question."

A smile flashed over his face and he shook his head. "Will you marry me, Leonie?"

Reaching for the back of his head, I pulled him to me and kissed him with all the enthusiasm and love and relief and excitement I felt. "Of course I will."

Thank you so much for reading Jonas and Leo's love story! These two were a challenge and joy to write! If you're wondering what happened to Wyatt Saint, don't miss his book, Almost Perfect. Catch a sneak peek at the end of the book! And don't miss the Reader's Guide to Jonas Bauer's Expletives—these were so much fun.

Make sure to sign up for my newsletter to get all the updates on the Back to Silver Ridge Series and more (Including a free book!): http://www.clairecainwriter.com/newsletter

A READER'S GUIDE TO JONAS BAUER'S EXPLETIVES

Thanks very much to my friend Kate and her husband (a native German speaker) who helped supply Jonas' German exclamations. Here's a little list below so you can delight in this small example of how magical the German language is.

Mein Gott — My god

Meine Guete — My goodness

Liebe Guete — Holy goodness

Heiliger Strohsack — Holy moly (lit. Holy straw sack)

Donnerwetter! — Used to express extreme anger/disbelief (lit. thunderstorms)

Um Himmelswillen — For Heaven's sake

Weibsbild — Typical woman

Suesser — Sweetie

Liebling — My lovely

The one I wish I could've fit in:

Bei meinen dottergelben Bartspitzen: By my yolk yellow beard tips (most like "that's peculiar")

ACKNOWLEDGMENTS

Whew! The end of Silver Ridge (or at least, this series set there). This book was a challenge—I'd been anticipating writing Leo for quite a while, but doing the thing and doing her and Jonas justice were a learning experience, for sure.

Thank you a million times to my amazing editor Zee Monadee who wouldn't let me settle—who kept pushing to make Jonas and Leo even better. This book is SO much better because of you in about a thousand ways!

Thanks to Emma Robinson for her cover design.

Thanks to my awesome beta readers Emma and Caroline—your feedback is so valuable, I can't even tell you! Go squeeze one of your adorable children and pretend it's me enthusiastically hugging you back. Special thanks to Kate for reading *and* supplying the German content—I loved getting to add some authentic German to Jonas! Any errors with the German herein are mine alone.

Thanks to Jamie McGillen, without whom I probably would've given up. Thanks to Julie, who is the literal best.

Thanks to Matthew for letting me verbally process my plots and problems and supporting me even when I whine about how I've written myself into a corner.

And thanks to my children, who are used to seeing me write in every possible moment, and all the more as they've been home for every. single. second. of the writing of this book, written entirely during the quarantine.

Finally, but very much at the top of my list, thanks to the readers who've shown support for this series. Thank you for reading, reviewing, and sharing these stories! You blow my mind.

ABOUT THE AUTHOR

Claire Cain lives to eat and drink her way around the globe with her traveling soldier and three kids, but is perhaps even happier hunkered down at home in a pair of sweatpants and slippers using any free moment she has to read and cook. Or talk—she really likes to talk. She has become an expert at packing too many dishes in too few cabinets and making houses into homes from Utah to Germany and many places in between. She's a proud Army wife and is frankly just really happy to be here.

You can also join Claire's facebook reader group for exclusive content and fun: https://www.facebook.com/groups/clairecain/

Website: http://www.clairecainwriter.com

E-mail: Claire@ClaireCainWriter.com

Newsletter sign-up for new releases, exclusives, and freebies: http://www.clairecainwriter.com/newsletter

Calla

I'd landed late afternoon and happily missed the hour-and-fifteen-minute drive from Salt Lake City thanks to the new private airport. My pop into the grocery had taken me ten minutes, max, but here we were, driving through town, and the January sky had already dimmed. Streetlights flipped on as we passed, and twinkle lights lit up trunks and branches of the trees lining the sidewalks.

Quaint. Beautiful. A little piece of my frozen heart thawed a touch. Not enough to feel the wretched thing stubbornly beating there, but enough to feel something like warmth as we crawled by the old Silver Ridge Lodge, then the massive, surprisingly pretty hotel that'd helped put the place on tourist destination lists since it opened a few years ago.

Once on the road out of town, he asked, "Have you stayed at this place? I haven't taken someone this far up before."

He didn't glance back as he drove, for which I was thankful.

At least he was mindful of the twisting canyon road he'd turned onto. Out of the bustling town and into the canyon, the light disappeared even more as we followed the road cutting between two of the Silver Ridge mountains. The larger was Silver Ridge Peak, but I couldn't remember the river's name that slipped by next to us.

"I haven't. Seems pretty new."

The only reason I'd been able to find an open StayBnB so last minute during peak ski season was thanks to total luck and perfect timing. I'd been scouring the website, checking back every few days, when it popped up. I hadn't even looked that closely, just told Mr. Warrick Saint I wanted his place for at least a thirty-day stay.

He'd accepted immediately, thank goodness. When I'd landed, I had a message from the owner. "*Sorry for the inconvenience. My brother Wyatt will be meeting you today. I will check in first thing tomorrow, but please let Wyatt know if there's anything you need this evening.*"

Warrick and Wyatt? I'd forgotten the kitschy Utah trend of naming everyone in a family with the same first letter. Two brothers wasn't so bad, though.

That little train of thought failed to distract me from the knot tightening in my stomach. By now, the sensation had become an old friend. Was I even alive if I didn't feel nauseated from anxiety with a side of impending doom?

"Looks like this is it?" Jarrod asked, as though I'd know.

We'd skirted a fenced-in field for a few miles after leaving the canyon and now sat on the abandoned-looking road in front of a high wooden arch with a sign that said "All Saints Ranch."

"Yep. The directions said drive up to the main house, then turn right and we'll see it." *Crap, I hope we see it.*

I'd chosen this place primarily because it was the only option. The bonus of its secluded location had seemed like a stroke of genius. No crowds from in town. No curious neighbors. But *wow*, this place was out here.

"Here's hoping the Saints, whoever they are, aren't psychopaths and murderers!" He chuckled heartily at his joke. "Just kidding. They're totally nice. You're safe with them."

The knot in me doubled in size.

Maybe Jarrod did know the Saints. Maybe they'd paid him off to lure unsuspecting women up to their murder cabin.

You booked this online, genius. Oh yeah.

But was I a complete idiot? Obviously, yes. More so than most people, though? Had I just set myself up to get axe-murdered by some country bumpkin Utahan cattle ranchers? Aside from Kristoffer, no one would know I was here. No one would find my body.

No one would be asking. If anyone did ask, they'd all be people who'd crack champagne and toast your demise.

I scrunched my eyes shut, banishing that barrage of thoughts. *Not helpful, brain! Get yourself together!*

Jarrod drove the long stretch of road flanked by fenced pastures all the way to a large farmhouse. A sprawling two-story home, it looked huge as we approached. Coach lamps lit the front to show stonework and wood—it had already grown too dim to see the full design. But it looked nice. Definitely nicer than something a murderer would own... right?

"Fancy," Jarrod said as he turned right. "The Saints are good people, though. You'll be fine."

A little gust of relief swept through me. The building sat less than a quarter mile away, and it had that same warm glow as the main house. Warrick, or Wyatt, or whoever, had turned on the outside lights, and it looked like a few inside too.

Another shard of ice dropped off and melted in me. My chest warmed at the cozy-looking cottage. Well, from what I could tell, it looked like a barn, and the description had said it was a converted small barn. Hopefully, I wouldn't freeze to death, but based on the smoke rising out of the chimney, the fireplace worked.

That I had no idea how to make a fire and no one to do it for me would be... interesting. Maybe the owner could teach me. I'd have to face any number of things I didn't know how to do on this trip, and that was part of the point, wasn't it? To haul myself out of this rut, if not to actually find myself.

"Well, all set here, I think. Oh, good, looks like somebody's here to greet you. I would'a felt weird just droppin' ya here in the middle of nowhere." Jarrod exited the car and popped the trunk.

I swallowed, pushed out an exhale, and braced myself. The next few minutes could get weird, but I'd handle it. And then I could go inside—and hopefully not get axe-murdered—and finally, finally cry myself to sleep.

The trunk slammed before I shut my door.

"Here ya go, Miss Mayhem."

Crap. Definitely recognized me—my stage name was pretty conspicuous. I'd traveled and booked under my real name, but no one knew me as anything but Miss Mayhem. *That* name was too notorious. It'd served me well the last decade as I clawed my way into pop icon status, but I'd always been just on the edge of disfavor. Too bold. Too revealing. And lately, too wrapped up in the horrible mess with Candy and repeated failed records.

Fortunately, this guy didn't seem all that fazed.

"Thanks, Jarrod. Can I have you sign a quick non-disclosure for me? I know it's odd, but I have to—"

"Say no more, say no more. I've done it plenty of times."

Thank Goodness. I swiped into the app on my phone, asked for his full name, and presented him with the signature block. This wasn't the way I normally did things. Who cared if a cab driver knew where I was staying? But I couldn't afford a crowd here, and I couldn't afford anyone knowing anything. The bad news could follow me into a cave, and I didn't need to do anything but simply exist to fuel the fire these days.

"Thank you. I don't mean to be a jerk, but I will have to use that if anything leaks. I—"

"Don't worry. I can keep my trap shut. Want me to stay 'til you get inside?" He glanced back toward the house.

Whoever had been here to greet me had disappeared. The front door to the little cottage stood wide open and light spilled out, so someone was still in there.

"Nah. I'll be fine." *Or I'll get murdered.* Tomato, tomahto.

"If you're sure..."

Ah, sweet Jarrod. Trying to keep me from showing up as a celebrity victim on a true crime podcast.

"I'm sure. Thanks again for the drive, and the, well, you know." No idea why it felt weird to reference the NDA he'd just signed, but it did.

He nodded, and without another word, loaded back into his car and left.

I grabbed the handles to both giant rolling suitcases and pulled them with me, thankful the dirt driveway was frozen solid. This would be just lovely when the ground thawed in a few months. Who knew if I'd still be here.

I heaved the two bags up the short staircase right to the door, with my purse and canvas bag of groceries over one shoulder, then knocked. *No answer.* But there was definitely someone in there, and I'd checked the reservation—I was only ten minutes late. So... I went in.

"Hello?"

Inside, the light was soft, and warmth from the glowing fire emanated down the hall. That scent of real wood burning made it feel immediately cozy, though I hadn't seen more than the entryway. It felt welcoming. Well, aside from that whole missing host thing.

"Hello?" I projected my voice a little more.

A crash of some kind sounded farther in, followed by a low muttered curse.

I left the door open but abandoned my suitcases. If I had to make a break for it, I didn't want to have any barriers. Granted, where I'd break to would be a problem considering we were miles from anything. I straightened my spine and pulled my shoulders back, then shuffled inside, the rubberized soles of my leather boots not making a sound on the stone floor of the entryway.

Just as I reached the end of the hallway, a towering figure arrived, backlit by the lights behind him.

"Shoot. I'm sorry." He stepped to the side and waved a hand for me to continue into the living room. He then followed me into the brightly lit space. A fire roared from the stone fireplace in the center of the room. It wasn't huge, but everything in it looked plush, clean, and comfortable, decorated in creams and natural colors with little pops of deep teal.

Thank Goodness! No way would a serial killer have teal throw pillows.

"I'm Wyatt. I think my brother mentioned I'd be meeting you today?"

He moved to the counter of the small kitchen, where a stack of papers and a set of keys waited. He still hadn't actually looked at me, which was fine by me. If he never did, he wouldn't recognize me, and that made life that much easier.

The voice, though. He had a very good voice. I had a thing for voices, which made some sense, considering I now earned my living with mine. Well, and my body, but that thought had grown more and more depressing lately.

But his voice? Rich and low, a little rumbly. Like if I put my head on his chest, the sound would fill up his whole body and spill over into mine, too. *Except that's a really weird thought to have about a potential murderer's voice.*

He was tall. Not towering, but I was five-ten, so it was a rare man who full-on towered. But he had at least four inches on me, which I appreciated. Granted, he did have boots on to give him a little lift—brown leather cowboy boots from the looks of it.

Wait, do I need cowboy boots? Probably. But now's not the time, brain!

His shoulders were broad inside a canvas-looking jacket, and he seemed built, but he also wore the outer layer plus some kind of plaid something that stuck out from under it, so he might've been hiding a giant beer belly and it'd be hard to tell.

Unlikely, based on this view, my rude, lascivious little brain whispered as I took note of his jeans and, honest to goodness—wait, really? Brown leather chaps. I wanted to laugh, but they looked... good. I'd never gone for the cowboy rough rider look but *hi.* Maybe I'd been missing out.

They framed his—

He looked like—

He broke my brain.

The probably-not-a-serial-killer brother-of-the-host chap-wearing cowboy-man straight up wiped my mind.

I cleared my throat, despite years of being reprimanded for the habit, grasping for the thread of the conversation. "He did, yes."

"Good. Good." Then finally, he looked up.

That didn't help one bit, because my chappified brain only saw crystal-blue eyes on a face so rough and handsome, so unpolished and yet overtly beautiful, I let out a weird little gust of air and forgot completely about hiding my face from him.

Get your copy of Almost Perfect today.

www.ingramcontent.com/pod-product-compliance
Lightning Source LLC
Chambersburg PA
CBHW051206190726
48288CB00006B/1831